Two Rivers

Cygnet Brown

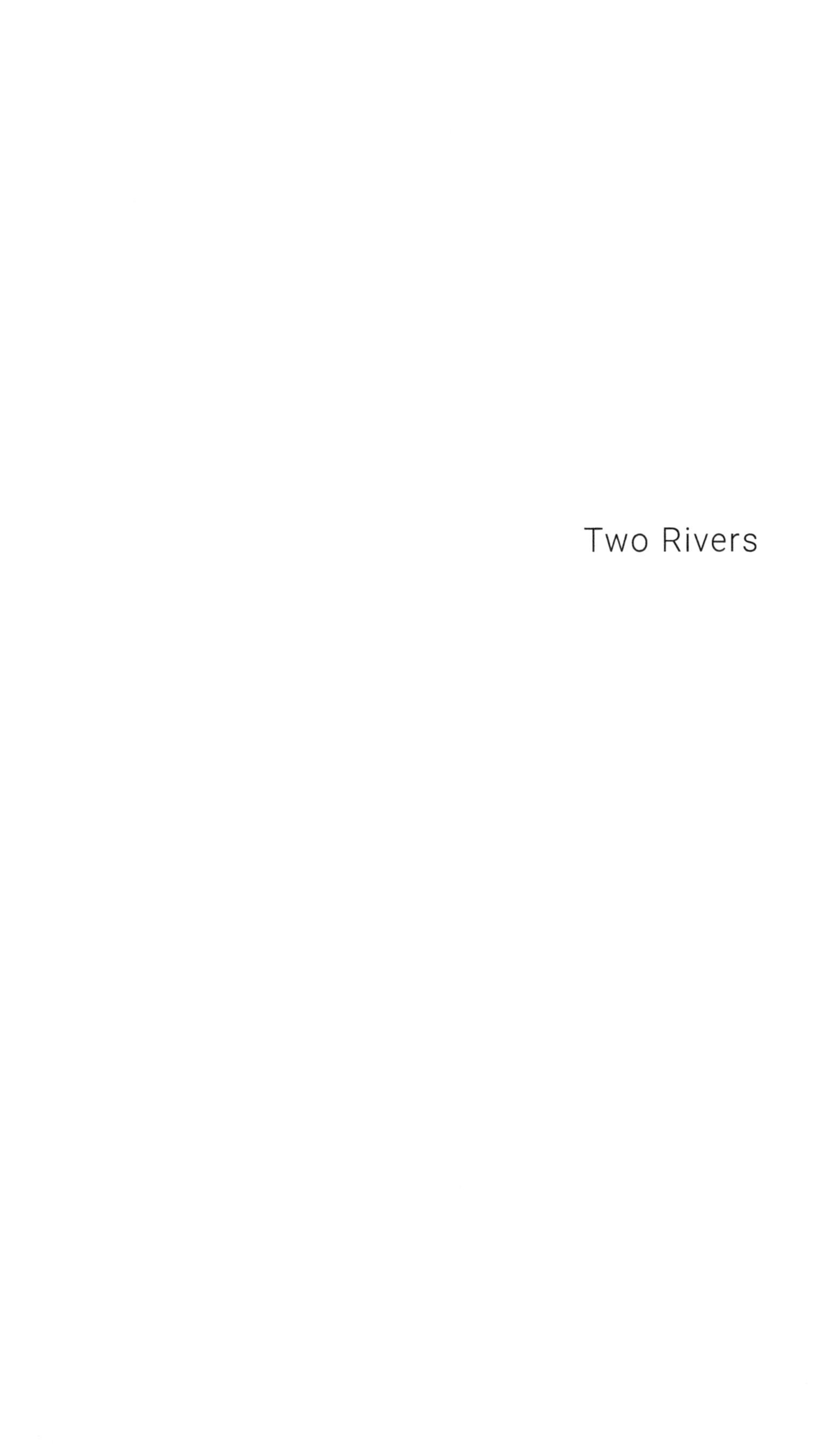

Two Rivers

Chapter 1-Rebecca

Rebecca Miles put down the wooden bucket that she carried on a stump and looked downstream at the first bright orange rays of the sun on the horizon. She always liked to get here around sunrise to get water so that she could watch the one pleasure of her day. The sun had not yet shown its bright orange face on the horizon. The sky to the east was a brilliant pink and purple while around it and along the stream, the sky and the creek and the trees were all still every shade of gray. The water lost its grayness and in the brilliance of the sun, it adorned itself with the reflection of the sky's blueness. As the rays grew brighter, the vegetation began to dress in day colors. The tree leaves put on their many pale hues of green in the young leaves, and the tree trunks were clothed in many shades of brown.

"Where are you, Rebecca?" she heard her mother calling from the cabin on the hill behind her.

"I'm coming, Mother!" she exclaimed and rushed to dip the bucket into the stream and as she did so, the hem of her skirt dipped into the water and siphoned the water onto the fabric up to her knees.

"Oh, blast it!" she declared. She pulled her dress from the water and yanked up the bucket and hurried back to the house.

"I say," her mother exclaimed as soon as she saw her daughter coming up the path. "I don't know how you can dawdle so. Winter's coming and there's so much to do, and you're out there daydreaming. Land sakes, girl how is it that every morning you end up soaked to the skin up to your knees? Now go in there by the fire and dry yourself off at the hearth while I get this last bucket of water on to boil. There's a bowl of porridge on the table if you can take the time to get your head out of the clouds long enough to eat it.

It was the middle of summer, and her mother was already talking about winter coming, but Rebecca knew better than to argue with her.

"Yes, Mama," she said.

Rebecca went into the house and stood by the fire. The heat from the fire and the cold dampness on her dress combined to form steam in the air.

"Guess who I saw a few minutes ago?" her father said as he came in the door.

"Who?"

"Your sweetheart, Isaac Thorton."

"He's not my sweetheart!"

"Ah, you don't fool me! You've been sweet on him ever since you first met him a couple of years ago."

"I ain't. . .I mean, I'm not sweet on him."

"William. . ." his wife said. "Don't tease the girl. Wash up. Your breakfast is almost ready. Rebecca, you know better than to say ain't. We may live in the woods, but we don't need to talk like heathens."

The Miles family went to the McCray farm every Sunday for the Concord neighborhood church services. Once a visiting itinerate preacher had come through. He was on his way up to Waterford from Warren but because of bad weather he was unable to continue his journey. Since it was Sunday, he went ahead and held a service for the religion starved neighbors at Concord. Most of the time, however, on all other Sundays they listened to Phillip McCray read from the Bible. Afterwards they had dinner at their own homes, but after dinner, Elizabeth McCray sat down with the children and taught them to read and write by using the Bible. She also had lessons in basic ciphering as well as in discussing the word for the week. The word for the week this past week had been "ain't" and how the children shouldn't use it because it was for ignorant people, and they weren't ignorant.

"Yes, Mother," Rebecca exclaimed.

"Is your dress dry? Did you finish your breakfast?"

"No ma'am I mean yes, ma'am. I mean yes, the dress is dry, but no, I haven't finished eating yet."

"Rebecca, you hurry and finish your breakfast and then bring the bedding out to be washed. The water in the kettle should be hot enough by then."

"Yes, ma'am." She took a bite of the porridge and swallowed and then took another bite.

As soon as her mother was out the door, she set down her wooden spoon and stared out the window.

It seemed like every day from before sunup until long after dark all there was to do for nine months of the year was work. In the morning, there were the daily chores of making the beds, sweeping the floors, helping get breakfast, and one of her jobs was getting the water from the stream. On Mondays, she had to haul even more water from the creek so that they could do the weekly clothes washing.

On Tuesdays, she had to help with the ironing which wasn't so bad in the winter, spring, or fall, but she certainly hated the heat of the old iron in the summer. Wednesdays she helped with the mending. It seemed that her father was always tearing his clothes out in the fields.

Every year it was the same. As soon as the maple trees were tapped in the spring, even before the sap stopped flowing, he was out clearing more land by first clearing out the underbrush and then cutting a ring all around the tall trees and then grubbing out around the stumps and creating hills in the black peat-rich soil around the dead trees and planting corn, squash, and beans. When that was done, it because a battle to keep the wild animals out of the gardens.

One would think that the worst problems they had would be the panthers and bears that roamed the woods, but that was not the case. They had more problems with the squirrels and the birds getting the newly planted seeds. Later, it would be the deer and raccoons feasting on the young plants. At least they wouldn't go hungry for meat. Every day, during the summer there were enough squirrels to feed every person and dog in the house.

On Thursdays. she and her mother did the churning. There weren't that many cows in the woods yet. They had one and the McCrays down the road had two along with a team of oxen. Isaac Thorton was the MvCrays' nephew, so it seemed that everyone around here had enough milk all the time during the summer. It was during the winter months that milk became scarcer. In the fall, her uncle David Miles was coming down from the Millcreek area and would bring his bull down the Indian trails and the bull would spend several days with the cows so that there would continue to be milk for everyone to drink or to churn into butter. For now, there was not so much milk available for them to sell any of their milk. First, they had to clear more of the forests, plant not only corn, beans, and squash but also some of the land in field grasses, wheat, and rye. Everyone knew that it would be many years before they could make a living at anything besides trapping or from rafting lumber downstream to Pittsburgh.

As Rebecca churned the day's milk, her mind wandered to thinking about her neighbor Isaac Thorton.

Isaac was Martha Thorton's eldest son. He was now twenty-four years old and the tallest of the brothers. He was several years older than Rebecca, but they often spent time together when they both took their cows to graze in the same pasture. Rebecca knew that it had been often whispered by other members of the families that she and Isaac would probably get married, but she didn't like the idea that her life was all planned out for her. She figured that she should have some say concerning the person she was or was not going to marry. She just might choose the traveling tin peddler if it weren't for the fact that he was thirty years her senior.

Chapter 2-Isaac

The fishing line plopped into French Creek. The small wooden bobber floated on the water as the current tried to drag it downstream. The line grew taut. The wooden bobber disappeared into the stream's muddy depths. Isaac Thorton pulled back on the fishing line attached to his bamboo pole.

He eased the line toward the shore. Within a couple of minutes, he had an average-sized bass on shore.

The fish reminded him of Rebecca Miles. Everything reminded him of Rebecca lately. Everyone around him too. They kept asking when were they going to finally tie the knot. The thought gave him a sick feeling in the pit of his stomach. The finality of it all. The idea of "death till you part" seemed like death to any dreams he had of doing anything different with his life.

Isaac added the fish to his stringer.

Thinking about Rebecca and staying here in this part of Pennsylvania made him feel like he couldn't breathe. He sucked in a breath and threw the line back into the water.

He needed to get away. There was a whole world out there and he was stuck here in this corner of Pennsylvania. He knew there was so much more to the world. Just last spring, his cousin Andrew wouldn't stop talking about going down the Mississippi River to see New Orleans. Isaac wondered what it would be like to travel downstream until they reached the ocean.

Isaac was like his father in that respect. He wanted to explore what else was out there before he settled down. Perhaps there was another woman out there who met his fancy that didn't live around here, but he would never know until he saw for himself. He didn't want to have to settle, not yet anyway.

As if thinking about Andrew made it so, Isaac saw something moving up the creek. As it grew closer, he saw the wooden boxy shape of the watercraft and then the men as they dipped their poles into the stream propelling the boat forward.

At the same time, he heard a rustle behind him. He turned to see his younger sister Mary.

"It's Cousin Andrew Mayford! I'll go tell the families!" Mary dropped the bucket she held and raced to the house.

Andrew's sister and Isaac's brother had married and lived back east. Matthew Thorton had married Lacey several years earlier after Matthew got his law degree from Harvard where he was now practicing law so in reality, they weren't actual kin, just in-laws, but since all the other cousins called him a cousin, the Thortons always called him that too.

For the past several years, every spring, before the river and creek were too shallow to navigate, Andrew always came up from Pittsburgh with supplies. He only came once per year with supplies that the McCray, Thorton, and Miles families needed. Andrew's canoe was loaded down with store goods of all kinds. These were the store goods that the families had ordered last year from Pittsburgh and intended to pay for with some of their furs.

Andrew and his boatman poled their way to the boat dock and threw the tie rope to Isaac who threw it over the pole onshore.

The families gathered at the dock. Andrew stepped up from the boat onto the dock. Greetings were shared all around.

"How was your trip?" Uncle Philip McCray asked.

Andrew turned to the older gentleman whose hair was now sprinkled with silver streaks. He shook his hand. "Everything was fine. No problems to speak of. We did have to deal with a few sandbars, but overall, the water was high enough for traveling."

"How's your mother and father," Isaac's mother Martha asked.

"They're fine. They send their best. Father has a guest from back east. We'll talk about that later. Let me show you the goods I brought."

Andrew helped the women down onto the boat deck and they went into the shed on the deck that served as the storage area for the most perishable items.

Inside were bolts of linen, needles, and thread, a couple of iron pots, and iron for Robert McCray, the community blacksmith to make tools for all the families. Andrew stepped aside and allowed them to examine what he brought. He handed the bill of lading to his Uncle Phillip who had arrived from the field.

"Who's your father's visitor from back east?" Phillip looked over the document the young man handed him.

Andrew continued speaking as family members removed most of the other items from the bottom of the boat. Soon there was just the metal in the bottom of the boat that Robert McCray would forge into metal projects to use around the neighborhood homesteads.

"Captain Meriweather Lewis is visiting," Andrew answered.

"Is that a fact? I thought he was President Jefferson's private secretary."

"He was, but the president asked him to take on a very different project. I assume he's taking advantage of Captain Lewis's experience in the military."

"Do you know what that big project is?" Phillip McCray asked.

"Well, the United States has purchased a huge tract of land from the French and the President wants him to lead an expedition into that land and explore it and report back to Washington their findings."

"Is that a fact?"

"Yes, and he's asked me to be part of the crew that will lead them down the Ohio to the Mississippi to St. Louis."

"You haven't been to St Louis, have you?"

"No, but I have been as far south as Louisville, Kentucky near where Lieutenant William Clark is stationed. That's where Captain Lewis plans to recruit most of the men that he wants to take on the expedition."

"Are they all to be military?" Isaac asked.

"I don't think so." Andrew replied. "Why do you ask? Are you thinking about coming along?"

"Well, I have gone most of the way to Louisville before," Isaac said.

"Isaac what about. . ." Martha Thorton began, but her husband, Luke put his hand on her shoulder.

"He is of an age to make up his own mind, Martha," Luke replied.

Isaac watched his mother nod in resignation. She knew that his father was right. Isaac was a lot like his father. He wasn't one to settle for civilization. He had a wild side that needed to be dealt with.

Mary, however, was not deterred. She asked her brother. "What about Rebecca?"

"I don't have to ask her for permission, Mary. We don't have any understanding."

"Understanding for what?" Isaac heard Rebecca's voice behind him.

"For anything. I was just telling them that we don't have an understanding beyond friendship."

"No, we don't," she retorted. "Is there something you want to do that I wouldn't approve of?"

He told her.

She shrugged, "Suit yourself. As you said, I have no say in the matter, but don't expect me to be waiting around for you."

"Of course not," Isaac replied.

Isaac saw his mother shake her head. He knew that she had always liked Rebecca and had expected them to marry someday.

Well, he thought. *These were no longer the days of arranged marriages. A marriage between us will not be decided by our families either. If family had been the ones who decided their marriage, I doubt that my father and mother would never have married if they had to depend on their parents to decide for them who they would marry. They were a completely unlikely couple and yet somehow their relationship works. Everyone I know married for love and I am no different.*

Isaac was going and there was nothing any of them would be able to do to stop him.

3

Chapter 5-Rebecca

He hadn't even asked me what I thought about him leaving, she thought.

Not that she cared, she thought she watched him load his bag onto Andrew's flatboat. He then picked up one of the poles and pushed the boat away from the shore. Because they were going downriver, the current quickly caught the boat and soon rounded the bend and out of sight.

At that moment she realized that her hands were fisted at her side. Disgusted with the betrayal of her true feelings, she immediately went home where her mother cooked beans for the noon meal.

Rebecca might have seemed sad to her mother because she said to her, "Don't worry. I am certain he will return."

"It doesn't matter," Rebecca took a piece of her mother's cornbread, covered it with butter, and slathered it with honey. "Whether he comes back or not is no concern of mine."

She wanted nothing more than for that to be true. She had enough to do without worrying about Isaac Thorton.

She bit into the moist bread and a little of the honey dripped onto her chin. She used her finger to wipe the sticky liquid from her chin and then took the bread with her as she went outside.

The dog days of summer had been the same for Rebecca as they had every year since she could remember. Summers were short here in north-western Pennsylvania and that meant that they had to hurry to get all the work done that had to be done before the frost killed everything in the garden and the fields.

Rebecca spent many of her days helping her mother with the pickling, jam making, and drying the apples they cut up and spread out to use in the winter for pies and other apple-rich desserts.

The only day that she wasn't working from dawn to dusk on Sunday when her strict Presbyterian father insisted that they spend the day resting in prayer and Bible reading. His prayer often looked like snoozing to Rebecca, but she wasn't going to say anything.

One Saturday afternoon in September a rider rode in on horseback along the road that meandered along the South Fork of French Creek. The horse that the man rode had a lazy movement that showed that he was in no hurry to get where he was going. As he came closer, Rebecca could see that he was a good-looking young man around Isaac's age.

"Hello, Miss," the rider said as he arrived at where Rebecca stood. "Am I nearing a settlement?"

'Yes," Rebecca answered. "Concord is just beyond that curve and that grove of trees. What brings you this way?"

"I'm traveling preacher, Miss." My name is William Christian."

His clothes were dusty, and his horse perspired from the miles he must have traveled that day. However, his hair was neatly tied back in a clean ribbon. His clothes were unusually clean, and he bore no odor of a young man on the trail for a long time.

Rebecca had seen circuit riders before. She knew that the ministry of a traveling preacher covered a large geographic region called a circuit. This circuit was distinguished by a name that was drawn from a local town, river, or other physical feature. The one in northwestern Pennsylvania was called the French Creek Circuit. She had heard from previous itinerants that circuits were also known by the length of time it took him to complete a single round. Circuits varied from two weeks to six weeks and were from 120 to over 600 miles in length, but most circuits were four weeks and from 100 to 500 miles long. Each of these regions included many communities where a minister had appointments or previous commitments to preach. The traveling preacher, on the scheduled day, appeared in the area and held a religious service. Young itinerants were encouraged to "never miss an appointment. The itinerant conducted from ten to over thirty meetings on each circuit. When a Methodist minister was appointed to a region, the Church handed him a list of "preaching places. William Christian was the new itinerant of this area.

Rebecca invited him to the house where her father sat on the porch cleaning his musket. While the two men talked and Rebecca stood by the window indoors, she listened and learned more about the young itinerate minister.

As a minister, William Christian traveled varying distances between these meetings. A Methodist leader traveled from five to nine hours many days. A traveling minister lodged with hospitable families, at taverns, or with Methodists. Sometimes a minister was treated with contempt by an entire community and was denied boarding. Reverend Christian took over this circuit because an irreligious family in western New York discovered that their guest was a Methodist preacher and asked him to leave as soon as possible. The pastor of the circuit decided that he wasn't as called as he thought he was and promptly quit.

"That's unusual," Rebecca's father said. "That type of reception was unusual. Circuit-riders are usually welcomed by citizens of this area."

During his yearly rounds, the minister became acquainted with most of the homeowners on his circuit. If a family was not saved, the Methodist itinerant· "spoke of religion" and "preached at them".

The growth in most circuits was steady but occasionally expanded rapidly through the influence of a revival. When a circuit became too large for a single minister the Church created a new circuit resulting in a loss in membership.

The Methodist Church expanded since its organization in 1784. Circuits, the scene of itinerant activity, were constantly in the process of growth, and circuit riders often experienced satisfaction when they preached and added members to the Church or founded new congregations.

"It's not pioneer work, here," Reverend Christian said. "It's not as if I am the first Methodist preacher who ever trod this soil."

Rebecca's father, though a Presbyterian, was grateful to have any religious services so he didn't mind that William Christian was a Methodist preacher.

Rebecca knew that the Methodist influence in a community became evident when the members built a church in their town. She wondered what her father would say if he were to settle in their community. A house of worship represented the acceptance of the denomination by a portion of the local population. Would he, a Presbyterian attend a Methodist church?

A long time would pass before that happened here. Only when membership increased could Methodists erect a meetinghouse. A local church didn't always need to construct a building. They simply possessed the structure of a less successful denomination. Further east, many Anglican parishes were vacated during the American Revolution.

Here in this area, Rebecca was sure that it would be a long time before Concord would be ready to open a church of any kind. In most instances, Methodists built churches in the larger communities. The pattern for construction varied according to the needs of the local congregation. Methodists raised money for churches through subscriptions. The first meetinghouse was often no larger than a cabin until the members could build a more expansive church. Sometimes they were held in abandoned barns.

There were still too many Presbyterians and Baptists and not a large enough population locally for the Methodists to have enough of a congregation to build a church. Denominational competition was a characteristic of American Christianity of this time during the early nineteenth century. Itinerants were often active participants in religious controversy. Methodists rejected products of the Enlightenment, including Deism; and they also attacked what they considered false doctrines within the Christian Churches, including Calvinism. New England circuit was where Calvinism was the predominant faith. Proselytizing was common between Methodists and members of these other groups.

Because they believed in God-sanctioned Methodism, the Methodist preachers felt justified in discarding the teachings of what they considered lesser churches.

The battleground between the denominations was the circuit. Methodist ministers became alarmed when Baptist preachers capitalized on a Methodist revival and drew new converts "into the water." Many preachers encountered problems in their dealings with this popular church. Presbyterian, Congregational, and other denominational ministers were frequently subject to Methodist attack, but William Christian tried not to do that here in Concord because he knew that Mr. Miles was a stanch Presbyterian. However, the religious faiths of this era were equally guilty of seeking converts from among the neighboring churches. William Christian admitted that he freely disputed with members of other denominations, but not here.

Like other ministers of the denomination, Reverend Christian wore conservative clothing. He carried clothing for every season and wore them according to weather conditions. Like many preachers, William Christian possessed only one suit of clothing including a shad-belly coat and a vest. Like every other Methodist preacher that Rebecca knew, Reverend Christian owned a watch, an umbrella, and a heavy overcoat for bad weather. He wore boots and owned one pair of shoes that he reserved for wearing at Sunday service. He possessed a wide-brimmed hat that protected against the weather.

Like other Methodist itinerants, though he kept his clothes clean, Reverend Christian's clothing had been exposed to the elements and as a minister, he was too poor to purchase additional articles of dress. William Christian set out poorly clad and nearly penniless on the circuit.

"My coat was worn through," he exclaimed, "and I had not a whole undergarment left. As for boots, I had none. He had patch upon patch and had a blanket with a hole in the middle in place of his overcoat."

Mama Miles, Isaac's mother Martha, and the other women of the community agreed to make William some new clothes for his meeting clothes.

He was also equipped with saddlebags. The saddlebag pockets contained his possessions including a Bible, a church hymnal, tracts, religious books, and the clothing for inclement weather.

Luke Thorton's family as well as Philip McCray's came for service that Sunday. Luke Thorton asked him, "Why did you decide to become a Methodist preacher?"

"Well, truth be told, Individuals thought me an enthusiast," he exclaimed, "because I talked so much. I just figured that if I was going to be talking, I should use it to promote the Lord's work."

Rebecca noticed that the families looked at her and wondered if this might be the young man who would ask for her hand in marriage. Rebecca wondered the same herself. She wondered what it might be like to have a preacher husband.

Since William Christian arrived, Rebecca hadn't thought about Isaac Thorton.

Chapter 6-Isaac

Isaac and the rest of Lewis's crew continued down the Ohio River. As the next two months continued, it seemed more like a vacation to Isaac than an expedition. During the next two months, Lewis and his men spent nearly a week in Cincinnati, then visited the fossil beds at Big Bone Lick, Kentucky, and reached Clarksville in Indiana Territory, where Isaac and the rest of the group met Clark and several young men from Kentucky who didn't need any convincing to come with them on the expedition.

They had arrived at Fort Massac on November eleventh where Captain Clark and other volunteers joined them. Isaac and Andrew were allowed to go up on the fort's catwalk and look down at the Ohio River. The fort site commanded a strategic view of the Ohio River. Though they were on the frontier, the area had a long and sorted history.

The Spanish explorer Hernando de Soto and his soldiers were said to have built a fort nearby as early as 1540. Maps from the early 18th century show an "Ancien Fort" ("Old Fort") near this location.

The French built Fort Massac in 1757, during the French and Indian War. The fort was originally called "Fort de L'Ascension." The name was changed in 1759, to honor of Claud Louis d'Espinchal, Marquis de Massiac, the French Naval Minister.

The fort was ceded to the British in 1763 and abandoned the next year. Chickasaw Indians soon destroyed it. In 1778, during the American Revolutionary War, Colonel George Rogers Clark, William Clark's brother, led his regiment of "Long Knives" into Illinois near the site of the fort at Massac Creek. The fort was rebuilt under the same name in 1794, during the Northwest Indian War.

On November 13, 1803, Isaac and Andrew met 27-year-old George Drouillard at Fort Massac where he had been working as an army translator. Captain Lewis hired him on the spot.

While sitting by the campfire that evening, Droullard told them about himself.

"I was born on September twenty-seventh in 1775. My father was Pierre Drouillard, a French Canadian and my mother was Shawnee. I was baptized Pierre at Church of the Assumption in Sandwich Ontario, across the Detroit River from Detroit, Michigan, but my parents never called me Pierre. Everyone calls me George."

"It doesn't bother you that I am half-Indian. Does it, Isaac?" Drouillard asked.

"Not at all, I have an older brother who is half Lenape."

"Is that a fact?" Drouillard asked.

"It certainly is. He now lives in Boston and has been trying to live that fact down by practicing law there. He's married to Andrew's sister."

"Sounds like a complicated relationship."

"Not to us it isn't," Andrew replied. "I'd like to hear more about your mother's family."

"The Shawnee people live in the Tennessee River Valley. They were three thousand strong before white settlers pushed them out, some Shawnees moved to Alabama and Georgia, and others to Pennsylvania. The northern Shawnee fought on the French side against Britain in the French and Indian War. After Britain won that war in 1763, many Shawnees moved to Quebec. Others settled west of white settlements, but left there to cross the Mississippi and settle around Cape Girardeau."

When I was young, my mother and I moved with Shawnee relatives to the Cape Girardeau area, where I grew up. She died when I was still young. My father, in 1776, married Angelique Descamps in Detroit, and I was later close to my stepsiblings in the Detroit area. Growing up around Cape Girardeau, I learned to speak Shawnee, French, English, and Plains Indian Sign, and to hunt and live off the land."

Isaac spoke to him in French and then also in Shawnee.

"You speak my native tongues well, I see," George replied. "I now understand why they brought you along. How about you, Andrew."

"Me? No, I'm just along for the company. I came this far with Captain Lewis because he was heading to the Mississippi. I plan to go to New Orleans or Natchez or somewhere downriver. I do speak a little French though."

"So, what brought you to Fort Massac?"

"I have been working for Captain Daniel Bissell."

"What made you decide to come with us?" Isaac asked.

"Captain Lewis is paying me twenty-five dollars per month. He paid me thirty dollars in advance to catch up my account with Mr. William Swan."

The next day, Captain Lewis gave Douillard his first assignment to go to Southwest Point, Tennessee, and escort soldiers who had volunteered for the Corps of Discovery to wherever the Corps would decide to set up camp around St. Louis.

The next day, Captain Lewis hired another man named Richard Warfington. He stood five feet ten inches tall, had brown hair and black eyes, and had a fair complexion.

"So where are you from?" Isaac asked him as they shared a meal that evening.

"I was born in Louisburg, North Carolina, and joined the U.S. Army in 1799."

After hiring Droullard and Richard Warfington, the now enlarged group continued down the Ohio River. Captain Lewis wasn't feeling well so he took a dose of pills which contained ten grains of calomel and fifteen grains of jalap provided by Dr. Benjamin Rush. He gave him the medications back in Philadelphia before Captain Lewis went to Pittsburgh where Captain Lewis purchased equipment for the expedition.

On November 14, the newly formed Corps of Discovery members arrived at a great chain of rocks that stretched across the Ohio River. They had reached the river's mouth. Those rocks indicated the ending of the river

A settlement of gravel, sand, silt, and clay formed a delta. As the men entered the mouth, the oarsmen directed the boat to the right side of the river where the water was slow and deep. This marked the beginning of the next stage of the expedition.

At this junction sat the military installation of Wilkinson-Ville. The settlement was established about 1787 as an outpost of Fort Massac.

That evening the expedition camped on the point between the Ohio and Mississippi Rivers. Lewis and his group had already rowed, poled, dragged, and occasionally sailed their boats a total of 981 miles in 76 days, including rest stops

Now major changes were to be made in the group. On November 18, the captains ordered the group to cross to the west bank of the Mississippi. Andrew would soon be leaving the group to travel down the Mississippi.

Captain Lewis started teaching Captain Clark how to use the equipment to make celestial observations to determine latitudes and longitudes. Captain Lewis had learned this skill from Andrew Ellicott and Robert Patterson back in Pennsylvania, and now he was teaching Captain Clark Their calculations were incorrect, but Clark, with some previous experience in surveying, "made a partial survey of the point"—a surveyor's "station"—and measured the widths of the two rivers.

"You seem to know this area pretty well," Isaac said to Captain Clark.

"I was here three different times back in the 1790s and in 1795 I even drew a map of the confluence." Captain Clark said.

"Which is why you, William Clark, are my top choice for this mission," Captain Lewis replied.

"My brother George built a fort four miles down the Mississippi from here," Captain Clark said. "My family knows this area very well."

"Is the fort still there?" Isaac asked.

"I believe there are some remains of it," replied Captain Clark.

"I wish we could check it out," Isaac said. He knew that Andrew was heading downriver, and Isaac wanted to be with him for as long as possible.

"I would love to see the place too," said Captain Clark. "Let's go!"

"I don't see why not," replied Captain Lewis. "It isn't that far. Who would like to come with us? It will give us a chance to work with some of our equipment some more."

The two captains and eight men paddled a canoe along with Andrew and his boatman's boat down the Mississippi to the abandoned post, Fort Jefferson.

"I have so many memories of this place," Clark said as he jumped from the bow of the boat and stepped onto the shore when they reached the fort built by his brother in 1780 three miles south of the mouth of the Ohio River on the Mississippi.

"My brother prophesied in 1779 that a fort in this area would become a trading center on the American river system," Captain Clark said. "It's a good thing he wasn't an Old Testament prophet because he would have been stoned."

"Why didn't the fort succeed?" Isaac asked.

"Patrick Henry, the governor of Virginia at the time, made the initial proposal for a fortification on the mouth of the Ohio in 1777, in a letter to the Spanish governor of Louisiana, Bernardo de Galvez.'

"Spanish, I thought that Louisiana was owned by the French," Andrew said.

"Yes, the French owned it, then the Spanish owned it and then the French owned it again, and now, thanks to the Louisiana Purchase, we own it."

"I see. So, what happened to the fort?"

"Patrick Henry proposed the fortification to protect trade and supplies between Virginia and Spanish Louisiana from British interference. Henry proposed this idea to my brother, who saw it as a fortification for frontier protection and conquest of British Indian allies. He later pressed Henry's successor, Thomas Jefferson, on the importance of a fort along both rivers, to control commerce and stop British supplies. In January of 1780, Mr. Jefferson formally approved the fort with the formal stipulation that the land must be purchased from the Chickasaws, who erroneously identified as Cherokees. Jefferson also wrote to Joseph Martin that the ground at the mouth of the Ohio River on the south side belonged to the Cherokee, and we would not meddle without their leave. My brother ignored this provision, as he would not buy the land from the Chickasaws or gain their consent to build the fortifications. This fort was built just north of Mayfield Creek. His miscalculation and disregard of the Chickasaw doomed the project to failure."

"Oh, I get it. The Chickasaw became a major problem."

"Indeed, they did. In 1782, four Chickasaw chiefs sent a letter to American military post commanders in the west to open peace negotiations, stating 'What damage was done by reason you settled a fort in our hunting ground without our leave and at that place you suffered most from us'". The Chickasaw eventually signed a peace treaty with the Spanish that respected Chickasaw territorial integrity but kept them at war with the Kickapoo."

"So, the Chickasaw finally agreed to a treaty?"

Well, yes, but this fort was isolated from the rest of civilization so there were logistical problems, and the inhabitants were unable to get supplies when they needed them because Indians stole those supplies. Many of the people ended up sick and starving. The fort was abandoned after a Chickasaw siege fourteen months after it was built."

As the members of the expedition floated closer to the site, they could see from the river the remains of the blockhouse of the old fort. They pulled the canoe onto the bank and then tied Andrew's flatboat onto a nearby tree. They fought their way through the overgrown brush to the block house's location.

The old fort consisted of the charred remains of a blockhouse and charred wooden fort walls. The walls were broken down and rotted.

The Chickasaw burned most of the buildings, but a couple that hadn't burned still stood. Their roofs were rotted and caving in and small fast-growing trees were already growing up through their roofs.

After they looked around the fort, they made their way back to the river and the boats.

"Well, I guess this is goodbye, my friends," Andrew said as he reached the shoreline.

"I guess it is," Isaac said. Suddenly he felt alone, probably more alone than he ever felt in his life. His only connection with the family was now going to parts unknown. "Will I ever see you again?"

"It's very possible," Andrew replied. "It's hard to keep members of our family separated for too long."

Isaac thought about how his father had been separated from the family for many years only to stumble upon his younger sister, Elizabeth, at Valley Forge. Blood did seem to be a magnet for anyone within the clan.

"Good luck to you, cousin," Isaac said and offered his arm to Andrew.

Andrew grabbed Isaac by the elbow and the two of them embraced.

"Good luck to you too, my friend," Andrew replied. "Now don't get yourself shot by any Indians. Do you hear? Your mother would never forgive me for talking you into going on this trip!"

Isaac chuckled. "You don't have to worry about me. Good luck."

Andrew nodded. "Just take care, you here?"

Isaac nodded and watched Andrew get into his boat. Andrew and his boatman poled away from the shore. As soon as they were out in the current, they stopped poling and allowed the boat to drift down the Mississippi. Andrew stood at the end of the boat and the boys kept their eyes on one another until Andrew's boat rounded the first bend in the river.

Isaac blinked away tears in his eyes and felt tightness in his throat.

Would he ever see his cousin again? He had heard the rumors of highwaymen and hostile natives along the southern end of the Mississippi. They could be trouble for Andrew.

Andrew's parting brought to him for the first time the idea that he too was going into the unknown. Would he ever see any of his own family again? There were, of course, potentially dangerous natives, and there were also unknown animals that could attack and kill him as well.

Isaac pursed his lips with determination. He would not let anyone see the tears that dampened his eyes and threatened to spill out onto his face.

"I guess we had better be going as well," Isaac said. He stepped back into the boat and grabbed his oar. The other men followed him in and the group of them headed back upstream to their camp. They returned to the camp opposite the Missouri side of the Mississippi

Isaac knew that it wouldn't do him any good to dwell on his homesickness. He threw himself into the activities of the camp.

The men spent the days hunting and fishing for their daily meat while the captains continued learning how to use their equipment to determine coordinates that they would need to use over the course of the trip. This was a good place to practice because the coordinates were already known. Lewis taught Clark what he knew about the equipment, and they studied their location on the eastern side of the Mississippi.

Isaac noticed that the captains developed a daily routine that involved obtaining their compass course readings that indicated the estimated distance on each course. This assisted Clark in mapping and might have been intended to assist future travelers, Isaac didn't know. Courses other than due north, south, east, or west were expressed by the number of degrees the course varied from either due north or due south. The bearing was taken with one of the three pocket compasses that Captain Lewis purchased from Whitney, as well as his plain surveying compass. Lewis and then Clark took a bearing at the beginning of this specific course, sighting on the point for which they were headed and then they sighted back at the end of a course toward the point at which it began. One thing Isaac did know was that the captains' distances were still just estimates.

On his boat, Lewis carried a brass sextant, like many of his scientific instruments. He purchased the sextant from Thomas Whitney of Philadelphia. He also carried a special case in which he carried "Arnold's" chronometer, of the most improved English construction that he purchased from Philadelphia watchmaker Thomas Parker.

On the western side of the Mississippi, they found a Shawnee and Lenape camp. The Lenape that Lewis encountered here was a splinter group that had left the main body in Ohio in 1789. This group had followed some Shawnees across the Mississippi to the Cape Girardeau region. They were part of the Absentee Shawnee, a group that supported peace during the American Revolution and began moving in small groups to the Cape Girardeau region in the 1780s. Both tribes had received land grants from the Spanish administration in 1793.

The Shawnee greeted them and offered a place at their campfire.

"You look familiar," one of the older chiefs said to Isaac.

"I am told that I look like my father when he was young," Isaac replied.

"And who was your father?" the Shawnee asked.

Isaac spoke to the man in the Shawnee tongue. "My father was Head of Stone and helped negotiate with the Shawnee and Lenape back at Fort Pitt."

"Ah, yes, I remember your father. I remember your uncle too. Philip McCray. That was his name. Wasn't it? "

Isaac nodded. "You are correct. Philip McCray is my uncle. Both are as grey-haired and strong as you are and doing well."

One of these Shawnee took a special interest in Seaman, Lewis' dog. He called the dog to him and gave him a piece of jerky.

"Fine dog. I would gladly pay three beaver skins for him," he said.

Lewis shook his head and patted the dog on the head. "I won't sell Seaman for any price. I bought him for his abilities. I am certain that be an asset during this journey."

Isaac also knew that Captain Lewis didn't want his dog to end up on the Shawnee fire's spit at dinner time. The Indian would be shocked to know how much Captain Lewis had spent on the animal. He was more valuable monetarily than the three beaver skins the man was offering.

Captains Lewis and Clark checked out the sand bar at the mouth of the Ohio and found a willow growing in its center.

"What an excellent location for a fort on this side of the Mississippi. It's very defensible. I can see up the Ohio many miles and up and down the Mississippi."

Isaac found George Shannon down by the Mississippi fishing.

"Where did you get the pole?" Isaac asked.

"There is a stand of bamboo up past that oak tree," George pointed as he flipped the tip of the pole. "Do you think you'll catch. . ." before Isaac got out asking if George thought he could catch something, something pulled hard on his line.

Other members of the camp came to the shore to watch George struggle with his pole and line. George fought it for a good half hour before he brought in a catfish, the biggest that Isaac had ever seen."

"That fish is big enough to feed the entire camp tonight!" Isaac exclaimed.

"With some to dry for the future," Captain Clark replied. "That was some good fishing, George."

They gorged on George's catfish that night. What they didn't eat, they cut up and dried the meat over a smoky fire.

After exploring the area for a couple of days, on the twentieth, they started up the Mississippi. Since Captain Lewis was certain that Captain Clark knew what he was doing, Captain Clark took over the responsibility of keeping track of the daily measurements of the river and the weather. Captain Lewis continued writing about the flora and fauna that they observed.

That morning, John Colter killed a heath hen, and they made soup of it for their noon meal. It tasted like chicken. After lunch, they arrived at Tywappity Bottom where a man dressed in buckskins waved them down.

"We don't get a lot of people on this part of the river going upriver this time of year," the man said. "What brings you up this way? My name is Findley, John Findley. I own one of these houses here."

"We're glad to meet you," Captain Lewis spoke for the group. "How strong is your community?"

There are fifteen families in our settlement." Mr. Findley replied.

"The settlement seems extremely close to the river. "Don't you ever worry about the river flooding in the spring?"

"No, we haven't had trouble with flooding so far. The river bottom here seldom overflows. At least it hasn't during the four years since we arrived here."

Isaac looked around. Poplar and white oak grew on the land on both sides of the river. This was the first poplar or white oak they had seen since they started up the Mississippi River. No cane grew near the river.

The banks abound with sand rush which grew much thicker than Isaac had yet seen. Captain Clark measured one of the stalks and it measured over eight 8 feet in length. It rose in a single stem without branch or leaf and according to the boat's pilot, the rushes stayed deep green throughout the winter. Both horses and cows seemed to thrive on it.

The fact that the bank on the opposite side of the river was lower than this side might have explained why the Findley settlement didn't flood.

The Corps of Discovery spent the evening visiting the Findley community and continued upstream the following morning.

More boats traveled on this part of the Mississippi than Isaac had anticipated despite what Mr. Findley had said, but they were all moving downriver.

Nathaniel Pryor, one of the new men Clark hired in Kentucky had gone out to hunt but had not yet returned to the expedition, even though they shot several guns to let him know how to locate the boats. Nathaniel still had not shown up after seven the next morning,

Captain Clark frowned and shook his head. "He knows the area and knows where we're going. He's bound to catch up with us sooner or later."

They landed at Cape Girardeau that afternoon. The settlement was named after Jean Baptiste de Girardot, who established a temporary trading post in the area around 1733. He had been a French soldier stationed at Kaskaskia between 1704 and 1720 in the French colony of La Louisiane. The "Cape" in the city name referred to a rock promontory overlooking the Mississippi River. As early as 1765 this bend in the Mississippi River had been referred to as Cape Girardot or Cape Girardeau.

At Cape Girardeau, Captain Lewis visited the commandant. He delivered letters of introduction from Captain Daniel Bissell. Isaac and George Shannon accompanied him on the visit.

Captain Lewis knocked at the front door of the commandant's home and a servant answered the door.

"No," he said, "the master is not home. He is at the racetrack."

The servant then gave directions to the track.

Captain Lewis sent George Shannon with orders to the company to set up camp to spend the night at a point just two miles upriver at Old Cape Girardeau.

Captain Lewis threw up his hands. "Well, Isaac, I guess that means we're going to the racetrack. I must put my credentials in his hands directly!"

Isaac continued to the racetrack with Captain Lewis. When they arrived at the racetrack, they found the commandant watching the drama by the track.

One fellow dressed in buckskins held the bridle of a black horse and was arguing with the judges. Another man stood nearby.

"My horse won that race. I was ahead of that other rider!" He exclaimed.

The fat judge shook his head. "I'm sorry. That's not the way that we saw it."

"Look, I know I won! My wife would kill me if she found out that I bet our best horse on a bet!"

The skinny judge with Franklin glasses handed him a bill sale. "We're sorry, but you knew what you were doing."

"I know I won and I'm taking his horse as payment for the bet."

"Oh, no you ain't!" the other man threw up his fists into a boxing stance. "I won that race."

This second man must have been the first man's competitor.

A crowd gathered as the two men started their session of the competition.

Isaac looked over at Captain Lewis and the captain shrugged.

"It is not unusual for the people at the track to be disorderly. Most of these participants—both riders and bystanders—were from Kentucky and Tennessee. They were men of desperate fortunes, but little too loose either character or property. They bet higher than most could afford."

"It certainly doesn't seem like a wise decision. Does it?"

"Well, these Westerners are a different lot, you must admit. It is not unusual for them to risk half or even all their personal property on a single wage. Their property, of course, is mostly just horses and cattle. No one around here has cash to speak of."

The commandant came to meet them. The commandant and Captain Lewis shook hands.

"How did you do?" Lewis asked the commandant.

"My horse lost the race, but I thought I would be alright when you consider that I had several other bets on other horses that I made. Today has been especially rough. On four horses I lost $200." The commandant waved off his losses with cheerfulness.

The Commandant Louis Lorimier was a man about five foot eight inches tall with dark skin, hair, and eyes.

"Ah, I'll get it back next time. Let's just watch the rest of these races."

They continued to watch the races. The commandant's son won a bet on another race for $600.

As the four men walked away from the racing grounds, Captain Lewis asked Commandant Lorimier, "How long has this settlement been in existence?"

"The settlement began eight years earlier and of that time the past two years were spent under the Spanish government. We already have a population of over one thousand people. The Spanish government let us use acreage based on family size. They called it head rights. The land was surveyed and recorded by the commandant's clerk. To be considered as owning the land, each family's claim had to be confirmed by the Crown of Spain. That was a requirement for gaining title."

"Have you lived around this area long?"

The commandant nodded, "I was once a trader with the Shawnee and Delaware. In the year 1781 a party under the command of General George Rogers Clark, of Kentucky, your second in command's brother, I believe."

"Yes." Captain Lewis nodded.

"That party burnt my store which stood at the mouth of a small creek a branch of the East branch of the Great Miami of the Ohio. I would think he would remember this. This branch formed one point in the boundary line between the Northwestern tribes and the U.S. made with them at Greeneville by General Wayne in 1795."

He further explained that the settlement of Girardeau dated back to 1793 when the Spanish government, which had acquired Louisiana in 1764 following the French defeat in the Seven Years' War, granted Louis Lorimier, a French-Canadian, the right to establish a trading post. This gave him trading privileges and a large tract of land surrounding his post. Lorimier was made commandant of the district and prospered from land sales and trade with the native peoples, such as the Ozark Bluff Dwellers and the Mississippian people.

"Is that so," Lewis replied. "What would you say your property's value was?"

"My property loss was valued at about twenty thousand dollars. This broke me as a merchant."

Lewis and Isaac looked around at the Commandant's large estate. The captain looked up at the commandant's house on the hill.

"It appears that you have entirely recovered your losses and are a man of very considerable property."

"Indeed, I have been blessed recently."

Lewis looked at Lorimier's hair. The man was sixty years old and had a head of wavy hair with scarcely a grey hair. His hair was black as ebony and was down to his knees and thick. His hair was kept in place by a leather girdle around his waist as was custom for Canadian traders. "I'd bet you once had a great mane."

"You would have won that bet," Lorimier informed him. "Once it was so long that it touched the ground when I stood up."

"Not that it's not magnificent now," Captain Lewis deepened the compliment.

"I'll tell, you what," Commandant Lorimier said. "How about if you come with me to the house and meet the family? I'm certain the wife has a fantastic meal ready."

Captain Lewis agreed.

They went on up to the house, and a woman opened the door.

"This is my wife, Susanna," Lorimier said.

Mrs. Lorimier was a Shawnee woman, but from her complexion, she was half-blooded only. Isaac guessed that she had been a very handsome woman when she was young. She was dressed in Shawnee leggings and moccasins but wore a linen dress and a jacket with long sleeves which was in a style worn by French-Canadian women.

The Lorimiers had a large family of very handsome children. Three were in their teens. Among these children was Louis Jr., a trader like his father, the one who had won the six hundred dollars in the horse race. His sons Auguste Bougainville and William had received appointments to West Point, and then Isaac saw Agatha, the Lorimiers' teenage daughter.

He was stunned by her beauty, this daughter of Lorimier was beautiful even though she wore plain but stylish clothes as were common in the East among the middle class.

The commandant encouraged Lewis and Isaac to stay for supper which they did. The lady of the house served the meal. They all enjoyed Mrs. Lorimier's roasted venison and vegetables.

"So, how far does this district extend?" Isaac asked as Mrs. Lorimier served the meal.

"The district extends from the grand bend of the Mississippi to the Apple River. The settlement extends back sixty miles as far as the St. Francis River. Sixteen miles west of Cape Girardeau is another settlement of German-Swiss and North Carolinians of German descent who settled along the Whitewater River. I think you would like them. They are sober, temperate laborious, and honest people. They erected two grist mills and a sawmill in an area where the population increases almost daily."

Lorimier's son Aguste Bougainville took Captain Lewis and Isaac to Old Cape Girardeau which was three miles upstream.

Isaac was disappointed that this was considered the frontier. He found it hard to believe that this community was so far from the hustle and bustle of the cities of the east. It didn't seem as wild as where he grew up in western Pennsylvania.

Thinking about home reminded him of Rebecca. What was she doing now? Was she thinking about him like he was thinking of her or had she moved on and met someone who kept her from thinking about him?

When Captain Lewis and Isaac returned to camp, they found the men had set up camp, but Captain Clark was very ill. Not only was Captain Lewis in charge of the expedition, but he was also the camp doctor. He went to care for Captain Clark, and Isaac went to join the other men at the campfire. Sergeant Charles Floyd immediately asked him to share with them what he had seen in Cape Girardeau.

On November twenty-fourth, Nathaniel Pryor who had been absent and lost for the last two days was found wandering along the river. He was exhausted from his wanderings but otherwise fine. They continued northward on the Mississippi.

They arrived in Kaskaskia on the twenty-ninth of November and in preparation for traveling to St. Louis, Lewis left Clark in charge of the boat. He did not take Isaac with him this time. Lewis remained there until December 5 when he took a horse back to Cahokia, while Clark and the party moved onto Cahokia.

December 6 and 7 were dark and dreary and a continual cold rain made everything miserable. Late on the seventh, they set out for St. Louis. Clark told them that the town was just two and a half miles upstream. The party would remain at Cahokia until Lewis finished his business in St. Louis.

Lewis rejoined the party on the ninth. He had gone to St. Louis and visited with the Spanish Commandant Carlos Dehault Delassus, lieutenant governor of Upper Louisiana. The Commandant would not grant permission to ascend the Missouri without permission from his superiors. Having already decided to winter at Wood River and knowing that the region would be transferred to the United States in the next few weeks, they ignored the commandant's reservations and continued northward toward their winter camp.

They passed St. Louis, the capital of Spanish Upper Louisiana on December 10. The village was not quite forty years old but was already the center of the fur trade for a huge region drained by the Missouri River. Although the town was not founded until France had lost control of Louisiana to Spain, it was essentially French in language and culture and the French fur magnates dominated St. Louis. Of course, after the American takeover, that would no doubt change.

St. Louis was founded on February 14, 1764, Pierre Laclede Liguest sent René Auguste Chouteau, regarded as his foster son, across the Mississippi with a party of workers to begin construction of the post, named for Louis IX, king of France, who had been canonized for his part in the Crusades. By the end of that year, forty families had settled in the new village, including many French people from east of the river unwilling to live under British rule. Later, under the Spanish government, the officials were residents, ethnically French, and the French fur trade dominated the economy. The Spanish withdrew Laclede's monopoly and competitors rushed in, but the founder still prospered. In May 1780, the Spanish garrison and the townspeople beat off a British-directed Indian attack, part of the western operations of the American Revolution. By 1799, the town had a population of 925, and by 1803, the population was just over a thousand inhabitants.

Winter was upon the expedition. A strong northwest wind blew during the night of December 11. Isaac could smell the snow in the air. Under frigid conditions, they set out the morning of December 12 at the usual time and passed the head of the island on which they had camped the night.

On the opposite side of the river from their camp, the mouth of a creek flowed into the Missouri. This Creek was called Wood River. Immediately after they passed the landing, the wind increased to a storm with wind, snow, and hail. Just in time, they had arrived at their winter camp's location on Wood River.

Soon after they landed, two canoes of Potawatomi Indians camped up on the other side and landed, formed their camp and three of them in small canoes came across when the waves were so high and the wind blowing fiercely that the group expected the canoes would fill with water or turn over, but it didn't. When the Indians arrived, they were all drunk, but their canoes had no water in them.

Captain Lewis sent hunters out to hunt. Soon the hunters returned with game including turkey and possum, enough to feed them meat for the next couple of days. They reported that the country was beautiful and loaded with game.

Separating Fact from Fiction

Much of what I have written about the Corps of Discovery, more commonly known as the Lewis and Clark Expedition, came directly from the journals written by Meriweather Lewis and William Clark as well as other members of the expedition. However, like any decent novelist, I have taken a few liberties in the details. I was going to separate the various players in this part of the book, but I realized that instead, it should be written as a single long story of who these people were and their contribution to The Corps of Discovery.

Jefferson wanted this expedition because they had newly acquired the Louisiana Purchase in 1803 and he wanted to get an accurate sense of this new land and its resources. He also hoped to find a "direct and practicable water communication across this continent, for the purposes of commerce with Asia". He placed special importance on declaring U.S. sovereignty over the Native Americans along the Missouri River. Lewis and Clark did well in their diplomacy with them.

When Jefferson began to plan for the expedition Lewis was his first choice to lead the expedition. Lewis' personally chose William Clark for his second-in-command. When he reached Kentucky, Lewis recruited Clark, then 33 years old, to share command of the expedition.

This real expedition was considered one of the most important expeditions ever conducted by Americans. The first part of the group left Pittsburgh, Pennsylvania with Meriwether Lewis on August 31, 1803, and met up with Captain William Clark in the fall of 1803.

Meriweather Lewis had joined the Virginia militia, and in 1794 was sent part of a detachment that was involved in putting down the Whiskey Rebellion that we witnessed in In the Shadow of the Mill Pond, Book V of the Locket Saga. In 1795, Lewis joined the United States Army. By 1800, he rose to captain and ended his service there in 1801.

On April 1, 1801, Lewis was appointed as Secretary to the President by President Thomas Jefferson, whom he knew through Virginia society in Albemarle County. As Jefferson's president, Lewis lived in the presidential mansion, and frequently spoke with prominent political figures along with men of the arts and scientific circles. He compiled information on the personnel and politics of the United States Army, which had seen an influx of Federalist officers made by outgoing president John Adams in 1801.

Though Isaac, my main character, did not go all the way to the Pacific, the Corps of Discovery continued their exploration. After crossing the Rocky Mountains, the expedition reached Oregon (which was disputed land beyond the Louisiana Purchase) and the Pacific Ocean in November 1805. They returned in 1806, bringing with them an immense amount of information about the region as well as numerous plant and animal specimens.

In 1807, Jefferson appointed Lewis as governor of the Louisiana Territory, and he settled in St. Louis. On September 3, 1809, Lewis set out for Washington, D.C. He hoped to resolve issues regarding the denied payment of drafts he had drawn against the War Department while serving as governor of the Upper Louisiana Territory, leaving him in potentially ruinous debt. Lewis carried his journals with him for delivery to his publisher. He intended to travel by ship to Washington from New Orleans but changed his plans while floating down the Mississippi River from St. Louis. He disembarked and decided instead to make an overland journey via the Natchez Trace, the old pioneer road between Natchez, Mississippi, and Nashville, Tennessee and then east to Washington. Lewis had written his will before his journey and had attempted suicide on this journey but had been restrained. Lewis died of a gunshot wound on October 11, 1809, at the Grinders Stand tavern 70 miles south of Nashville. It is unsure to this day whether it was suicide or murder because those close to him knew that Lewis was clinically depressed. Upon hearing the news neither William Clark nor Jefferson questioned the coroner's report that Lewis died of suicide.

The second in command in The Corps of Discovery, William Clark was born on August 1, 1770. A native of Virginia, he grew up in pre-statehood Kentucky. He was the younger brother of General George Rogers Clark, William had served in the Army for four years, participating in the campaigns of General Anthony Wayne in the Northwest Territory before resigning his commission in 1796 to attend to the family business. Because of the Army seniority system, Clark received a second lieutenant's commission instead of a captaincy when he rejoined the military as Lewis's second-in-command. But he and Lewis concealed this from the members of the expedition, who always referred to him as Captain Clark. Along with Meriwether Lewis, Clark successfully led the Lewis and Clark Expedition of 1804–1806 across the Louisiana Purchase to the Pacific Ocean.

After the expedition, he settled in what became the state of Missouri. There, he served in the militia and as governor of the Missouri Territory. After Missouri statehood, from 1822 until his death in 1838, he served as Superintendent of Indian Affairs. He was a planter and slaveholder. He died September 1, 1838.

Not including the infant Jean Baptiste Charbonneau and Lewis' dog Seaman, George Shannon, born in 1785, was the youngest member of the Lewis and Clark Expedition. He was born in Pennsylvania and joined the Corps of Discovery in August 1803, as one of the men from Pittsburgh recruited by Lewis as the captain waited for the completion of the voyage's vessels there.

During the expedition, Shannon got lost on two occasions. The first incident was dramatized in his book and occurred on August 26, 1804, when he was sent to retrieve two pack horses. He was separated from the party for sixteen days and nearly starved. He went without food for twelve days except for some grapes and rabbits. At first, he thought he was behind the expedition, so he sped up thinking he could catch up. Then, getting hungry, he went downstream to look for a trading party he could stay with. Finally, John Colter was sent to find him.

Shannon got lost again August 6, 1805, at Three Forks. He had been sent to explore one of the forks. He rejoined the party after three days by backtracking to the forks and following the trail of the others.

In 1807, he was with a party led by Nathaniel Pryor that was attempting to return the Mandan chief Big White to his people. He was wounded in an encounter with the Arikara and lost a leg. For this, he received a government pension.

Three years later, he assisted in Nicholas Biddle's history of the expedition. Still later, Clark asked him to join a fur trading enterprise, but Shannon chose to study law instead. By 1818 he began his law practice in Lexington, Kentucky, and later ran for senator from Missouri. He was buried in Palmyra, Missouri in 1836.

Though a member of the Corps of Discovery, John Colter is best remembered for explorations he made during the winter of 1807–1808 after the expedition ended, when he became the first known person of European descent to enter the Yellowstone and to see the Teton Mountain Range. Colter spent months alone in the wilderness and is widely considered to be the first known mountain man.

John Colter, along with George Shannon (and our main character Isaac) joined the expedition while Lewis was waiting for their vessels to be completed in Pittsburgh and nearby Elizabeth, Pennsylvania. The skills he had developed from this frontier lifestyle impressed Meriwether Lewis, and on October 15, 1803, Lewis offered Colter the rank of private and a pay of five dollars per month when he joined the expedition.

As noted in our story, the expedition arrived at the Mississippi River in November and in December established its 1803-04 winter camp at Wood River, north of St. Louis. While Lewis and Clark were away from camp preparing for the journey, Colter and three other recruits disobeyed Lewis' orders and left camp to find whiskey. When they returned, Lewis disciplined Colter and the others with ten days' confinement. Soon thereafter, Colter was court-martialed because he threatened to shoot Sergeant John Ordway. After a review of the situation, Colter apologized and promised to reform. He was reinstated.

He turned out to be one of the best hunters in the expedition and often went out hunting alone. He had an uncanny ability to locate passes through the Rocky Mountains and a knack for bartering with various tribes. This attribute earned him his later role with Manuel Lisa.

Always healthy, he was often one of the few hunters allowed to leave the camp during periods of illness and recuperation. In an event that saved the expedition, Colter encountered Tushepaw Flatheads and through non-verbal peace communications was able to persuade them to abandon their search for two Shoshone who had stolen twenty-three head of horses and get one of them to help the expedition locate and accompany them to the Snake River, Columbia River, and subsequently the Pacific Ocean. Once at the mouth of the Columbia River, Colter was among a small group selected to venture to the shores of the Pacific Ocean, as well as explore the seacoast north of the Columbia into present-day Washington state.

After traveling thousands of miles, in 1806 the expedition returned to the Mandan villages in present-day North Dakota. There, they encountered Forest Hancock and Joseph Dickson, two frontiersmen who were headed into the upper Missouri River country in search of beaver furs. On August 13, 1806, Lewis and Clark permitted Colter to be honorably discharged almost two months early so that he could lead the two trappers back to the region they had explored.

Colter, Hancock, and Dixon ventured into the wilderness with traps, ammunition, and small tools gifted to them by the expedition such as knives, rope, hatchets, and personal utensils. The route of this trapping party is not known. It is speculated that unfriendly Blackfeet in the region of the Lower Missouri and a lack of horses forced the company to seek their fortunes in the tributaries of the less-prosperous

Yellowstone Valley, a region inhabited by the friendlier Crows. The partnership lasted only two months. Colter and Hancock had a falling out with Dixon in the winter of 1806-07 at Three Forks, Montana.

Colter was back in civilization in 1807 near the mouth of the Platte River when he encountered Manuel Lisa, a founder of the Missouri Fur Trading Company. Manuel was leading a party, including several former members of the Lewis and Clark Expedition, towards the Rocky Mountains. Among them were George Drouillard, John Potts, and Peter Weiser. Colter decided to return to the wilderness, even though he had spent just a week from St. Louis. At the junction of Yellowstone and Bighorn Rivers, Colter helped build Fort Raymond. Lisa later sent Colter to search out the Crow Indian tribe to discover opportunities to establish trade with them.

Colter left Fort Raymond in October 1807 and established trade with the Crow nation. Over the winter, he explored what would become the Yellowstone and Grand Teton National Parks. He explored Jackson Hole below the Teton Range, later crossing Teton Pass into Pierre's Hole, known today as the Teton Basin in Idaho. After heading north and then east. He returned to Fort Raymond in March or April 1808.

The following year, in 1808, Colter traveled with John Potts into the region near Three Forks, Montana to negotiate trade agreements with local nations. While leading a group of Flathead and Crow Indians back to the trading fort, Colter's party was attacked by Blackfeet. The Flatheads and Crows managed to force the Blackfeet into retreat, but Colter suffered a leg wound from either a bullet or arrow. This wound was not serious because Colter quickly recuperated and left Fort Raymond with Potts again the next year.

In 1809, another altercation with the Blackfeet resulted in Colter's capture and Potts' death. They encountered several hundred Blackfeet who demanded they come ashore. Potts was killed, but Colter went ashore, and was disarmed and stripped naked. After a council, Colter was told to literally run for his life and was pursued by a large pack of young braves. Though a fast runner, after several miles the naked Colter was exhausted and bleeding from his nose but far ahead of most of the group with only one assailant still close to him. He then managed to overcome the lone man. Colter killed the brave with the brave's own spear. Colter took the brave's blanket and continue running until he reached the Madison River. He hid in a beaver lodge to escape capture. He traveled at night for eleven days until he reached a trader's fort on the Little Big Horn.

In 1810, Colter returned to Three Forks to help construct a fort. After two of his partners were killed by the Blackfeet, Colter left the wilderness for good and returned to St. Louis.

In St. Louis he married a woman named Sallie and purchased a farm near Miller's Landing Missouri, now New Haven Missouri. Around that time, he visited William Clark and gave him detailed reports of his explorations. During the War of 1812, Colter enlisted and fought with Nathan Boone's Rangers. The circumstances of his death are uncertain. One report was that Colter supposedly died of jaundice on May 7, 1812. and was buried near Miller's Landing. Other sources indicate he died on November 22, 1813. His legacy was retold by Washington Irving and Nicholas Biddle who characterized him as a man intimidated by regular society.

The member of the Lewis and Clark Expedition who lived longer than any other was Patrick Gass. He was born on June 12, 1771 in Falling Springs, Pennsylvania. His parents, Benjamin, and Mary Mc-Lene Gass moved the family around several times before finally settling in western Maryland.

From 1777-1780, Patrick Gass lived with his grandfather. He joined the military In 1792 at 21 years of age, and he fought the Indians who often attacked settlers in the western frontier of the colonies. He served at Bennett's Fort in Wheeling and in August, General Anthony Wayne led the offensive that ended confrontation with the Indians in the area.

In 1794, Gass returned to Mercersburg and became a carpenter's apprentice for two years. Near the end of his apprenticeship, the 1796

Peace at Greenville jumpstarted settlement in the western territories. Gass worked as a carpenter until 1799 when a war with France threatened. Gass immediately re-enlisted in the 10th regiment under General Alexander Hamilton but received his discharge in June of 1800 when the tensions dissipated.

Gass re-enlisted and in May 1801, joined Captain Russell Bissell's company stationed at Kaskaskia, Illinois. From there, he volunteered to join Lewis and Clark along with John Ordway and Charles Floyd. He joined as a private and was promoted to sergeant after Charles Floyd's death. Gass maintained a journal, but his poor education hindered his ability to write and express the events of the day well on paper.

When the expedition returned in 1806, Gass's friends encouraged him to publish his journal, but because he lacked editing skills, Gass employed a schoolteacher, David McKeehan, to prepare it for printing. McKeehan agreed, and the pair decided that Gass would receive 100 copies of the final work and own the copyright. The balance of the printed editions would belong to McKeehan. Zadok Cramer published the book. The country was excited to read about the newly returned expedition and the discoveries and knowledge the explorers brought back. Clark's and Lewis' own accounts weren't published for another seven years.

After his journal's publication, Gass returned to military service in Kaskaskia. He served as the assistant commissary until the beginning of the War of 1812. He fought in several battles, including Lundy's Lane, where a splinter from a falling tree cost Gass one of his eyes. He rejoined the fighting in 1814 and fought in Pittsburgh and Niagara to protect the country against invasion from Canada.

Gass was discharged during the spring of 1815 at Sachet's Harbor. He finally settled in Mansfield, Illinois. Unfortunately, Gass's adventurous nature did not agree very well with civilization, and he took to drinking and telling anyone who would listen about his war stories and experiences with Lewis and Clark. He tended a ferry in 1815, then worked in a brewery. Gass used his experience as a carpenter to help

John Brown build a Baptist meeting house. He then found work hunting stray horses and working at a mill. Gass's father died in 1827, leaving Patrick a negligible inheritance to survive on.

In 1829, the 58-year-old Gass moved in with John Hamilton. Gass fell in love with Hamilton's 20-year-old daughter, Maria, and they married in 1831. Maria bore Gass seven children in 15 years, but one died in infancy, and another died of smallpox. The family moved to Brooks County. Maria died of measles in 1846, leaving Gass to raise five children by himself. Gass had earned 160 acres and $96 a year as his pension from the army, but he lost the land because he did not pay his taxes nor did he cultivate it, and the pension money was hardly enough to provide for his family. In 1856, Gass called a meeting to lobby for better pensions for soldiers and the families of dead soldiers who fought in the War of 1812, but the army rejected the group's resolutions.

While Gass never had to beg, he often struggled to feed his family. He was so intensely patriotic, that he offered to fight for the north during the Civil War when he was 87. Patrick Gass died at ninety-nine years old on April 2, 1870.

One of the captains' favorites was George Drouillard. He had been born in Canada and was the son of a French-Canadian and a Shawnee mother. He met Lewis at Fort Massac where Captain Daniel Bissell employed Drouillard when Lewis recruited him for the expedition. Drouillard was known for his general skill as a scout, hunter, woodsman, and interpreter. Indeed, he was one of the best hunters of the expedition and often accompanied the captains on special reconnaissance missions.

Born in 1773, by 1803, Drouillard was a civilian interpreter, scout, hunter, and cartographer and was hired by Lewis and Clark for these skills which he did well.

After the expedition, Drouillard became a partner in Manuel Lisa's fur-trading ventures on the upper Missouri and Yellowstone Rivers having joined the Missouri Fur Company in 1809. Drouillard, many believed, was killed in 1810 in Montana while trapping beaver, in an attack by the Blackfeet or Hidatsa.

Although several died within a few years of the expedition, Charles Floyd was the only member of the expedition to die during the expedition. Floyd probably died of a ruptured appendix and consequent peritonitis. The ailment was not even recognized by medical science until twenty years after the expedition, and the first successful surgical treatment didn't occur until 1884. Probably no physician of the time could have done much more for Charles Floyd than the captains did. A purgative like Rush's pills, their usual remedy for digestive disorders, could only have hastened Floyd's death, but this is probably what Dr. Benjamin Rush himself would have prescribed if he had been present—along with bleeding—which would have accomplished nothing. Floyd was buried near Sergeant Bluff on the Iowa side of the river, near the present town of Sergeant Bluff, Woodbury County, Iowa.

Within present Sioux City, Woodbury County; later travelers often remarked on the site, and George Catlin painted it in 1832. By 1857, the Missouri River had undercut the bluff, and the grave inadvertently opened and some of the bones were lost. Citizens of Sioux City moved the bones to a new burial site. In 1895, the bones were again examined, and a concrete slab and a one-hundred-foot monument was erected in 1901. The Floyd River still bears his name.

John Ordway was born in 1775 the youngest of ten siblings, Ordway was one of the sergeants from the United States Army who stepped forward to volunteer for the Corps of Discovery. Ordway exercised many responsibilities on the trip, he issued the provisions, appointed guard duties, and kept the registers and records. John Ordway also kept a detailed journal about Native American life during the expedition.

After the expedition, John Ordway married Gracey Walker and became a successful landowner in what became New Madrid County, Missouri. He raised peach and apple orchards and became very prosperous. He died of unknown causes in 1817 at around 42 years of age. The circumstances of his death and his exact burial place are unknown.

Nathaniel Hale Pryor was born in Amherst County, Virginia, about forty miles southwest of Charlottesville and Monticello, in the foothills of the Appalachian Mountains, but no records remain of his birth. He was a cousin to Charles Floyd and was born in 1782. His family moved to Louisville, in frontier Kentucky, when he was eleven, and he joined the expedition on October 20, 1803, at Clarksville, Indiana as one of nine recruits from Kentucky. In 1798, he had married Margaret Patton, but since Lewis had instructed Clark to take only unmarried men on the expedition, his recruitment suggests that either Margaret had died, or else the two were divorced by that time.

Pryor had some talent as a carpenter. During Camp Dubois' construction he supervised the men assigned to saw planks, and he oversaw the repairs of two Indian canoes they purchased shortly before they departed from Fort Clatsop. He accompanied Lewis and explored the lower Marias River in early June 1805. On April 1, 1806, he and two privates explored six miles up the Quicksand (today's Sandy) River, which meets the Columbia at Troutdale, east of Portland, Oregon. Later that same year, traveling down the Yellowstone River, Clark assigned Pryor to lead a command trying to take horses to trade for supplies at Fort Assiniboine in Canada. He was often prone to shoulder dislocation throughout the expedition, once at Fort Mandan on November 29, 1804, and August 23, 1805.

At the end of the expedition, Nathaniel Pryor was promoted to the rank of second lieutenant in the First Infantry. He left the army in 1810 to become a trader but had some unfortunate encounters with Indians.

Governor William Clark licensed him to trade with the Winnebago Indians, and he quickly established a profitable business, including a smelting furnace at Julien Dubuque's lead mines in Iowa. Clark asked him to try to locate Tecumseh, or the Prophet, which roused the "hostility and enmity" and murderous intent of the Winnebago nation following the Battle of Tippecanoe.

It was winter, and while an Indian woman in Pryor's house distracted his executioners, he fled across the Mississippi on the ice. The Indians killed two of his men, stole all his personal property and trade goods, and destroyed everything else. Later he filed a claim against the government, on the grounds he did not know of the Indian unrest, but modestly limited his demands to the actual value of the lost goods, $5,216.25. Writing in his behalf to Secretary of War James Barbour fourteen years after the event, his friend Franklin Wharton called Pryor "a man of real, solid, innate worth," whose "genuine modesty conceals the peculiar traits of his character." He was, Wharton also said, "a brave and persevering officer in the attack on New Orleans."

Pryor re-enlisted and saw action in the Battle of New Orleans during the War of 1812. In August of 1813 he was commissioned first lieutenant in the Forty-fourth Infantry. One month later, he was promoted to captain and saw action in the Battle of New Orleans on January 8, 1815.

In June 1815, he was honorably discharged from the army and returned to the Indian trade, opening a post on the lower Arkansas River, among the Osage. Like his previous commercial ventures, this one saw limited success. In 1821, Pryor established another trading post on the Canadian River, married an Osage woman, and served several years as an unofficial, unpaid interpreter and mediator for her people. He was highly respected by Indians, military authorities, government officials, and others. In 1830, Governor Clark appointed him as a temporary sub-agent for Clermont's band of Osages at $500 per year. He failed to step up into a permanent appointment.

In 1827, William Clark made Pryor a sub-agent and interpreter to the Osage tribe based on his influence among the Indians and his knowledge of the Osage language. Pryor died in June of 1831, at about age forty-nine.

Corporal Richard Warfington was born near Louisburg, North Carolina in 1777 and joined the U.S. Army in 1799. His enlistment information stated he was five feet ten inches tall, had brown hair and black eyes, with a fair complexion.

The issue on August 4, 1804, where the captains were in a quandary as the keeled boat and pirogues traveled between future Nebraska and Iowa was a real event. They were well downriver from the Mandan–Hidatsa villages, from which was where they intended to dispatch the keelboat back to St. Louis that summer or fall of 1804. The man that they had assigned to lead the return party back to St. Louis, Corporal Richard Warfington, had joined the army five years earlier and his hitch was up that day. He could choose to leave the service and hitch downriver with the next passing flotilla of fur traders and leave the returning barge without a commander. Fortunately, Warfington agreed to stay on. This meant he would spend the long, cold winter at Fort Mandan.

His crew of four men (I made Isaac a fifth man), plus two former Corps members, left on April 7, 1805, to return the keelboat downstream as the permanent party faced their canoes and pirogues westward. Warfington had charge of the precious journals and other records of the first year's travel, botanical specimens, and preserved animal specimens—plus a live prairie dog and six live magpies. He also had to keep an eye on deserter Moses Reed and repentant mutineer John Newman. The keeled boat took only about 47 days—until 23 May 1805—to travel downstream the distance that had taken 173 days, including pauses to visit the Yankton and Lakota Sioux, the year before.

In January 1807, Lewis wrote to Secretary of War Henry Dearborn, recommending that Warfington receive a bonus even though he did not serve in the permanent party. After that, Warfington wasn't heard from again except for Clark's listing him as being alive in the mid-1820s. We're not aw

John Shields was the one exception that the Corps of Discovery made and was the only married man on the expedition. Shields had the skills needed on the frontier to maintain their guns throughout the expedition. He proved invaluable.

Besides being married, Shields was the oldest enlisted man on the expedition until Jean-Baptiste Lepage enlisted at Fort Mandan. He was a relative of Daniel Boone and lived with Nancy, his wife of thirteen years, and his daughter in Kentucky on the Ohio River downriver from Louisville. Clark likely knew Shields before the expedition. At the end of the expedition, Cark requested of the Secretary of War additional compensation to Shields for his weaponry repair skills.

Shields was not a military man and did not adjust readily to the Corps of Discovery and he sided with Reuben Field when Field defied Ordway's orders when in February 1804, both captains were doing business in St. Louis, and John Ordway was left in charge. Shields later gave a formal apology after Field's court-martial.

At Fort Mandan, Shields' smithing skills ranged from gunsmithing to horseshoeing. Shields and Willard stumbled onto an ingenious way to obtain supplies for the corps. Because the local Indians valued metal tools, the blacksmiths got permission to cut a burned-out shove into small squares and made these into hide-scrapers which the Native Americans gladly traded corn to obtain. The two blacksmiths also mended farming implements.

A Mandan chief asked him to make a war ax for him of the chief's design. Shields didn't believe the design was practical, but who was he to argue with a war chief? When others saw the ax, they too wanted axes made by Shields and Willard. They procured enough corn for the party for the winter and beyond.

As the Corps traveled, Shields regularly joined the hunters. He was one of the Corps' best shots. At the Great Falls later that month, though, Shields found himself on the business end of a hide scraper. Lewis assigned Patrick Gass, Joseph Field, and Shields to prepare the iron boat for launching. First, they scraped elk hides, and Robert Frazer was enlisted to sew the leather to the metal frames. Shields was as skilled with wood as he was with iron.

Shields hid most of his gunsmithing tools at the Marias River. Perhaps they were his personal tools of the trade, left behind for safety, but his gunsmithing abilities were even more necessary during this second year on the frontier.

He was a man of integrity and repaired their guns often. On April 7-8, 1806, Shields repaired Captain Clark's personal Pennsylvania rifle. He renewed the mainspring on Lewis' air gun in June and on July 1,

1806, he repaired many of the men's guns. Clark named the Shields River east of Livingston, MT, for the gunsmith one of the few place names honoring enlisted men that continues to this day.

When he arrived home, Shields learned that Jonathan Clark, the captain's brother, and business agent in his absence, had sent his wife 21 bushels of corn and four dollars. Jonathan Clark's papers do not show whether he continued to assist Nancy Shields throughout her husband's absence. Even though our story has Isaac doing the deed, Jonathan may have delivered a buffalo robe that John Shields sent home from Fort Mandan for his wife. (Of course, I moved Nancy Shields' location upriver from St. Louis so that Isaac could be the one to deliver the buffalo robe.)

In 1807, the Shields family and several of John's siblings moved with Daniel Boone's brother Squire to Indiana. They settled around Corydon, where John met his first grandchild before his own death in 1809.

The other blacksmith was Private Alexander Hamilton Willard. He was born in July 1777 in Charlestown, New Hampshire. He was recruited to the Corps of Discovery from Fort Kaskaskia from Captain Amos' artillery. He had enlisted in a U.S. Army artillery company in 1800.

He received the harshest punishment in a court martial on July 12, 1804, when he laid down and fell asleep while on duty on the trail. Normally the punishment would have been death, but both captains showed him mercy and punished him with 100 lashes divided evenly over four straight days at sunset. and he was detailed to the return party in April 1805. Willard later served during the War of 1812.

After the expedition, on February 14, 1807, Alexander married Eleanor McDonald. She gave birth to their twelve children. They lived for many years in Platteville, Wisconsin. He died in March 1865 and was buried in Franklin Cemetery in Franklin, Sacramento County, California.

Private John Whitehouse was born to James Whitehouse and Sarah Vaughn in Fairfax Virginia in 1775. His family moved to Kentucky when he was nine years old. A private in the first infantry at Fort Massac under Captain Daniel Bissel, he enlisted into the US Army at twenty-three in 1798 and was recruited to the expedition in 1803, when he was twenty-eight years old. He was initially expelled from the expedition for misconduct but was allowed to return after repenting. He kept a journal and often acted as a tailor for the other men.

On the expedition, Whitehouse was a hide-curer" or a tailor and frequently made and repaired clothing for the other men. He kept a journal throughout his time on the journey, which was published in 1905. Captain Clark gave him the title of 'Corporal', but later had it taken away due to misconduct at Camp Dubois.

After the Lewis & Clark Expedition, Whitehouse faded from the historical record. In 1807, he was arrested for debt. He was released to rejoin the army to fight in the War of 1812, only to desert in 1817. His later life and death remain unknown.

Private Hugh Hall was a resident of Carlisle, Pennsylvania when he joined Captain Robert Purdy's Company of the Second Regiment US Army Infantry at Fort Southwest Point, Tennessee when he volunteered for the expedition in 1803.

He was among a group of six or seven men who got drunk on New Year's Eve 1804 and was court-martialed twice for drunk and disorderly conduct and was punished. He redeemed himself over the next several months and became part of the permanent party. After the expedition, he had problems with his land warrant. Although he took possession of land in Indiana Territory after March 1807, he later assigned the warrant to another person.

While in the St. Louis area on April 11, 1809, Hall borrowed two dollars from Lewis, becoming one of the last expedition members to see his former captain alive. It is not known if Hugh Hall was married or had children. He was listed in the 1820 census as a farmer living alone in Washington County, Pennsylvania. Hall is thought to have died between that year and 1830 because he was not found on any census records.

Thomas Proctor Howard was born in Brimfield, Massachusetts in 1779. He began a five-year enlistment in the U.S. army at age 22, and by 1803 had been posted to Southwest Point, Tennessee. The blue-eyed Howard was one of a group of eight men assigned to the expedition from Captain John Campbell of the Second Infantry Regiment. Clark rejected four of the eight who, he judged, were "not such I was told was in readiness . . . for this Command." He accepted only Howard, Hugh Hall, John Potts, and Richard Warfington. At Camp Dubois, Howard was one of Clark's couriers. He carried a letter to Lewis at Cahokia on January 27, 1804.

Howard was the last among the eleven members of the expedition to be court-martialed. He committed his crime at Fort Mandan on the bitterly cold night of February 9, 1805, when he was given permission to go to the Mandan village but returned after hours and scaled the wall to get in. When a Mandan saw him, he did the same. Lewis gave the Mandan a piece of tobacco after he explained that he could have been killed for scaling the walls. Because of Howard's "bad example", he was detained by the guard and court-martialed for his offense. At sundown the following day he was sentenced to 50 lashes, but his sentence was referred to the mercy of the commanding officer. By that point, more than eight months into the expedition, Howard must have shown enough redeeming qualities to justify suspending his sentence, because the trail's record was omitted from the Orderly Book. That alone would have been enough to garland his reputation as an indispensable member of the Corps of Discovery.

On July 25, 1805, within the Missouri River Canyon Lewis named a creek after Howard that came to be known as Sixteen Mile Creek.

Thomas Proctor Howard and William Werner went to the Salt Camp on the ocean to bring back a salt supply on January 23, 1806. When they had not returned by the twenty-sixth, Lewis feared they were lost. Fortunately, they returned safely two days later and explained that the bad weather made it difficult to travel with the salt. On July 28, 1806, he was one of the two riflemen who greeted Lewis and his detail as they neared the Missouri after fleeing from the fight on the Two Medicine. Howard and another man had gone ahead of the canoes to hunt, and he had killed two deer.

In 1808, Howard married Genevieve Roy, an illiterate French woman. They had two sons together. Howard died in St. Louis, probably early in 1814. Howard's small estate remained unsettled until 1826, when all its papers were signed with Mrs. Howard's "X." One of his boys, Joseph, worked as a trapper for William Ashley on the Upper Missouri for about twenty years.

Private John Potts was born in Germany in 1776. The Corps of Discovery recruited him from Southwest Point from Captain Robert Purdy's company of the Second Infantry Regiment. Potts was a black-haired, black-eyed Hessian miller. On January 4, 1804, at Camp Dubois, he and William Werner got into a fight after dark. After the disciplinary action, Potts was never again a disciplinary problem in the expedition. He was one of the hunters, often sent out with other hunters.

When Clark went forward searching for Shoshones north of the Three Forks of the Missouri in July 1805, he took Potts, York, and Joseph Field along. Hiking overland in Montana, the moccasin-clad men's feet were injured with prickly pear cactus.

On their return from the Pacific, in April 1806, Potts was with Clark when took men to explore Oregon's Willamette River. Potts was under his command when the Corps split up to cross Montana that July. At Long Camp on May 30, 1806, Potts nearly drowned when his dugout canoe was swamped in the Clearwater River.

After the expedition, in 1807, Potts, George Drouillard, Jean-Baptiste Lepage, Peter Weiser, Richard Windsor, and John Colter went to work for Manuel Lisa who led an expedition up the Missouri and built a trading post named Fort Raymond, at the mouth of the Bighorn River at Yellowstone. After its completion in November, Potts trapped around the fort.

Lisa sent one employee, Edward Rose, to trade with Crow Indians. Three others, all Corps of Discovery veterans, Colter, Drouillard, and

Weiser, traveled hundreds of miles to trade and tell Indians about the new fort. Rose spent the winter living with Crow people and giving away his trade goods. He returned to Fort Raymond without any furs.

Rose got into a fight with Lisa and then took it out on Potts when Potts ran to stop the unfair fight. Lisa ran out to his keelboat, boarded it, and pulled away from shore. Rose then ran outside and trained the fort's swivel gun on the boat which was everyone's means of getting home. Ten to fifteen men tried to tackle him. A few days later, Rose left to marry a woman of the Crow tribe.

John Potts was recovering from his beating while John Colter was recovering from a leg injury he received during a Blackfeet attack, and the two of them became trapping partners. Potts rented two horses from the company. Once they recovered, in late summer 1808, they headed toward the Missouri headwaters where they knew beavers were prolific.

To prevent confrontation with the Blackfeet, they trapped in the morning and evening and lay low during the daylight hours, but one day they were in a canoe checking traps on the Jefferson River when Colter heard trampling that he insisted could be a Blackfeet war party. Potts said he was certain it was a bison herd, so they continued their work.

In his memoirs, Colter described what happened next. Several hundred Blackfeet warriors surrounded them on both sides of the river and insisted that the two men ground their canoe. On the bank, a warrior took Pott's rifle, but Colter grabbed it and returned it to his friend. Re-armed, Potts moved the canoe away. He was immediately struck with an arrow. He yelled for Colter to escape, and Potts shot at least one other Indian. This helped Colter in his escape but ensured Potts' demise. The Indians dragged Potts' body onto the bank and hacked him to pieces. Colter ran for his life.

Private George Gibson was born in Pennsylvania, but he was living on the Kentucky frontier when William Clark recruited him in 1803. On the expedition, Gibson was one of the best hunters. On occasion he played the fiddle for the Corps of Discovery. He also served as an interpreter, most likely through sign language.

Gibson survived one of the Lewis and Clark Expedition's most painful wounds. Gibson's injury occurred on July 18, 1806, along the Yellowstone River. He also survived the failed attempt to escort Chief Sheheke home to his Mandan village. But Gibson's own life was cut short by syphilis or perhaps the era's deadly medication for it (mercury poisoning). His demise could also have been a combination of the two.

Gibson had contracted syphilis from a Mandan or Hidatsa woman, who probably contracted it herself from an infected British or Canadian trader. He was treated with mercury which only treated the symptoms. This disease progressed through five stages including death. Gibson was frequently ill during the winter of 1805-06 probably due to this disease.

In 1807, George Gibson joined fellow Corps members, Pryor and George Shannon, and 45 other men to return Chief Sheheke home to his Mandan village. During the Arikara Indian attack that cost Shannon his leg, Gibson received a flesh wound from which he recovered. He returned to St. Louis, where the following year, he married Maria Reagan. In January 1809, Gibson became very ill. He died sometime before July 10, 1809, when William Clark assisted Gibson's wife Maria in settling her husband's estate.

A Maryland resident, Private John Collins served at Fort Kaskaskia under Russell Bissell when he volunteered for duty with the Corps. He built a reputation at River Dubois camp in the winter of 1804 as a thief, a liar, and a drunk. He had little respect for authority he was a slow learner. He earned 50 lashes before the Corps left St. Charles in late May, and his back could scarcely have healed before, at the end of June, he was sentenced to another 100 lashes for stealing whiskey and drinking on sentry duty. Collins eventually worked his way back into the captains' good graces, enough so that in September 1805, Clark named a creek in the Bitterroot Mountains after him.

In July 1804, the officers tested his honesty when they assigned him as the Superintendent of Provisions for his squad responsible for their daily provisions. In mid-October that same year, Clark appointed him as a member of the court martial of Private John Newman.

After his initial misconduct, John Collins kept a low profile. While among the Lemhi Shoshones in late August 1805, Clark sent him on a short errand in the company of an Indian because Collins had at least some proficiency in Plains sign language. His name seldom came up in the journals anymore, except as a hunter. When they reached Weippe Prairie in 1805, Captain Clark named a significant watercourse after him.

Immediately following the expedition, Collins sold his land warrant to George Drouillard and partnered with Pierre Cruzatte and headed up the Missouri River to join John McClellan's trapping expedition. In 1807, that group set up a post west of the Rocky Mountains in future Montana. Of McClellan's original forty-two men, thirty were killed by Indians over the next three years. His life until 1822 is unknown.

In 1822, St. Louis fur trader William Henry Ashley advertised for men to accompany him to ascend the river Missouri to its source and be employed there for up to three years. Collins signed and went with Ashley that year. The following year, Collins was with Ashley's party heading up the Missouri when some Arikara confronted them after a different group of white traders killed a chief's son and another Arikara man. Collins was among several of Ashley's men who were killed in that attack.

Privates Reuben and Joseph Field (Joseph was a year and a half older than his brother.) were among the best hunters of the expedition, but Reuben was possibly the better shot. He was, at least, at Camp Dubois on January 16, 1804, when Clark's men set up a shooting match with some residents. At stake was a pair of leggings. Clark recorded that Reuben came in first. Reuben had some trouble getting used to military ways. At Camp Dubois during early March 1804, he refused Sergeant John Ordway 's command to stand guard on regular rotation. Reuben repented, and never was in trouble again.

Reuben and his brother did not hunt together and were usually paired with other hunters. One of Reuben's specialties was making exploratory side trips up rivers that flowed into the Missouri. On June 3, 1805, Reuben and Joseph hiked seven miles up the Marias River and did not find the waterfall that would confirm they were on the Missouri. After their report, the captains divided men into two large parties to go simultaneously up the Missouri and the Marias. After they found the falls and the arduous portage was in progress, Reuben was sent up the Sun River with Drouillard not only to hunt for meat, but also to bring back elk hides to cover the iron boat.

After the expedition, Reuben and Joseph may have joined the 1807 civilian component of Chouteau fur men going up the Missouri. Joseph was killed in the Arikara battle that prevented Chief Big White's immediate return to his Mandan village, and cost George Shannon a leg. After his brother's death, Reuben decided to join the army only to learn that the down-sized peacetime army had no openings available.

The following year he married or thought he did. He and Mary Myrtle were wed by an itinerant frontier minister, and later heard whispers about the man of the cloth's credentials. Writing his will in 1822, Reuben made sure to protect his wife legally by willing his entire estate to her. He and Mary were childless. He died not long after the will was made, but in the meantime he and Mary, childless, moved to Jefferson County, Kentucky, and began to farm with the help of four slaves.

Little is known about Private Richard Windsor, other than the fact that he was recruited at Fort Kaskaskia from Captain Russell Bissell's company of the First Infantry Regiment. Windsor was an experienced woodsman and productive hunter throughout the expedition.

On May 26, 1805, Lewis named a creek Windsor's creek. It is now known as Cow Creek in Blaine County, Montana, a few miles from where the Nez Perce crossed in 1877 when chased by U S Army General Miles. On the night of July 26, 1806, the night after their horses had been stolen, Windsor and three other men were asleep after their first day floating down the river in two bull boats. A wolf bit Pryor's hand then attacked Windsor and Shannon shot it.

After the expedition, in 1807, Windsor joined several Corps of Discovery veterans in Manuel Lisa's expedition to build Fort Manuel, a fur post on the Yellowstone River at the Bighorn's mouth. He worked safely from Lisa's Bighorn post for two or three years, then returned to Missouri. He rejoined the army and served until 1819. Clark, in 1825-1828, recorded that Windsor lived along the Sangamon River in Illinois.

Private Silas Goodrich's origins are unknown including whether he had prior military service. He was one of the finest fishermen in the Corps of Discovery. After the expedition, Goodrich joined the Army.

When Private Robert Frazier joined the expedition whether he had been in the army is unknown. At first, he was not part of the permanent party but was transferred from the intended return party on October 8, 1804, to replace Moses Reed after the latter's expulsion. Frazer kept a journal and received special permission from the captains to publish it. But the publication never took place, and the journal is lost. Only Frazer's map of the expedition has survived. He died in 1837.

Private John Bratton was one of the nine young men that Douillard brought from Kentucky. In the spring of 1806, he was incapacitated for several weeks by a mysterious back ailment, perhaps the longest serious illness experienced by any member of the Corps of Discovery. An Indiana sweat bath finally cured Bratton. After the expedition, he served in the War of 1812.

Half French and half Omaha Indian, Pierre Cruzatte was a master boatman and fiddle player. Unlike the contract French boatmen, he and Francois Labiche were enlisted members of the expedition's permanent party. Blind in one eye and nearsighted in the other, Cruzatte accidentally shot Lewis while the two were hunting in August 1806. However, Lewis let bygones be bygones when he later paid tribute to Cruzatte's experience as a riverman and integrity. Cruzatte's fiddle playing often entertained the Corps of Discovery.

Originally from New Hampshire and born in 1784, Private John Dame was recruited at Fort Kaskaskia from Captain Amos Stoddard's artillery company, Dame is mentioned only once in the journals. He was a member of the return party.

Recruited at Fort Mandan, John Baptiste Lepage was a French-Canadian fur trader.

Private Francis Labiech was picked as part of the party because of his experience as a trader with the Indians along the Missouri. Like Lapage, he was a member of the permanent party. When he returned to St. Louis in September 1806, Labiech's service did not end. He and other former Expedition members were enlisted to travel with Meriwether Lewis to Washington, DC as escorts for Mandan Chief Big White and Yellow Corn and his son, a delegation of Osage chiefs, Pierre Chouteau; and interpreter René Jessomme, his wife, and his two children.

Labiech lived in St. Louis with his wife Genevieve Flore and 7 children between 1811 and 1834. In 1827, he signed a contract with Pierre Chouteau of St. Louis to serve as a boatman, voyageur, and winterer. for the American Fur Company. Tax records in St. Louis show he was there in the 1820s, and records of the fur trade show that he was still working in the mid-1830s when he was about 60. His absence from the Missouri 1840 census suggests that he had died by then.

Hue McNeal from Pennsylvania may have been in the Army prior to joining the expedition on April 1, 1804. A man with that name was on the Army rolls as late as 1811.

Private John Newman was born in Pennsylvania in 1785 and was recruited at Fort Massac from Captain Daniel Bissell's company of the First Infantry Regiment. Newman was expelled from the expedition following his court-martial for having uttered repeated expressions of a highly criminal and mutinous nature. He remained with the expedition doing hard labor until sent back with the return party to St. Louis in April 1805. He died in 1838.

Little is known about Private Moses Reed's origin and background. He attempted to desert in August 1804, was apprehended, tried, convicted, and expelled from the expedition and was sent back with the return party to St. Louis in April 1805.

Private John Robertson was born in 1780 in New Hampshire and recruited from the regiment of Artillery of Captain Amos Stoddard's artillery company at Fort Kaskaskia. Robertson initially joined the expedition as a corporal, but Robertson admonished him for having no authority over his men and when he failed to break up a fight at Camp River Dubois, Clark demoted him to a private. Robertson was most likely the first man to leave the expedition. On June 12, 1804, Joseph Whitehouse recorded in his journal that a private belonging to Captain Stoddard's company of Artillery was sent back to St. Louis with a trading party encountered coming down river. Presumably Robertson returned to his artillery company because there is no further record of him.

William Werner fought with John Potts at Camp River Dubois and was convicted of being absent without leave at St. Charles, Missouri. Other than these incidents, the journals reveal little more about him.

Peter Weiser was born in 1781 in Pennsylvania. He had been recruited from Captain Russell Bissell's company of the First Infantry Regiment at Fort Kaskaskia. Weiser descended from the noted frontier diplomat Conrad Weiser. After the expedition he joined Manuel Lisa's fur-trading venture up the Missouri.

William Clark had praised John B. Thompson for being a valuable member of the party, but virtually no other information about Thompson was in the journals. Thompson may have been a surveyor before joining the expedition.

Private Ebenezer Tuttle was born in 1773 in Connecticut. He was recruited at Fort Kaskaskia from Captain Amos Stoddard's artillery company. Tuttle was a member of the return party in April 1805. The only mention of him in the journals is in the Detachment Order of May 26, 1804.

Private Isaac White had been born in 1774 was part of the Massachusetts Regiment of Artillery Recruited at Fort Kaskaskia from Captain

Amos Stoddard's artillery company, White was a member of the return party to St. Louis in April 1805. The only mention of him in the journals was also in the Detachment Order of May 26, 1804.

York-African American Slave of Captain Clark was born in Virginia in about 1770 to Clark slaves Old York and Rose. Both York and William Clark were thirteen when York became William's personal slave. In the Virginia society in which Clark grew up, it would not have been uncommon for a Caucasian boy to have an enslaved boy as a personal servant. It also appeared that he had wife back in Kentucky.

Although most slaves weren't allowed to carry weapons, York used a gun to shoot game on the expedition. Clark, in his journal, recorded the Indians' fascination with a man whose blackness would not wash off. Instances occurred where Indians inspecting York and trying to scrub his skin to see if his blackness was natural. The Arikara called him "great medicine".

When the expedition reached the west coast, Lewis and Clark held a vote to decide where the men would stay for the winter. York was allowed to vote along with all the others, though the concept of an enslaved man voting would have seemed preposterous back East.

No known documents establish that York had ever been freed. Clark, however, in a conversation with the writer Washington Irving in 1832, Clark did claim to have freed York. There is no clear record of what happened to York. Some accounts have him dead before 1830, but there are also stories of a Black man, said to be York, living among Indians in the early 1830s. Another account says that Clark legally inherited York in 1799. The journals indicated that he was large, strong, and perhaps overweight. He carried a rifle during the expedition and performed his full share of duties like the other members of the Corps of Discovery. Some stories say that York was freed in 1811 and operated a wagon freight business in Tennessee and Kentucky.

In recognition of his contribution to American history, in 2001, President Bill Clinton named York as honorary sergeant of the US Army.

Lewis described the interpreter, Toussaint Charbonneau, as a man "of no particular merit," while both captains acknowledged the indispensable service of his wife Sacagawea provided the Corps of Discovery.

This famous member and only female member of the expedition was born around 1788, probably near Lemhi, Idaho. The daughter of a Shoshone chief, Sacajawea, the Indian woman wife to Toussaint Charbonneau, mother of Jean Baptiste Charbonneau, was a Shoshone Indian woman. As a child, she was kidnapped by the Hidatsa and sold to the Mandan tribe. While with the Mandan, Toussaint Charbonneau bought Sacagawea and he made her his wife. On February 11, 1805, she gave birth to a son – Jean Baptiste. On the expedition she acted as interpreter, who traveled thousands of wilderness miles from the Mandan-Hidatsa villages in the Dakotas to the Pacific Northwest.

During the expedition, she proved to be a significant asset for searching for edible plants, making moccasins and clothing, as well as allaying suspicions of approaching Indian tribes through her presence. A woman and child accompanying a party of men indicated peaceful intentions.

Jean Baptiste Charbonneau, son of Charbonneau and Sacajawea. would grow up to have a varied and lengthy career on the frontier, starting with his role as the youngest member of the Corps of Discovery. Clark nicknamed him Pomp or "Pompey," and named Pompey's Pillar or Pompey's Tower on the Yellowstone after him in 1806. Clark offered to educate the boy as if he were his own son.

The Charbonneau family disengaged from the expedition party upon their return to the Mandan-Hidatsa villages. They traveled to St. Louis in 1809 to baptize their son and left the boy in the care of Clark, who had earlier offered to provide him with an education.

In 1823, Jean Baptiste Charbonneau attracted the notice of the traveling Prince Paul of Wurttemberg, who took him to Europe for six years. On his return to the United States, Jean Baptiste became a mountain man and fur trader. He later became a guide for such explorers and soldiers as John C. Frémont, Philip St. George Cooke, W. H. Emory, and James Abert. He eventually settled in California and died in Oregon while traveling to Montana in 1866.

Born in 1776, Peter Pinault was the son of a French-Canadian trader and a woman of the Missouri tribe. He was listed as a member of the corps as of May 1804. He probably returned to St. Louis with Corporal Warfington.

Lewis' dog, Seaman, a Newfoundland dog, was a member of the Lewis and Clark Expedition, the first trip from the Mississippi River to the Pacific coast and back. He was the only animal to complete the entire three-year trip. Captain Lewis purchased Seaman in 1803 specifically for the expedition while he was in Pittsburgh, Pennsylvania, while the boats for the voyage were built. He chose the Newfoundland breed because they do well on boats, are good swimmers, and can assist in water rescues.

After the expedition, Lewis returned with Seaman to St. Louis. Upon Lewis' premature death, Seaman refused food and died of grief.

Though Chief Big White didn't go west with them, he did accompany Lewis and Clark to Washington. Returning Chief Big White to his people, however, became a major problem to the captains in their later capacities as governor and Indian superintendent. Because of Sioux and Arikara hostility, he did not reach home until 1809.

Sadly, the Mandan did not believe his tales of the wonders he had seen. He lost much of his prestige and influence. His long absence had allowed rivals to supplant him. He was killed in a Sioux raid on his village in 1832.

Chapter 12-Isaac

On March tenth, the captains invited Isaac to attend the formal ceremony of the transfer of Louisiana territory from France to the United States. The ceremony was held at the home of Charles Gratiot.

As their canoe came around a bend, the house came into view.

"That's the biggest house I've ever seen this side of the Mississippi!" Isaac exclaimed. "It's the biggest house I've seen anywhere.

It was bigger than Andrew's parents' home in Pittsburgh. This house was built of white limestone and stood two stories high. The house had a circular front entrance with steps leading up a cliff to the mansion at its summit. At the door at the top of the stairs, a servant led them into the room inside.

Isaac may have gasped at the house from a distance, but he was even more impressed with the interior entrance area.

A male servant motioned them inside. The inside was equally opulent. The circular entrance stairs went up either side into the second story of the main part of the house. An ornate chandelier's candles were lit and nearly filled the space of the portico above them. A series of many paned glass doors in the back of the room led to the main house. The floors of the room were squares of black and white marble. White-painted chairs were placed around the room's periphery to seat dignitaries. In front of them was a pedestal with papers on it.

The ceremony began. Well-dressed men and frontiersmen alike gave speeches and signed papers. Isaac knew he would be telling his children and grandchildren about this grand affair in the years to come.

Afterward, the captains and Isaac borrowed horses to ride up the Missouri River to stop a Kickapoo war party from attacking the Osages. On the way upstream, they stopped at the camp for a night because it was on their way to the Kickapoo encampment.

Sergeant John Ordway oversaw the camp during Isaac's absence.

The captains and Isaac knew something was amiss when they entered the camp when they found no man on sentry duty. As they came to the captain's office where Sergeant Ordway was stationed, they discovered that firewood was not stacked. They smelled the stench of unburied feces. In the office they found Ordway writing in the daily report journal.

Upon seeing the officers, Ordway immediately came to attention.

"What's been going on here, Ordway?" Captain Clark asked.

"I am sorry sir. Some of the men refuse to work. They refused to dig new latrines because they said it was busy work. They couldn't see any need for them because we'll only be here a couple of months at most. Why do we need another latrine when what we have is sufficient? These men just wanted to sit around the fires and gather wood for those fires. Some of them just walked away and went hunting without asking permission."

"All right then, "Captain Clark turned toward Isaac. "You go let the men know I expect them to muster in the parade ground in five minutes."

"Yes, sir," Isaac replied.

The men scampered into a formation. Most of them looked like they had just rolled out of bed and many of them had.

Captain Clark walked up the line and back down. Rueben Fields snickered, and Captain Clark stopped in front of him.

"So, Fields, you think this is funny? Sergeant Ordway said that you refused a direct order from him to stand guard this afternoon. What do you have to say for yourself, Fields?"

"I, I..."

"That's a better answer than others you could have given," Captain Clark replied. He walked up and down the line again. This time the men lowered their eyes. Isaac felt sorry for them, but he was also happy that he had gone with the captains to the signing.

"I'm disappointed with the way that all of you behaved while I was gone. Therefore, I must confine all of you to camp. None of you will leave the camp for any reason for ten days. No visiting the locals. No visiting the whiskey shops. The only men with permission to leave the camp are those who have explicit orders to go hunting. Is that clear? If neither Captain Lewis nor I are here, you will follow the orders of the non-commissioned officer we put in charge during our absence. Is that understood?"

"Yes sir," was mumbled by several men along the line.

"I didn't hear you," Captain Clark exclaimed.

"Yes, sir," they said loudly and in unison.

"Good, Sergeant Ordway has posted your orders on the bulletin board in front of the offices. I expect you to carry out those orders."

Captain Clark dismissed the men, and they all headed toward the bulletin board in front of the office.

On the twenty-fourth, Captain Clark ordered the men to rebuild the boat that they would be taking up the Missouri River.

"Thorton, I'd like for you to come with me to visit the nearby Indian camps. I saw smoke up on the bluffs this morning. I want to know who is camping nearby."

"Yes sir," Isaac nor did any of the other men ask why Isaac was allowed to leave the camp again even though he had just gone with Captain Clark. He could leave because he had not been one of the men who disobeyed the sergeant's orders.

In one camp they found three squaws and three children. They looked hungry, and their clothes were threadbare. Captain Clark left some of his hardtack and jerky with them. In another, they found a ten-year-old girl and her four-year-old brother. Their parents were gone and they had no idea where they had gone. He left the rest of what they had with them.

"Let's try our hand at a little fishing," Captain Clark said.

They caught several fish. They built a fire and cooked some of the fish they caught.

"As hungry as those other Indians looked, I'm sure we'll find someone who will need a good meal," Captain Clark said as he threw the string of remaining fish into his bag.

In a third, sitting in front of a hut of forest bush, they saw a man who Isaac could see immediately that Captain Clark knew but had not expected to see again.

"Well, well, well, if it isn't Simon Gerty."

"Hello, William Clark, I heard you were out this way."

Isaac knew that Simon Girty was one of the most hated Americans almost as hated as Benedict Arnold was. As a Loyalist in the Revolution, he led Indian war parties against the settlements of the Ohio Valley. He continued the same activity for many years as a British Indian agent. He may not have been any more active than other British agents, but he acquired among the Americans a special reputation, perhaps greatly exaggerated, for malice and cruelty.

Isaac had heard from his parents that Girty was also known by his Seneca Nation name, Katepacomen, or "Renegade Girty". He was a Pennsylvania-born loyalist and white chief of several tribes within the Shawnee-Iroquoian nations since 1777. Girty was known to oversee the brutal torture and murder of Col William Crawford in 1782. He was said to have served as the chief of a Miami tribe whose band of 400 warriors killed Major James Fontaine, the son of General Charles Scott during General Josiah Harmar's campaign.

Since the 1790s, Girty made his home in Canada, and he believed, probably correctly, that his life would not be safe in the United States. There is no other record of him crossing the border. Now that France sold this land to the United States, much to his dismay, Girty was back on American soil.

"I hadn't heard that you came down this way. I heard you were living in Canada."

"The weather up there is too harsh for me, so I moved down this way. How was I to know that the United States would purchase this side of the river from the French."

The old man grunted as he lifted himself from his seat by the fire, hobbled over to his woodpile, and threw sticks on the fire that were as gnarled as his fingers. Rheumatism was consuming him.

"I don't have any quarrels with you, Girdy." Clark reached into his bag and took out a bag of flour then threw his string of fish of the fish that he and Isaac had caught that morning in the Mississippi.

As they left the campsite behind, Isaac said. "That was remarkably forgiving and gracious. That man must have been one of the prime villains of your boyhood."

"A man can't hold grudges and sleep at night. Besides, that old man is already going through his personal purgatory."

As the days wore on, the signs of spring were everywhere. The weather turned warm, and Isaac no longer had to break ice from his water bucket in the morning. The green glossy and red buds of Spicewood, a member of the myrtle family appeared. The male cottonwood tassels grew larger than a large mulberry and the shape and color of that fruit, and some of these tassels had fallen from the trees. The green blades of the grass began poking up through brown patches of weeds.

Every morning heavy fog lay thick around them blunting any sound around them and making the atmosphere seem unreal. A heavy rain with lightning and thunder stormed until midnight. Large insects that resembled mosquitos attempted to bite the horses, but the horses didn't seem to notice.

On April 4, the captains chose the final detachment. Isaac would remain part of Corporal Warfington's detachment. He was in the second squad.

This squad was led by Sergeant Charles Floyd. He oversaw privates Hugh McNeal, Patrick Gass, Reuben Fields, Joseph Fields, John B.

Thompson, and Richard Windsor. Also attached to the second squad were Richard Warfington, Isaac Thorton, Moses B. Reed, Robert Frasier, and John Newman.

Sergeant John Ordway would continue to keep the roster and detail the men of the entire detachment as necessary.

They packed provisions. Lewis settled the account with the contractor. Lewis Crawford, a trader at Prairie Du Chein with information about the Sioux and the Iowa Indians. Lewis sent a letter with him to give the message to Indians on the Des Moines River about the change of sovereignty in Louisiana. The following day, Crawford took his canoe downriver to get supplies for his trading post.

Snow fell on April sixth. The next day, they celebrated their upcoming departure with Captain Stoddard and fifty of his men. Six days later, the two Captains took off in Ramsey's canoe to go to St. Louis. On the thirteenth the captains arrived back at camp from St. Louis. Captain Clark raised the flag and gave the men lead, powder and extra whiskey.

On the eighteenth, Floyd and Shannon took horses to get Captain Lewis from St. Louis. They returned that afternoon. That same afternoon, Jean Pierre Chouteau arrived with twenty-two Indians. After staying one night both captains left with them for St. Louis. Ottaway was left in charge from April twenty-second through the twenty-fourth. This time, he had no problems like he had the last time he was left in charge. The captains returned by boat on the twenty-fifth.

They finished loading the boat and one of the canoes. Each boat now had twenty oars. They added a sail to the large boat to make the chore of fighting the current easier.

Once the boats were loaded, Captain Clark issued weapons to the men. The weapons included fifteen of the new Model 1803 rifles, the first ones issued. This weapon, the first rifle specifically designed for the U.S. Army, was .54 caliber with a thirty-three-inch barrel. The captains referred to them as short rifles, because they were considerably shorter than the civilian Kentucky long rifles that the Kentuckians carried. The captains had their own Kentucky long rifles, and some of the enlisted men who were already in the army brought long rifles with them. These Kentucky-type long rifles had been issued to them in their original units. Other enlisted men carried Model 1795 muskets, .69-caliber weapons based on an earlier French design, which were the standard infantry arms. The muskets, which were smoothbores, could be used as shotguns by substituting rifle shot for a single ball. All these guns had flintlocks.

Chapter 13-Rebecca

In March, the winds in northwestern Pennsylvania changed. Rebecca could smell that change in the air. One day the wind blew icy cold from the north. The winds blew and everything seemed to try to blow away with gale-force warm winds blowing from the south. These winds brought the smell of greens growing all around. Soon the rains, cold at first and interspersed with snowflakes became more temperate as April progressed, bringing forth leaves though dormant at the beginning of May. By the end of that month, the leaves were fully developed.

During this time, Stephen Cooper courted Rebecca in earnest. Stephen was working on the farm with her father when not romancing Rebecca. At the dinner table, Stephen Cooper and her father discussed developing the land around the house.

On Sundays when the new itinerate preacher came around, Stephen sat on the bench at the Miles home with Rebecca sitting beside him. Rebecca felt irritated when every time they walked into the church he he stayed uncomfortably close to her. After the service, he would next to her and nod at the other men as though he was telling them she was a prize he claimed.

When they were alone, Stephen seldom talked to Rebecca. With her father, he discussed plans for the farm. He never asked her opinions or what she wanted, but always insisted on taking the lead.

Rebecca's mother was ecstatic that another man desired her daughter's company. She was thrilled that he planned to remain part of the farm, and that her daughter wouldn't be far away if she married Stephen

Cooper. No one asked Rebecca what she wanted or that she had misgivings about Stephen's motives.

The trees were in full leaf one Sunday late in May, a Sunday when Stephen asked her to go for a walk with him.

"Alright," she said. She grabbed her shawl and met him outside.

The two of them strolled down toward the creek.

At one place where there was a slope and rocks in the path, Stephen put out a hand to help Rebecca over them, but rather than taking his hand, she stepped over them without assistance. They then went up the slope from the creek to a location where the spot overlooked the valley below.

They came to a place where spring flowers grew in abundance.

"This would be the perfect place for us to build our house."

"What are you talking about?"

"I'm talking about our marriage, of course. Your father gave us his blessing. I think we should get married next month, don't you?"

"No. Stephen. "You think you love this land. You love my father, but you don't love me. I am just an ornament to you. I'm not interested."

"We'll learn to love each other," Stephen said.

"Just by that statement, I can tell that you don't love me. You don't love me, and I don't love you. I'm not interested in being part of a dowery, I won't marry you."

Rebecca turned back down the hill. Stephen didn't follow but stayed watching her walk away along with the future he thought he wanted to have with her.

"Where's Stephen? Didn't he come back with you?" Rebecca's father asked as she put her shawl back up on its hook."

"He is up on the ridge," was all that Rebecca said. "I'll help you get supper ready."

Stephen didn't come in for dinner, nor did they see him the rest of the evening.

The next morning Rebecca's father went out to the barn to tell Stephen that breakfast was ready.

He came running back to the house.

"He's gone! He must have left while we were sleeping."

"He left?" her mother asked.

"Yeah, he packed up and left. Did he say anything to you about leaving, Rebecca?"

"No, he didn't."

"Did you say something to him, Rebecca?"

She had not told them that she had turned him down. "I think he left because I refused to marry him."

"You refused to marry him?" her mother said more like an accusation rather than a question.

"That's right. He and I are not compatible."

A month later, rumors flew that Stephen Cooper was seen near the village of Warren where he was courting yet another girl. Neither Rebecca, her father, nor her mother spoke about Stephen Cooper ever again.

Chapter 14-Isaac

Rain fell most of May fourteenth, so they delayed the start of the expedition up the Missouri River until four that afternoon. The men in boats and canoes finally set out from Camp River a Dubois at 4 o'clock and proceeded up the Missouri River under sail to the first Island in the Missouri. A crowd of well-wishers lined the river.

A pop pop pop of gunfire rang out from the crowd onshore, and Isaac ducked for cover within the confines of the canoe which he helped propel upstream.

Sergeant Charles Floyd laughed at him. "Silly boy, Isaac. Someone on shore shot a gun into the air!" he exclaimed.

They didn't go far that night and camped on the upper point opposite a creek on the south side below a ledge of limestone rock called Colewater. They made four-and-a-quarter miles that first afternoon. The party consisted of the two officers, one Frenchman, and twenty-two men in the boat with twenty oars, one servant, and seven French in a large canoe, a corps, and six soldiers in another canoe (this was the canoe that Isaac was in). The men were in high spirits.

They all felt apprehensive and excited about passing through this country. That night several of the men sat journaling about the beginning of their adventure. Everyone knew that the journey that they were undertaking was a historic event and they wanted it well-documented for posterity.

Isaac felt the determined and resolute character of each member of the corps, and the confidence which pervaded all ranks dispelled every emotion of fear and anxiety for the present. A sense of duty and honor existed, which would attend the completion of the object of the expedition.

The next day, Isaac was invited to experience sailing on the barge rather than paddling the canoe, but problems slowed them down. The river was muddy, and they couldn't see the bottom. The barge got stuck on logs several times during the day. The men were able to get the barge off and without injury though in one instance, for several minutes they were in danger. Too much weigh was in the stern. They redistributed the weight throughout the boat to prevent the boat from running afoul of concealed logs in the riverbed. The canoes couldn't keep up because it did not have enough men to maintain speed going upriver. The captains moved a few more men from the barge to the boat.

Now that Isaac wasn't fighting the currents, he was able to look out over the landscape. They were still in a somewhat civilized area because they saw some fields where farmers were clearing and plowing the land. The soil was extremely rich.

What would Rebecca think of this country? He wondered.

The spire of the small Roman Catholic Chapel of the town demonstrated that they had arrived at St Charles at noon.

St. Charles was the earliest white settlement west of the Mississippi and north of the Missouri. In 1787, Auguste Chouteau surveyed the settlement, and soon after the district of St. Charles was established. The parish church and the settlement were named for St. Charles Borromeo. When the Spanish took over the Louisiana town, they renamed it "San Carlos del Missouri". Already, by the time the Americans had purchased Louisiana, American settlers, including Daniel Boone and his family, were surrounded by the French inhabitants. This village was at the foot of a hill from which it took its name Petite Côte, French for "little hill". The village contained about one hundred homes and about four hundred and fifty, mostly French, inhabitants.

The people were poor, but they were kind. They told the crew that the country around them was beautiful with both prairies and timber.

Captain Lewis had business with the commandant at St. Charles, Don Carlos Tayon, a French-Canadian, and one of the original settlers of St. Louis, and the men of the camp were invited to spend their evening meal at the home of Mr. Francois Duquette.

After dinner, Isaac took leftover food to the men who were on guard at their campsite. Sergeant Ordway was on duty.

"Isaac, could you take a message for me to Captain Clark? William Warner, Hugh Hall, and John Collins are absent without leave. The three men who were supposed to be on guard tonight, but some of the other men heard that they planned to sneak out to the party anyway."

"Yes, I can take the message to Captain Clark."

Upon returning to the party where the men who were off duty were enjoying the presence of women at a dance, Isaac saw Captain Clark talking with Mr. Duquette.

"Captain Clark?" Isaac held out the sealed note to him.

"Thank you, Isaac."

Isaac passed the message onto Captain Clark.

Captain Clark opened the note and read it.

"Isaac, could you get Sergeant Floyd for me?"

"Yes, sir," Isaac replied.

Sergeant Floyd was talking with a couple of young women near the dance floor.

"Sergeant Floyd, Captain Clark wants to see you," Isaac said.

"Alright," he then turned toward the women. "If you'll excuse me."

One of the girls smiled at Isaac. "So you're part of the expedition?"

"Yes, yes, I am," Isaac talked to the women as he watched Sergeant Floyd approach Captain Clark and then head toward the four men who were absent without leave. John Collins had grabbed one of the young women and was dancing wildly with her.

Hugh Hall and William Warner were standing near the whiskey keg guzzling down the amber liquid.

"You gentlemen need to go back to camp," Sergeant Floyd said.

"Ah, you can't make us," William's speech was slurred. He poured another shot of whiskey. He threw back his head and downed it.

Captain Clark headed their direction and Isaac followed to back up the captain and the sergeant. With the three of them demonstrating a show of force, Willam Warner and Hugh Hall immediately responded.

"Alright, we're out of here." Warner said.

When Captain Clark joined them, William Warner and Hugh Hall left. Captain Clark motioned to John Collins to leave as well. Instead, he stopped dancing, and stood toe to toe with the captain.

"You ain't got no right to keep me from ths party, William Clark," After Collins called him by his first name, he then cussed him out.

Captain Clark ordered Isaac and Sergeant Floyde to take Collins under arrest back to camp.

The next morning, Clark had to court martial the three men and punish them by confining them. At 11 o' clock, the trial was conducted by Sergeant John Ordway, Joseph Whitehouse, Rueben Fields, Potts, and Richard Windsor.

The charges were read that William Warner and Hugh Hall were absent without leave. The prisoners both pled guilty to being absent from camp without leave. They were each sentenced to twenty-five lashes on their naked backs, but the court recommended they not be whipped because of good conduct to the mercy of the commanding officer.

At the same court, they tried John Collins. The court charged him for being absent without leave, for misbehaving in an unbecoming manner at the ball the previous night, for using bad language after returning to camp, and for using disrespectful language to the commanding officer. To the first charge, he pleaded guilty, but to the second two charges, he pleaded not guilty. After deliberating the evidence, the court determined that Collins was guilty of all charges. He was sentenced to fifty lashes on his naked back. Captain Clark agreed with the court's decision and ordered that John Collins' punishment be taken that evening at sunset in the presence of the entire company. William Warner and Hugh Hall's punishment was remitted as the court had requested.

One evening in the middle of May, Captain Lewis finally arrived at camp.

At muster that day, Captain Lewis inspected the men and the camp. He was pleased that he found his men in good health and with the work that Clark and his men had done while he was away. That evening, several members of the party went to church including Isaac. It would be the last Christian service any of them might ever attend.

Captain Lewis and Mr. Ducett set out from St. Charles at three the next afternoon. After every matter was arranged, the expedition proceeded on under a gentle breeze. The river's current was very rapid, the banks steep, and the river bottom was miry. At one mile a violent rain with wind out of the southwest. They landed on the north side of the river and camped. It rained most of the night. Three Frenchmen went to get George Drouillard and Alexander Willard who were returning the borrowed horses.

On the twenty-third, they started early in the morning. passed the mouth of the Osage River on the south side, about a mile and a half below the Tavern Cave. One mile above the cave was Tavern Creek. Just beyond the creek, they settled for the night.

The next day, they stopped at the Boone's Settlement. This colony of Kentuckians was named for Daniel Boone, who came there in 1799 when he received a land grant from the Spanish government. His son, Daniel Morgan Boone, had preceded him there in 1797 and convinced his father to come.

The Corps of Discovery embarked the next morning at 6 o'clock, having fair weather, and passed Boone's settlement lying on the North side of the river. This settlement was made by Colonel Daniel Boone, the person who first discovered Kentucky, and who was residing at this place, with several of his family and friends.

Isaac went with Captains Lewis and Clark up to the Boone house.

When Daniel Boone came to Missouri, he was 65 years old, and even now he looked spry for his age. He brought his wife, Rebecca, and several of his children with him. Daniel acquired 850 acres. They were in the process of building Boone's house. He had been appointed judge and commandant of the Femme Osage district in 1800 and held the post until the American takeover. Captain Lewis let him know that with the American takeover, his work for the Spanish government was ending. Rebecca Boone gave them homemade cornbread to share with the men of the expedition.

"Along with the meat you hunted, you should have enough for everyone to have their fill," Rebecca Boone replied as she handed the board holding the bread to Isaac.

"Thank you, ma'am," Isaac replied.

After leaving the next morning, the violent current broke one of the boat's ropes causing it to turn broadside. The current washed the sand from under her and she wheeled and lodged on the bank below three times before they got her back in deep water.

George Drouillard and Willard, two of our men who left them at St. Charles met them there. They camped about a mile above where they nearly lost the boat in an old French-style plantation house. The house was vacant.

"This is what they call a retrograde bend because the bend caused us to turn back east two miles from where we started this morning at the Boone plantation," Captain Clark said to Isaac.

The following day they came to the last white settlement on the river. The village was a French village called La Charette. The English called it St. Johns. They soon passed the River Boeuf where they met a boat laden with furs and deer pelts.

"Well, Hello there!" One of the men called over to the men manning the canoe that Isaac was paddling in. 'Where are you boys headed?"

"We're going to the Pacific!" Robert Frasier exclaimed.

"Is that a fact?"

"Where are you heading?" Isaac asked the man.

"We're returning to civilization after trading with the Indians." The man answered.

When Captain Lewis heard this, he invited the two men to set up camp with them.

The man who had been talking to the boys was Regis Loisel.

Loisel told them that he was born in the Parish of L'Assomption, Montreal, and came to St. Louis in about 1793. By 1796 he had formed a partnership with Jacques Clamorgan, which in 1798 became the reorganized Missouri Company. After that partnership ended, he formed a new partnership with Hugh Heney in 1801. Loisel had wintered that past winter with his partner Pierre-Antoine Tableau on the prairie up north on the Missouri.

That evening, he shared much information about the country where they were headed. He offered letters of introduction to his trading associates Heney and Tableau. He also informed them that he saw no Indians on the river below the Poncas.

The expedition camped that night near the small town. The people of the village were poor, the houses small, but they generously sent the expedition milk and eggs to eat.

The expedition set out the next morning during a gentle rain shower. The weather cleared up and stayed that way during the following day.

Now that they were past the organized villages, they developed a routine. Two men rode horses on shore, hunted during the day, and joined the corps in the evening. Whenever it rained, the river rose and when it stopped raining, the river receded, and the men had to lay out their provisions to dry. The men took turns hunting.

On May thirtieth, Whitehouse got lost in the woods during his hunting expedition and the French shot off their swivel cannon to get his attention. The river bottom lands were rich with cottonwood, sycamore, hickory, white walnut, and butternut. Isaac also saw a type of riverbank grape and various types of rushes. Sadly, the grapes wouldn't be ripe until they were long gone.

On the last day of May, two canoes strapped together filled with bear Skins and pelts came down from the Grand Osage. Aboard, was one French man who was half Indian, along with his squaw. These men had letters from Mr. Choteau who had gone to the Osage Nation. The message said that part of the Osage Nation had settled on the Arkansas River. The Osage did not believe the Americans owned the country, so they disregarded the St Louis agreement.

"So where are you from, sir?" It was the most common question asked of anyone on the Missouri River.

"Sir? You called me sir? Now that's a hoot, did you hear that Buster!" said one of the men and slapped his leg. "You just made my day calling me sir! Now to answer your questions, we came up from the Kansas River where we wintered and caught a great quantity of beaver."

"What happened to the rest of the beaver?" Isaac asked. He saw only a few pelts in the back of each raft.

"The darnedest thing has happened," said the men replied. "We lost most of them in a prairie fire."

Isaac wondered if they were telling the truth or if they were just telling a fish story.

"Just to let you know, the Kansas Nation is now out on the plains hunting buffalo. They hunted last winter on the Missouri."

They talked a little more and after eating the noon meal, the men in the double raft continued downstream.

At muster that day, Captain Lewis held a letter up. "Mr. Choteau has some information that I would like to share with you from the Osage. He says that originally the Osages lived on the upper Osage River. During the early 1700s the group known as the Little Osages moved away and settled on the lower Missouri River, near the Missouri Indians. Those remaining on the Osage River were known as the Great Osages. Late in the 1700s the Little Osages rejoined their kinsmen. By this time about half of the Great Osages had moved to the Arkansas River a couple of weeks west of here. They spoke the Siouan language of the Dhegihan group and have an economy based on hunting and horticulture."

On the morning of Monday June fifth, they went under a tree and mast got hung up in one of the overhanging branches. Ordway was manning the steering. The rope to the mast stuck in a limb of a sycamore tree and the stay broke like a twig. They camped on the south side of the river at the lead mines. The hunters came in with eight deer which they dried into jerky that evening. Lewis, Clark, and all the men burned their names into several trees.

The expedition continued upstream. They came to a sandbar with where greens were growing. York swam across and had gathered enough watercress and tongue grass for them to eat at the evening meal. There was good wind, but they couldn't use it because the mast was broken. They came to rapids which made Isaac's canoe lag the rest and didn't make it to the place where they camped for two hours. That night Clark said that he suspected that other tribes were on their way to war against the Osages nation probably they are the Saukee.

On June sixth, they mended their mast and set out at seven in the morning under a gentle breeze. They crossed an Island that they called split rock Island. The river had risen a foot during the night. While they traveled down river, they saw their first buffalo on the Missouri River. They next day, Captain Lewis took five men out that evening to investigate Moniteau Creek. They found a salt lick and creek, and they saw more buffalo and found dried buffalo chips and buffalo wallows near the river. They also found a den of rattlesnakes. They killed three of them and continued down river That evening, The hunters came in with the meat from three bears. They dried the bear into jerky for later when meat wouldn't be as plentiful.

Continuing up the river they came to the Osage River where the French said contained lead ore. They said that nearby there was an ancient Osage village. They continued upstream. It was beautiful prairie. Grassland, woodland, and river all melded into one continuous motion as they poled their way up the Missouri. At one place they found some high land with stone suitable to use for knife-sharpening whetstones. They saw wild goose plum and hazelnut trees. The fruits just forming on the trees.

On the twelfth they halted, and four canoes of cargo came down from the Sioux nation and with them was an old man who had been with the Sioux for twenty years and had great influence with them. His name was Mr. Pierre Dorion, Sr. He agreed to go north with them as an interpreter. William Clark had heard of Dorion before, for the trader had corresponded with his George Rogers Clark in 1780. Within a few years of that date, he had gone up the Missouri to the Yankton Sioux, where he married and settled down as a trader.

John Robertson had finished teaching several of the men of the company including Corporal Warfington how to handle the guns on the boat and he wanted to return to his unit. Because he had no further purpose in the expedition, he returned to Captain Amos Stoddard's artillery company on Dorion's boat along with the traders. Dorion himself went with the expedition upriver as their interpreter.

They asked him to return with them, hoping some of the Sioux Chiefs would return to Washington with them. Clark purchased 300 pounds of grease from them in exchange for the pelts the members of the expedition had collected.

On June fourteenth, they arrived at the mouth of the Des Moines River. The ground above the river was not mountainous but rose above the river. Below its mouth was a beautiful overgrown plain bottomland.

Isaac watched the two captains walk to the hill from the top where they had a beautiful prospect of surrounding country in the open prairie. The captains caught a racoon, and the hunters brought in a bear and a deer.

They passed a stream called Snake Creek. After supper that night, the men surrounded a campfire when George Drouillard asked, "Would you like to know why they call the river Snake River?"

"I would imagine they call it that because someone saw a snake on it."

"That would be a good guess, but there's more to the story. I heard from another trader that when he was in St. Louis that an immense snake lived in a small lake five miles upriver. It gobbled like a turkey and was heard for several miles."

Isaac swatted a mosquito on his neck and then another. They had come into a swarm of mosquitos. Soon all the men were swatting the biting insect. Some of the men covered themselves with cold ashes from the fire. Isaac just went to bed early to keep the mosquitoes from biting.

The following day, they had to tow the big boat in a low place on the river. They had to tow the boat after they passed an old French fort on the river. The water was too rapid to allow them to use their poles to propel them upriver.

Captain Lewis shook his head. "We need a heavier tow rope and more oars. I say we can make them from what materials are available here."

Isaac started seeing big ugly itchy welts on his legs. He knew that it was from the ticks that were in the area. They were unbearable. He dabbed the bites with mud from the river which did help a little. He also dabbed mud on the welts on his arms because the mosquitos were as bad as the ticks. Captain Lewis gave each of the men a mosquito netting to sleep under.

Hunting was good and the men brought in a lot of game. Despite the hard work of pulling the boats upstream, the men were in good spirits.

At one point, the water became extremely hard to navigate. The canoe that Isaac was in couldn't be poled or rowed so the men jumped in the water and pulled the boat while swimming.

On June twenty-second, they awoke to a violent rainstorm with wind, lightening that lasted an hour. The river rose more than four inches after the storm. The wind settled to a gentle breeze, and they were able to use the sail, but they had to be careful to avoid the snags that had washed into the river with the rain shower. The following day the river dropped eight inches. The river's water was swift, and the wind was blowing from the wrong direction, so they were unable to continue upriver and had to stay camped in the same location until they had more favorable conditions.

The next morning, Captain Clark decided to go out hunting himself to see what he could bring in. He left at six and returned to the boats with two deer and a bear at eight o'clock. He had brought the deer to the shore to clean when the bear showed up and he shot it.

They came across a coal bank and then some rapids they had to tow through, which happened for two days straight. On the last day of June, they saw the biggest wolf any of them had ever seen.

The mast broke again so the men stopped to fix it. There they explored and found the most signs of game that they had ever seen. They found tracks and bear, wolf, and waterfowl skat.

On the first of July, they located numerous raspberries and grapes growing near the river. The grapes, of course, were not ripe, but the raspberries were. They popped the berries into their mouths as fast as they could pick them. Isaac thought was nice that they didn't have to pick it for his mother to make preserves, but he really missed her preserves.

On July third, they halted at a trading house owned by some Frenchmen. They built the trading house to trade with the Kansas Indians. There the corps saw a fat gentle white horse. The trees were pine, black walnut, honey locust, oak, and western buckeye.

Independence Day was spent paddling upriver. In the morning they celebrated the day by shooting off the swivel cannon. They passed a bayou of a large Lake on the right side that appeared to have once been the bed of the river. It paralleled the river for several miles. They passed a creek they named Fourth of July Creek. Joseph Field was bitten by a snake on the side of his foot. Isaac applied bark of the slippery elm and Peruvian bark to reduce the swelling.

That night they camped on the lower edge of a plain where another old Kansas Indian village had once stood. The prairie here was beautiful with hills and valleys interspersed with timber. They ended the day by again discharging the swivel gun at the bow of the boat and gave the men an extra gill of whiskey. They dined that evening on corn they had purchased the day before at the French Trading Post. They called the creek near their camp Independence Creek.

The next day, Clark swam the horse across and up the river for two miles under the bank where the old Kansas town had once stood. War had reduced the Kansas nation and forced them back into places where they could defend themselves on horseback. He saw a lake in which one creek and several brooks ran into it from the hills. The lake had great quantities of sunfish and geese.

The boats passed some bad sand bars that were situated parallel to one other.

Here the boat caught on to a piece of driftwood.

Isaac watched in horror from his canoe as the boat caught on a piece of driftwood. The men on board yelled to one another as it turned around three times before they could get it heading upstream again.

Fortunately, the boat received no damage. At noon they arrived at a beaver lodge. Captain Lewis's dog Seaman drove the beaver out of the lodge. On the high lands the land was open with only a few trees. They camped on the left side under a high bank. Great quantities of summer berries, grapes and wild roses grew along the river.

The following day they passed a prairie named Reeve's Prairie. Isaac felt like they were traveling through paradise.

That afternoon while they were setting up camp, Clark gave the men a warning.

"Always be wary of your surroundings, boys. Just because it's peaceful now, doesn't mean that natives aren't out there somewhere watching us. Back in 1795, traders Benito and Quenache de Rouin were returning from the Kansas village. They were robbed and beaten but not killed by the Iowa. The two were left for dead at the mouth of the Kansas River. I wouldn't want that to happen to any of us."

The grassland stretched out for miles with only a few trees dotting the landscape. They saw several young swans.

Frasier became sick with sun poisoning. Captain Lewis bled him and gave him a saltpeter drink which revived him.

When they set out early the following morning, Frazer was much better. Sergeant Ordway met them at the mouth of one of the creeks. Five men became sick with violent headaches, and several had boils.

Isaac killed a deer standing on the bank from his canoe. The expedition camped at the head of the Grand River.

They stopped on July twelfth because the men were exhausted. After an early breakfast, Clark took five men including Isaac and went up the Ne Ma Har River about three miles, to an open level part of an immense prairie.

Clark went on shore and passed Several knolls to the top of a high artificial knoll. From the top of the knoll, Captain Clark and Isaac saw several small mounds in the level plain. They walked up a hill on the lower side of the plain and saw several artificial raised mounds. From the top of the highest mound, they viewed the expansive plains around them. They saw the beautiful Missouri river about eighty yards wide meandering through the level plain as far as he could see. Vivid green trees and shrubs bordered the river, creeks and runs. The mounds indicated to them that the area had once been widely inhabited.

The river's gentle current's headwaters started up near the Pawnee Village on River Blue, a branch of Kansas. Little timber grew near the mouth for one mile above, only a few trees, and thickets of plums and cherries were seen on its banks The creeks and small ravines meandered into the river were lined with some timber. Captain Clark got grapes on the banks. They were nearly ripe and. plums, crab apples, and wild cherry were also growing there. The wild cherries were larger and grew on a small bush. Captain Clark marked his name and the date near an Indian mark of animals and a boat.

Isaac couldn't help wondering what Rebecca would think of this place. He needed to stop thinking about her. She would probably be married by the time he returned. If that is, if he ever did return.

That night, Isaac awoke to hear Ordway admonishing Willard for being asleep at his post.

The next morning, Captain Clark tried Willard for sleeping on his post and the young man received 100 lashes. Though this seemed like harsh treatment, according to military rules at the time, Willard's offense was punishable by death. Hence, the captains judged this case, instead of a panel of enlisted men as would have been the case for a lesser offense. Isaac doubted they had any intention of inflicting so severe a penalty, but this impressed every one of them of the seriousness of such a lapse. A surprise attack could mean the deaths of the entire party.

Chapter 15-Isaac

August began with intermittent rain that lasted all day. The rain would stop then start again a few minutes later. Captain Clark rode on the French canoe that day and was as wet as the men. The country through was in every respect like that through which they passed the day before. The brooks had high water, black with mud from the rains that had recently fallen.

Along several brooks, trees grew along their banks as far as Isaac could see. On the hilly banks the trees were short pines and cedars. The trees in the river bottoms were ash.

They dodged more sand bars that day than usual, and more soft mud. The current moved slower than it had further downriver.

The expedition stopped to allow a herd of buffalo to cross in front of them. The large buffalo herd passed over high water and in some places the animals had to swim across. The herd was so large that it took the animals half an hour to cross, delaying the expedition by an hour. Clark took four men and killed four fat cows for their fat and all the meat they could carry on the small canoes.

An hour after they landed for the night, a large bear came so close to their camp that one of the men shot and killed it as it neared their fire. In the evening the hunters came in. They too had good luck with hunting and brought in several deer. They made a fire and laid the animal skins to dry. Two men attended to them, while the others made camp for the night.

Because they day was sunny and dry, they spent the next day on shore to dry out their skins and provisions. As Isaac helped spread out skins in the sun, he swatted flies that seemed to rise everywhere.

They set out the following morning. They didn't need to stop to cook the noon meal that day because they had cooked enough meat the night before. They only saw a few buffalo that day, but they saw many elk, deer, wolves, bears, and beavers. They also saw a few ducks, geese, a black-billed magpie, one golden eagle, many bald eagles, and red-headed woodpeckers.

Ordway and Willard went on early on the following day with a small canoe to hunt. They arrived at the camp where Isaac had just killed a rattlesnake. They killed a deer and an old silver-grey grizzly.

"Well, it's about time you showed up," Isaac said. "Put the game over there while I get you a plate of stew."

"You'll never guess the time we had," Sergeant Ordway said.

"Yeah," said Willard. "We had planned to reconnect with the party at midnight. However, the current drew us into a snag of branches, so we had no chance of getting out of it.

Willard continued while Willard took a bite of food. "The snag ran about halfway through when the stern of our canoe ran through an obstruction and snagged Willard and drew him out of the boat. The current was strong, but he was able to hold onto a branch. I took his oar and hauled the bow first one way and then the other to clear the canoe. He paddled to shore and ran up to the opposite shore of Willard. Willard called back to say that he was safe and asked me if I was okay."

Willard now took up the story. "Ordway said yes, but I could not hear him. I had made a raft of two small sticks I caught floating and tied my clothes on them. I said I would swim through this difficult part of the river and asked him to deal with the canoe. That's when we both saw the bear."

"Who shot him?" Isaac asked.

Willard continued. "Ordway was the first to come to his senses enough to shoot the bear."

The next morning, Isaac and Corporal Richard Warfington were called to the captains' tent.

"We've got a bit of a quandary here," Captain Lewis told the two young men in front of him. We're well downriver from the Mandan–Hidatsa villages where we intend to dispatch the keelboat back to St. Louis that summer or fall. However, it's just come to our attention that your hitch, Corporal is up today. Our problem is what are we going to do? Should we send you back or. . ."

"I would be willing to take command of the returning boats," Isaac replied.

"I guess it's up to you, Corporal Warfington. We would prefer that a civilian like Thorton here not take charge of the boat, but we don't have any control over your decision at this point. You can leave your service and hitch a ride downriver with the next passing flotilla of fur traders or stay with us. The choice is yours."

"Captain Lewis, I would be happy to stay with the expedition until you discharge the boat from duty. I was kind of looking forward to seeing more of this Louisianna Territory anyway."

"Splendid," Captain Lewis replied. "I'm glad to see that we aren't losing either of you men."

Mosquitoes were a menace that night. The men would have found a better location to camp, but they waited there because Reed had not returned from their hunting expedition. A thunderstorm drenched everything that night and filled the canoes with water. They had to unload the canoes and the wind blew sand in their faces.

On August sixth, a violent storm blew the flag from Isaac's canoe. They set out early to Counsel Bluff even though Reed was missing. He had not yet come back from hunting. La Liberte had also gone and had not returned. Many speculated that La Liberte would ever return. Waiting was not possible. The boats were still a few miles downriver from Counsel Bluff, and they had to hurry to their planned meeting with the local natives.

Clark dispatched Douillard, Reuben Fields, William Bratton, and Francois Labiche to bring back Moses B. Reed. Dead if he did not come back peacefully. They were instructed to go to the Ottawa tribe's village. They were to ask if the Indians had seen La Liberty and bring him to the Mahar's Village. They also sent a message to the Ottawa and the Missouri tribes requesting an audience with them. They requested a few of their chiefs to come to the Mahar's camp, where they would make peace between them and the Mahar and Sioux. As an offer of good faith, Clark gave them a wampum string and a carrot of tobacco.

The ninth dawned foggy and damp. The dense fog held them up until after seven-thirty. The river was low and covered with cottonwoods and grapevines. Captain Clark killed a turkey. They passed a bad place in the river where the river was shallow and marshy. The following day, they rowed and sailed twenty-four miles.

They passed a high bluff where Black Bird, the king of the Mahar, died of smallpox along with three hundred of his men about four years earlier. The hill where his people buried him was about three hundred feet above the river. Captain Lewis and Clark went up on the hill to see the grave and hoisted a flag above his grave to honor him and please the Indian tribe.

Chief Blackbird was known for his friendship with white traders and strong rule over his people. Under his leadership the Omaha rose to prominence on the eastern plains. Reports of his war deeds were mixed, but he seems to have had great authority because of his sorcery, especially in the deaths of the enemies who were killed when he poisoned them with poisons purchased from traders. According to stories, he was buried on the top of the hill, seated on the back of the horse he used to watch for friendly traders.

The boat and the canoes passed the mouth of a creek on the south side that the Indians called in the Mahar tongue *The Great Spirit is bad*. They had gone fifteen miles that day.

The following day they found grapevines laden with fruit covering the lower parts of the cottonwoods. Large willows also grew in the lowlands.

As they built their evening fire, Isaac heard a long low howl from the Indian camp that sounded like dogs barking.

"What's that? Isaac asked.

"That's a prairie wolf," Douillard said.

"That's a first for me," Isaac replied. He dropped his armful of sticks into the fire.

On the fourteenth the party searching for the Indians at the Mahar town to invite them to counsel returned. They did not find the Indians, but they found a village that had been decimated by smallpox. By nightfall, the other men who searched for the deserted man and to ask the Ottawa to counsel had not yet returned.

While Isaac waited with the rest of the men in camp, Douillard told him what he knew about the Omaha tribe. The Omaha tribe seemed to be closely related to the Poncas. Both spoke dialects of the same language, and both were horticulturists and hunters. The Omaha had settled in Nebraska by 1700. By 1750, they were primarily located in Nebraska, although they hunted and camped on both sides of the Missouri River. In the last decade of the eighteenth century, they caused trouble for the French traders who wished to ascend the Missouri River beyond the Omaha village to trade with the Arikara and Mandan.

The following day, Clark and ten members of the party including Sergeant Floyd and Isaac caught fish pike, salmon, bass, perch, red horse, small catfish, and a type of perch called on the Ohio "Silverfish". The party who had gone to the Ottawa still had not returned when the fishermen cleaned their catch.

Isaac noticed that Sergeant Floyd still had the cough from the cold that he had a few days earlier. He had dark circles under his eyes, and he seemed to trip over things like he didn't have much energy.

The next day they went fishing again as they waited there for the other Indians to come back. They spent their time repairing the mast.

They continued waiting for the men to get back from looking for the deserter.

August eighteenth was Captain Lewis' birthday. The Pawnee had returned from their hunt on August twelfth. On the 18th the party who had been sent in pursuit of Moses B. Reed who had been missing since the fourth returned with him, along with eight Indians and a Frenchman. The corps gave the men provisions to eat. They immediately had the trial of Reed. He confessed. The captains sentenced him to run the gauntlet four times through the detachment and the captains disqualified him from the permanent party. After the gauntlet, Reed was given one hundred lasses.

That night, the captains and the chiefs discussed the war between them and the Mahar. They postponed the further consultation until the next day. They danced that night until eleven o'clock, the perfect end of Captain Lewis' birthday.

On the nineteenth, The Captains held a council with the Ottawa, who wished to make peace with all nations.

Before Captain Clark went under the canopy where the meeting was to be held, Isaac was standing beside Sergeant Floyd when Floyd slumped forward and began to vomit.

"Isaac, take him back to his tent and help him. When the meeting is over, I'll ask Captain Lewis to look at him."

Isaac helped Charles Floyd to his tent. Charles' pains were sharp and localized to his lower abdomen. The pain arose abruptly and seemed to come and go in spasmodic waves. One minute he would seem to be doing better and the next, he was bent over in excruciating pain.

Charles was seriously ill. Fortunately, the corps had no reason to move from that spot because the captains negotiated a treaty with the Indians. These Indians appeared to be very friendly towards them. George Douillard stopped by Floyd's tent to see how his friend was doing. Charles Floyd had just had one of his attacks and Isaac was nursing dabbing the sergeant's forehead.

"Hey, friend, how's it going?" George looked down at Charles. Isaac could see the concern in George Douillard's eyes. "You don't look so good."

"I could be doing better," Floyd said weakly. "How are the speeches going?"

"Oh, you know how it goes, Captain Lewis delivered to them a long speech which was I Interpreted. The captains gave the head chief a medal, and to the other chiefs, he gave commissions; and he gave gifts to everyone including those "burning glasses" that he's so fond of."

The "burning glass," was a lens for focusing the sun's rays to start a fire. It was an item the Indians found useful and intriguing. Captain Lewis had purchased eight dozen of them in Philadelphia as gifts to the Indians in 1803. In the evening the Indians left the camp, seemingly well pleased.

After the Indians left, news had gone all around camp that Floyd was very ill and many of the corps stopped in to see how the sergeant was doing.

Clark was up for most of the night with Floyd, as was Isaac. No matter what they tried to do for him, Sergeant Floyd grew weaker and no better. At one point after midnight, Charles Floyd revived somewhat.

"I'm going away," Charles said. Isaac immediately knew that Charles believed that he was dying.

"Don't say that," Isaac touched him on the arm. You'll be fine."

Charles waved Isaac's hand away and looked intently at the captain. "Captain Clark, can you write a letter for me?"

"What do you want me to write?"

"Tell my family what I did for the corps. And Isaac, can you make sure that it gets delivered?"

Isaac didn't say a word. He just nodded.

By morning, his pulse was barely palpable, and nothing would stay on his stomach. Captain Lewis examined him and turned toward Isaac.

"Let's see if a bath will revive him," Captain Lewis said. He was the most medically trained of anyone on the expedition. Captain Clark and several of the men including Isaac lined a wooden box with animal skins to hold water and then heated water to put into the tub they created. They were just ready to put Charles Floyd into the water when Isaac tried to take his pulse.

"I don't feel anything," Isaac replied. He put his hand up to the man's nose. No breath could be detected. "He's gone."

After his death, they were gathering his things when Isaac picked up Floyd's journal. In the last entry It said

"Satturday augt 18th ouer men Returnd and Brot with them the man and Brot with them the Grand Chief of the ottoes and 2 Loer ones and 6 youers of thare nathion

They still had no information about the whereabouts of the Frenchman called Le Liberte. The commanding officers expect he has deserted."

"He never mentioned that he was ill," Isaac replied.

He wept.

They buried Charles Floyd at the top of a hill overlooking the river. Isaac believed that Charles would have liked this place. He had a beautiful view of this vast country. His grave was situated just below a small river without a name to which they named Floyds River and the bluff where they buried him, they named Sergeant Floyds Bluff. They buried him with military honors and fixed a cedar post at is head and his name, title, day of the month and year. Captain Lewis read the funeral service over him. After paying every respect to the body of this deceased man they lowered his body into the grave and covered his body with soil.

How many more would die before they completed their mission?

They returned to the boat and proceeded to the mouth of the little river and camped. It was a beautiful evening. Charles Floyd would have enjoyed that sunset. Isaac would miss him.

Chapter 16-Isaac

The next morning, Isaac dipped his oar into the water and pushed back the water in one smooth motion. He stared back at the lonely hill where they had buried Charles Floyd. He felt the emptiness of having had to leave behind a man that he had grown to respect.

Everyone was unusually quiet too as they set out early the next morning under a gentle southeasterly breeze. They traveled quietly all day as they dipped their oars into the glassy surface of the Missouri. They passed a deserted Mahar village near the mouth of the Great Sioux River. They made good time that day. They seemed to want to put miles between them and the reminder of their mortality behind them.

The following day, they came across a bluff that had iron pyrite and what looked to be copper along with other minerals. Captain Lewis decided to check out the quality of the minerals, Captain Lewis became ill from the fumes and the task of testing the cobalt, which appeared to be of soft Isinglass. The copperas and aluminum in the bluff were very pure. Purging the body with laxatives was the most effective way to dispel metallic toxins from the body, so Captain Lewis took a dose of magnesium salts to work off the effects of the arsenic.

Captain Lewis felt better than he had the night before so they continued upriver the following day. The river straightened out. Two elk swam near the boats and the men fired at them, but no one seemed to be able to kill them. Captain Lewis led a party of hunters out onto the prairie. Reuben Fields came up with the horses and brought two deer. He also killed a buffalo near two yellow clay bluffs Captain Lewis killed a goose, and Collins killed a small doe and said that they had seen several prairie wolves. After they camped, Shannon saw an elk on a sandbar and shot it through the neck. Captain Clark killed another deer, and Isaac caught a beaver.

The next morning, they passed a high blue clay bluff. Several small fiery balls rolled into the river from the burning coal and cobalt. They found great quantities of some type of currant. These currants grew on a scrub and resembled a damson plum and had a rich and fine flavor. Captain Lewis named it "buffalo berry". Clark and his servant and Isaac went on shore. He killed a deer and York packed it on his back. In the evening Clark killed two buck elk and wounded two others which he could not pursue by the blood as Clark's ball was so small.

They passed the mouth of the White Stone River. Here large points of land were covered with cottonwood and elm.

August twenty-fifth dawned to a cloudy morning. Captains Lewis and Clark decided to see the mound traders had told them about. They said it was evidence of another nation in that area. The captains selected Shields, Joseph Fields, William Bratten, Sergeant Ordway, John Colter, York, Corporal Warrington, Frasier, and George Drouillard to go with them. They left the canoe with two men and ascended to high ground. From that vantage point, the country was level and open as far as they could see except for a few rises in the distance and the mound which the Indians called *The Mountain of Little People or Spirits*. The mound had a conical form.

The Indians believed little people with big heads inhabited the area. They feared these little people would shoot them with bows and arrows if they tried to go near them.

At two miles further the dog Seaman was so hot that they allowed him to play in the creek when they arrived at the hill. Still affected by the debilitating effects of the cobalt and mineral toxins from two days earlier, Captain Lewis was exhausted from the day's heat. He needed water and the men with him were also thirsty. The first water they found was in a creek around the bend on the northeast side of the mound. Fortunately, the water was sweet and refreshing. Here, fruit was also in abundance. They picked grapes, plums, and blue currants. They camped in that spot all night.

The next morning, they investigated the mound further. This mound was located on an elevated plain that rose about the otherwise level prairie. The base of the mound is a regular parallelogram. From the longer side of the base the mound walls rose steeply. The mound joined with two regular rises, each in oval and half its height forming three regular rises from the plain. The main mound was narrower at the sides of its base. The structure looked manmade, but the earth and pebbles and other substances were uniform with the rest of the topography. The structure had to be a natural formation.

The prairie was open containing no timber and was level as far as the eye could see. The wind blew unobstructed over the plain. Insects of various kinds blew in the wind and a few were protecting themselves on the leeward side of the mound for shelter. Small birds were feeding on those insects. One of these birds was a small brown martin which they saw in vast numbers. They were so gentle that they didn't leave when the men came close to them. From on top of the mound, they saw a beautiful landscape with hundreds of buffalo feeding in before them in all directions.

The group joined the boat at nine in the morning. After they made jerky from the animals that they brought in, they prepared elk skins to make tow ropes before setting out. Drouillard and Shannon took the horses to hunt on the land while the rest of the men continued up the Missouri.

George Douillard returned from the hunt to tell them that Shannon and the horses were missing. George had walked all night to return to camp. While Douillard warmed himself by the fire with a cup of coffee, the captains sent Shields and Joseph Fields back to look for Shannon and the horses.

The next afternoon, an Indian swam to the canoe. The boats landed and two Mahar boys joined the other Mahar boy who swam to the canoe.

"We wanted you to know that the Sioux are camped nearby on the James River." One told them.

Another one said. "We also wanted you to know that our nation, the Mahar nation has gone to make peace with the Pawnee."

Captain Clark turned to Sergeant Pryor, a Frenchman, and the interpreter, Mr. Durion, to the camp to see and invite their great chiefs to come and counsel with them at Calumet Bluffs.

The Indian boys stayed with them all night. Captains Lewis and Clark both felt sick because they had eaten so much corn meal and plums. They camped below the Calumet Bluff in a Plain to wait for Sergeant Pryor and Mr. Durion, who were sent to the Sioux camp from the mouth of the James River. Before they landed the French canoe hit a snag and would have sunk had there been a load on it. Upon examination, the canoe was not fit to use, and they determined to send it back with the party that was going to return to St. Louis. Some of their load was wet so they moved what they could to the other boats. Shields and Joseph Fields joined them. They had not found Shannon or the horses.

That afternoon the men who had gone to the Indian camp returned and brought sixty Indians of the Sioux nation with them. Sergeant Pryor informed the captains that when he approached the Indian camp, they came to meet them supposing it to be Captain Lewis or Captain Clark to be of the party intending to take them on a robe to their camp.

The custom of carrying a distinguished visitor to camp seated on a buffalo robe supported by several men was widespread among the Sioux. The sergeant who had gone to their camp told the men in the camp that the Sioux had forty lodges about nine miles from the Missouri River up the Sacque River.

Their dwellings are made of dressed buffalo and elk skins, painted red and white, and are very handsome. They did not cut their hair like other Indians in the area. He said the women were homely and mostly old, but the young men were young and viral.

They met with several Sioux Indian chiefs—The Polsey, White Crain, Little Bowl, and Red Hand.

The James River was deep and navigable above the mouth where the sediments and sandbars lay. They learned from the Indians that this river passed the Sioux River and headed with the St Peters and a branch of Red River which fell into Lake Winnipeg to the north.

After breakfast, the captains sent Mr. Darion to the other side for the Chiefs and Sioux warriors. The man returned at ten o'clock with the chiefs. The captains spoke to the Indians and expressed the wishes of the US government concerning their tribe.

They offered a few items to the chiefs and a small gift to each of the men present. They gave the main chief a commission, some wampum, and an American flag. They retired to dinner. Mr. Darion seemed unhappy that he could not dine with Captains Lewis and Clark. The seventy Sioux present wore buffalo robes. A few held muskets that they had traded for with the French. The remainder had bows and arrows and were decorated with porcupine quills. They wore strings of white bear claws around their necks. These bear claws were three inches long and were strung as close as possible to each other on a string.

Only four of the chiefs remained with the captains. They were stout men and stayed to themselves. These chiefs were dignified men, had a high degree of superiority, but loved to laugh. They were interested in the air gun. The warriors with them formed a circle around three fires and danced until late.

Because they had been up late the night before, on the last day of August the chiefs delayed their deliberations with the captains until half past seven. It was a solemn occasion.

The oldest chief stood and faced the captains, "My great father's two sons I see before me this day. You see me, and the rest of the chiefs and warriors. We are very poor, we have neither powder, ball, or knives, and our women in the village have no clothes nor do we have clothes for our children to wear. We wish that my father's sons would be charitable enough to give them some things, as his brothers gave him a fine suit of clothes with a flag and a medal or gave him permission to stop the first trading boat or canoe that would come up the river to trade with them. would make peace with or between the Pawnee and Mahar. as his nation, and I would bring chiefs from each nation to the seat of government next spring with me with my chiefs, and that my situation was such that I could not leave my nation to go before spring."

He continued, "I hope the Great Father's sons will hear me better than the English. Yes, they gave me a medal and some clothes whereas the Spanish gave me none. You have given me clothes and metal, but we are poor because the trader has not come to bring us goods for some time. I wish you would consider and give me something more to take back to our squaws at home."

Captain Lewis stood up. "I am sorry, but we are not traders. However, we have come to make the road open for the traders who will come. In a short time, plenty of traders will come to supply the wants of your people on better terms than ever you had before with them."

The old man sat down, and the second chief was named Mathuga. He spoke better English than the elder chief. "My father, White Crain, spoke with me yesterday and today it pleases me to see how you have dressed our old chief. I am a young man, I do not want to take much, but my father has made me a chief. I had much sense, but now I think I have more than ever. I agree with the old chief. Please share your goods with us. We are poor and in need of trade goods."

He sat down and a third chief stood, "I am Mandan. I am a young man and know but little, and cannot speak well, but what you have told the old chief I have heard."

As he sat down, a fourth chief stood.

He said, "My fathers I cannot speak much to you. You make our old chief higher than all of us. I am glad to see him so finely dressed by you & will agree to what you told him and will do everything you and he agree upon."

Yet another chief stood, "My brothers, the medal you gave me gives me the heart to go with my old chief to see my great father in that place you call Washington."

After a moment, he spoke again, "You see before you, my two fathers, you made my old chief so fine that I will not go to war but take his advice and bury the tomahawk and knife in the ground and go with my old chief to see my Great Father. When I was a young man, I went to the Spanish and did not like what they said as well as I like what you have said to us. I am glad you came to see Father's land and all his red children, and the flag you gave us. It is so large and protects our children from the heat of the sun. He says also that he is willing to make peace with his neighbors, but the fine metals that you gave us we will give or show them so that they need not take our horses. We have our horses and bows and arrows here, but we want a little powder and lead to kill the buffalo. Our horses are poor and cannot run after them as they will be able to in the spring. Theirs is one tribe of red men that have not their ears open, but the old chief and us will do the best we can for you, about the other nation and all others as far as in our power lies."

Now a warrior, rather than another chief stood up. He said, "I am glad to see how fine you have made the old chief. Before now I could not spare him, but now I am willing to let him go to see your Great Father. My father, we wish you would give us a little powder and a little of our Great Father's whisky. We will rejoice under the colors of our Great Father."

When all was over most of the warriors went back across the river. The chiefs remained till dusk, and the commanding officers showed them the air gun and many other curious items.

Old Mr. Durion, the interpreter, left and went with his son to the Indian nation. The commanding officers gave the Indians commissioners more tobacco and corn to take with them to their lodges. Near sunset, a blue crane flew over and attempted to land on the boat's mast. It missed and fell into the boat. One of the men caught it and gave it to one of the Indians. The chiefs got into a canoe and crossed the river arriving safely on the opposite shore. There they camped and immediately after their campfire was lit, rain began to fall and doused the fire. It rained intermittently all night. The men who did not participate in the ceremony with the Indians were fishing and had amassed a considerable quantity of fish. They gave some of them to the Indians who milled around the camp waiting for the chiefs to finish their business. Colter had not yet found George Shannon because they had not yet returned.

After the council, the Indians set off for their towns on the other side of the river. They waved and smiled back at the explorers like they were old friends.

The Corps of Discovery set out again under a gentle breeze blowing from the south. They passed the reddish yellow, brown, and white clay cliff of Calumet Bluff. Here, the highlands approached the river on each side with a gentle ascent. Opposite the bluff was a large Island covered with timber located close to the left side.

Isaac was relieved to be moving upstream again. Every thrust of his oar into the river led them that much closer to the Mandan villages and that much closer to the time when he would be going back down the river.

"Look there," George Douillard pointed toward a pile on the left.

On the left side of the river, they saw a beaver house that stretched one and a half miles. Captains Lewis and Clark and two men investigated this lodge that created a small pond. They caught fish there like they did every day along the river.

The following day, a thunderstorm occurred. They heard several gunshots which they assumed were from their hunters Douillard, Reuben Fields, and Collins. They saw a breastwork of an ancient fortification shaped into an oblong form, situated on strong and well-chosen ground near the water. These works had to have been erected hundreds of years earlier. Isaac had seen similar breastworks back in the Allegheny Mountains and had heard of many others already on this journey. He heard one of the Indians say they even existed in the Rocky Mountains on the west.

By noon the wind blew so hard that the boats could not continue. The wind blew until after four. They gave up trying to continue that afternoon and camped at that location for the night.

The next morning when they set out, it was cold. Isaac saw his breath. Winter was coming. Would they be able to make shelter before winter arrived?

Captain Clark found three kinds of seeds that he prepared to send to his brother with the returning party in the spring.

Along the river, they saw signs that Colter was following Shannon. He had not overtaken him yet.

The cold wind continued to blow on the fourth of September. They passed the mouth of the Niobrara River and a Ponca village near its banks.

The Poncas were a Siouan-speaking tribe, whose language was nearly identical to the Omaha. They were horticulturists living in earth-lodge villages but made seasonal tribal hunting trips far out onto the plains. They did not meet with Lewis and Clark because they had been on their seasonal tribal hunting trip.

The following day, a Wednesday, was warmer because the wind blew from the south. The wind blew hard when they set out early. They set up a jury mast and sailed. They saw a large gangue of turkey and what they thought might be a grouse. They passed Poncas Creek which came into the Missouri on the left side. On the right side was a cliff. Between the Missouri River and the cliff was Poncas Creek which native had many springs containing salty mineral water. They saw several wild goats on the cliffs as they passed by. They then saw black-tailed deer. Captain Clark sent Shields and Gibson to the Poncas Towns on Poncas Creek. Up that creek was a beautiful plain and the Indians were out hunting buffalo. The Poncas raised no corn or beans.

Gibson killed a buffalo in the town. They saw a campfire that indicated that the two men Colter and Shannon, who were absent for several days were ahead of them. The corps had used the last of their preserved meat and the men had killed three buck deer and two elk. They made jerky from the deer, elk, and buffalo they had harvested during the past few days.

They passed a tall steeple-shaped rock that they called Old Baldy. That day they had their first sighting of an animal that the French called a prairie dog. Later in the day, they killed a rattlesnake with a prairie dog in its stomach. They filled some of the prairie dog holes with five gallons of water. They forced one of those rodents out and captured it.

The prairie dog's mouth resembled a rabbit, its head longer, its legs were short, and its toenails were long. Its tail was like a ground squirrel which the animals would shake to make a chattering noise. Its eyes were like a dog's eyes. Its color was gray, and its fur was soft.

On the eighth of September, they sailed all day and passed the place where Jean Baptiste Trudeau had wintered the winter previously. The plains they passed were blackened and smelled burned. They saw many buffalo and white wolves. That day, Captain Lewis killed a buffalo as did another one of the hunters. They also brought back another deer.

George Drouillard brought Isaac a plate of buffalo ribs and sat down beside him.

"Thanks, George," Isaac replied as he took the plate. He then tore one of the ribs from the rack and bit into the meat. The tender juices of the meat trickled down his chin.

"This is perfect," Isaac replied. "It's as good as my mother's cooking."

"It certainly as good as anything my mother would make," George replied.

So, do you know anything about this Trudeau fellow?"

"Matter of fact, I do. I heard he came to St. Louis from Canada in 1774 and now serves as a schoolmaster there. By 1795 he started making these trips into the Indian country. He speaks in the languages of several of the river tribes. In 1794 he headed the expedition of the Company of Explorers of the Upper Missouri to reach the Mandan villages. The Spanish lieutenant governor appointed him to the post. The Sioux blocked Mr. Trudeau from reaching the Mandan, so he wintered here. I'm told he first wintered here in 1794–95.'

The next day they saw a man coming down the bank on horseback. It was Shannon who had been with the horses. After sixteen days alone on the prairie with the horses, he finally met up with them.

Isaac got him some cold buffalo from the night before and he wolfed it down.

"Thank you, guys, I didn't know if I'd ever eat again," Shannon then took another bite, chewed it, and swallowed the meat before he continued. "I haven't eaten anything but some grapes and a rabbit. I didn't have any musket balls, so I shot the rabbit with a hard stick instead of a musket ball. I used all my bullets during the first four days. I saw footprints that I thought were from some of you guys, but I guess it had been from some Indians. I pushed ahead as much as I could until I became too weak to travel and determined to lay and wait in the event that a trading boat would happen by. I kept one horse as a last result for food. The other horse had failed me, and I had to leave it behind. The horse will likely starve to death this winter because I had no bullets or anything to kill him for meat.

The weather was overcast and gray for the next several days and the walls on either side of the river were also gray. On the fourteenth, they hoped they would see an old volcano MacKay had told them was in the area. They found no evidence of volcanic action. The burning deposits of coal or lignite may have led Mackay to this belief, which would have been based on what Evans had told him. Mackay had never been on this part of the Missouri River.

That day Shields killed a prairie rabbit and Captain Lewis was excited as he examined it. Its eye was large and prominent, and its eyeball was circular, deep-sea green, and was one-third of the eye width. The remaining two-thirds of the eye was a ring of bright yellowish-silver color. The ears were very flexible and located on the upper part of the head and very near each other. The animal moved them with great ease and quickness and folded them on his back or raised them whenever the rabbit wanted. The front outer fold of the ear was a reddish brown. The inner folds or those which lie together when the ears are thrown back occupied two-thirds of the ear width and were white except one inch at the tip of the ear was black. The hinder fold was light gray. The head, back shoulders, and outer part of the thighs are grey. The sides where the belly saw were lighter becoming gradually whiter. Its belly and breast were white and shaded gray. The tail was white, round, and blunted at the point. The fur on it is long and extremely fine and soft. When the rabbit ran, it carried its tail straight behind the body. The body was much smaller and longer than the rabbit in proportion to its height. Its teeth were like those of a hare or rabbit. Its upper lip split. It ate grass and herbs. It lived on the open plains and was extremely fast. The animal never burrowed or took shelter in the ground when pursued. It could jump as much as twenty-one feet. These prairie rabbits ran more easily and bound with greater agility than any animal that Isaac had ever seen. These animals lived solitary lives and seldom associated with others of their kind.

Captain Lewis skinned the hare and a goat that Captain Clark also shot that day. He stuffed them, bones and all, so they could send them east along with the other goat Lewis had stuffed to send back to Washington.

The following day they passed the area where Shannon told them he had waited for the trader Mr. Courtin because he thought the corps had gone on without him. They came to the mouth of the White River. The captains sent some men up this river to investigate that river. They camped that night at the side of a bluff. The expedition members still believed that Courtin, a trader with the Teton Sioux, the Arikara, and the Poncas, was traveling on the river behind them.

At dawn, at muster the next morning, Captain Lewis made an announcement.

"Captain Clark and I have realized that we won't be able to send our French detachment back to St. Louis until next spring. Captain Lewis looked right at Isaac as he made the next comment. "I know that some of you were looking forward to returning, but we are not to the Mandan village yet and winter will be coming soon so sending you back would not be expeditious."

Isaac was disappointed that he would not go home as soon as he had hoped. He wondered if Rebecca would even remember him when he returned.

Hunting was good this time of the year. Two days later, as they came to a river bend, they began traveling with numerous buffalo, elk, and goats feeding on the plains. Grouse, larks, and prairie chickens were common. They passed an island of willows below the Tylor's River which came into the Missouri River above the gorge of the river bend. They saw innumerable plovers and brants taking flight. The catfish in this part of the Missouri were small and not as plentiful as the lower parts of the river. The shore on each side was lined with rough gritty stones of different sizes. Cedar also was common along the river.

Isaac developed a serious abscess on his thigh and was in a lot of pain. Captain Lewis did all he could to relieve him including a drawing poultice. The fact he wouldn't be going home before winter made the abscess seem even more painful.

One morning a thick fog detained them until after seven when the sun began to dissipate the overcast clouds. They continued northward the following day. The wind from the southwest did not seem as strong as it had been.

They passed more herds of buffalo and passed an island where the Indians grew corn, beans, and squash.

Here, they came to a fort, Fort aux Cedres, built by Régis Loisel, in the winter of 1803. The buildings had already begun to gray, but Isaac could tell that they were constructed of and fenced with cedar. The fort was sixty-five to seventy food square with a sentry box in two angles cornered the pickets thirteen and a half feet above the ground.

Regis Loisel gave them a tour of his trading post. The trading house was forty-five and a half by thirty-two and a half feet and divided into four equal compartments. One compartment was for merchandise, and one for a common hall, for pelt storage with two pelt presses. The last compartment was for his sleeping quarters. The roof was covered with buffalo hides. The chimneys were stone, clay and wood. The Indian camp around the fort was for the Sioux who came to trade with Mr. Loisel. After they left, they passed a creek and islands of corn, beans, and squash.

The next day they passed an Indian camp where they saw cedar poles sticking high out of the ground. They soon saw that the Indians tied their dogs to these poles, and the dogs dragged their possessions from one camp. to another.

Reuben Fields found a creek the following day so they named it after him. Three Sioux boys swim across the river to let them know that a band of Sioux called the Tetons had eight lodges on the next creek and another sixty lodges a short distance further up the creek. The men gave the boys two "carrots" of tobacco to carry to their chiefs with instructions for them to speak with the captains the following day.

Before moving on, the next morning, they had selected some clothes and a few medals for their chiefs that they expected to meet. As they passed an island, Colter ran out of the plains and down the bank.

"What's wrong?" Isaac asked the young man who was apparently out of breath from running.

"The Sioux have taken my horse."

They took him on board and continued upriver.

A little further upriver, they saw five Indians on the bank who asked to come on board.

"We are friends," Captain Lewis said to the Indians, "but we cannot stop. We intend to continue upriver."

It was important to let the Indians know that they weren't afraid of them. He continued. "One of our men had a horse that was sent by our Great Father. We will not speak to your Great Chiefs until the horse is returned."

They came to the mouth of a small river where trees along the river had burned. They camped about two miles up this river that they named Teton. Captain Clark went on shore and smoked with a chief named Buffalo Medicine who waited for them there.

"I know nothing about the stolen horse," The chief told them.

"I want the Great Sioux Chiefs, to council with me tomorrow," Captain Clark said. The chiefs stayed on board all night.

The next morning, September twenty-fifth dawned fair with a breeze from the southeast. They raised the flag. Isaac helped set up an awning on a sandbar at the mouth of the Teton River to council under.

At about 11 o'clock, the two head chiefs arrived. Captain Lewis offered them food which they took, and the chiefs gave the captains some meat.

Mr. Durion tried to interpret the language, but he struggled with the translation.

"I speak Omaha, Pierre Cruzatte said. "Omaha is my mother's tongue. You have some Omaha prisoners here. If you have an Omaha who speaks Teton Sioux, we can communicate."

They found someone who spoke both Sioux and Omaha, so the captains communicated through the Omaha prisoner and Pierre Cruzatte.

At noon, the council began. First, the chiefs smoked the peace pipe with Captains Lewis and Clark. Captain Lewis delivered a written speech to them as did Captain Clark explaining their purpose entering Sioux waters. The men of the corps marched in formation in front of the captains and the chiefs.

Next in the ceremony, Captain Lewis gave the head chief, Chief Black Buffalo, a medal and Captain Clark gave them to the other chiefs.

"Come aboard the boat and see the many amazing items that we have."

Onboard the boat, the captains gave the chiefs half a wine glass of whiskey. They tipped back their heads, emptied the glasses and through the interpreters they asked for more. They took up the empty bottle, smelled it, and made many simple gestures and soon became belligerent.

Captain Lewis shook his head. One of the chiefs was noticeably drunk.

"Not so close to the edge," Captain Clark warned but it was too late. The drunk man went over the side of the boat and into the muddy river.

The Omaha prisoner told Pierre Cruzatte something and Pierre addressed Captain Clark.

"Captain Clark, he says that he heard the chiefs saying that they were planning to harm us."

"Thank you," said Captain Clark to the Omaha prisoner.

As soon as they landed, three young Sioux seized the cable of the canoe and one of the warriors hugged the mast.

The chief made extreme arm gestures toward the tarp under which were the trinkets the corps had to share with the various tribes.

He began speaking rapidly in his language. The Omaha translated to Pierre and Pierre translated to Captain Clark. "He says that if the corps want to continue through Sioux waters, they must pay more tribute."

"Alright," Captain Clark said and took out another medal for the chief. The chief pushed it away and pointed to a keg of whiskey near the tarp.

"No," Captain Clark replied. "I think we've shared enough of that with you."

The chief stood face to face with Captain Clark. Isaac didn't need an interpreter to know that the insults the Sioux now gave were personal to Captain Clark and that he intended to do him injury.

They had prepared for this possibility because of what they were about the Sioux. Captain Lewis had ordered all the men always to carry their weapons while in Sioux waters.

"To arms, men," Captain Clark ordered. He drew his sword. All the men around him drew their weapons and pointed them not at the warriors, but at the chief.

The grand chief then took hold of the cable and motioned for his men to leave. The warrior got out of the canoe and the second chief walked about twenty yards back. All had their bows strung and guns cocked and directly pointing at Captain Clark.

Captain Clark held his hands out, palms down. "Now, gentlemen, we come in peace. We didn't come here for a fight. We're just passing through." Clark spoke to them all but primarily addressed the chief who let the rope go and walked to the Indian party of about one hundred warriors.

Clark again offered his hand to the main chief who refused it while all this time the Indians pointed their arrows directly at Captain Clark. Captain Clark proceeded to the canoe and pushed off and had not gone far before the main chief and Chief Buffalo Medicine walked into the water and requested that they be let on board. Clark took them in, and they continued about a mile and anchored near a small island that Clark named The Bad Hundred Island. The captains placed a guard on shore to protect the cooks and a guard in the boat and fastened the canoes to the boat to keep anything from being stolen. The two chiefs stayed on board all night.

On the twenty-sixth, the expedition moved on. The river was lined with short Indians with small legs who requested the corps to let their women and boys see the boat. They asked for the corps' friendship. Many men, women, and children were on the bank watching them as they passed. These people were short with thin legs.

The men's bodies were greased. They blackened themselves and had headdresses made of hawk feathers. Their clothes were covered with skunk skin robes with pockets to hold their tobacco. Their women appeared very well, with fine teeth, high cheekbones, and dressed in petticoats made of animal skins and robes with the flesh side out and the hairy side turned back over their shoulders. These women did all the laborious work for husbands who frequently had several wives.

Captain Lewis and five men went on shore with other chiefs, who appeared to wish to become friendly. They asked the corps to remain one more night to watch them dance. In the evening Captain Clark walked on shore and saw several Mahar women and boys in a lodge and was told they were prisoners recently taken in a battle in which the Teton killed a number and took forty-eight prisoners.

Later, Clark advised the chiefs to make peace with the Mahar and give up the prisoners, if they intended to follow the words of the Great Father. They promised that they would. Clark and Isaac went into several Teton Sioux lodges. They were stretched on poles and made of dressed buffalo skins. These tents formed a three-quarter circle.

At about five in the afternoon, ten well-dressed men approached Captain Clark. They offered him a buffalo robe. They sat down in front of him and requested that Clark get into the robe. He did, and they carried him to their council tents. They set Captain Clark between the two chiefs and about seventy men who were seated in the circle in front of the chief.

They smoked the peace pipe under an awning made of forked sticks and covered with swan's down. The Spanish flag and the one the captains gave them the day before were displayed on either side of the council area. A large fire was made on which a large dog was cooking, and in the center about four hundred pounds of buffalo meat which the Indians gave to the corps. Soon after Clark took his seat, the young men went to the boat to bring Captain Lewis in the same manner as they brought Captain Clark. Soon after, an old man rose and spoke approving what the captains had done. He requested that the white men take pity on them.

The great Chief then rose and spoke and with solemnness took up the pipe of peace and pointed it to the heavens, the four corners of the earth and he made some motions and presented the stem for the captains to smoke.

After smoking the pipe and a short speech to the tribe, the captains were requested to take the meat, and dog meat to the captains to eat. They returned to smoking until dark when all was cleared away and a large fire built in the center. Several men with tambourines highly decorated with deer and hoofs to make them rattle, assembled, and began to sing and beat.

The women came forward highly decorated with the scalps and trophies of war of their fathers, husbands, and relatives, and danced the war dance, which they did with gusto until midnight when they informed the chief that they intended to return on board. They offered women to the captains, which they refused. Four chiefs accompanied the captains back to the boat and stayed all night.

Captain Clark and Isaac watched with horror as one warrior whipped two squaws who appeared to have fallen out of the dance. When the warrior approached, all the women fled into the night. They kept four or five men on guard walking around the camp and singing. Everyone seemed to be in good spirits that evening.

Clark talked to twenty-five Mahar squaws who had been taken prisoner. They said that the Tetons had destroyed forty lodges and killed seventy-five Mahar men and boys. There were forty-eight prisoners in all. The chiefs had promised him that they would deliver the prisoners to Mr. Durion who was with the Yankton Sioux and then gave their Mahar interpreter a few awls to give to the prisoners. Clark saw wild ground potatoes made into a paste-like hominy in a bowl that held up to two quarts of liquid made of a big-horned animal called a big-horned sheep.

The next day, most of the party went to the village five or six at a time throughout the day. The chiefs desired that the expedition stay that day. The chief of the lodge said that another lodge was coming that day with six hundred men and seven chiefs. The chiefs and their sons went on board several times that day and dined with the officers.

Sergeant Gass informed Sergeant Ordway and Isaac that when he was at the village that day, he counted eighty lodges which contained ten persons each. Two-thirds of the Indians were women and children.

The lodges were portable. The Indians drew them on sleds from one place to another with their dogs. They harnessed ones carrying about 80 pounds with ease.

They all watched the women work and dress buffalo skins for clothing and lodges. The women were very friendly. The vessels that they carried their water in were deerskin pouches. Some were making wooden bows for hunting.

The chiefs promised the captains that they would send the prisoners back to the Mahar people.

Another dance occurred that evening. At dark the officers and seven or eight of the party went over to the dance and see them dance and carry on nearly as the evening before. At first, the men danced and made speeches following them, the women then danced. The dance lasted until midnight, at which time the members of the expedition returned to the boat and brought with them two chiefs.

As they came on board, the man at the helm failed to secure the main canoe to the boat. The canoe swung round in the current and came full force down against the bow of the barge and broke the cable of it. They found they were loose in the river. The captains roused all of the men and got them safe to shore. The Indians hearing the commotion expected that the Mahar Indians had come to attack the corps. They all ran to assist the corps on the bank of the river and fired several guns for an alarm only.

"It's alright." Captain Lewis called out to the tribe. "We just had some problems with the boats."

Because they continued to fear for the lives of the members of the expedition, some of the Indians remained with them the rest of the night. The corps examined the boat that met with the stroke and found that the canoe had sprung a leak at one place. They corked it, bailed the canoe, and examined it for damage. They were relieved that there wasn't much damage, but they lost the boat's anchor. Ordway was on duty when this happened and remained on guard the rest of the night.

The following day they tried several ways to replace the anchor that they had lost but had no success.

The main chief, Black Buffalo, who was still on board and intended to go a short distance up river with them, was informed that the men were looking for the anchor. He grabbed the cable so the boat couldn't leave. He told Captain Lewis, who was standing at the bow, that they wanted more tobacco.

Chief Partisan demanded a flag and tobacco, but Captain Clark refused to give him any. After much negotiating, the captains gave a carrot of tobacco to Black Buffalo which he shared with his men. Captain Clark jerked the cable from them and sailed under a breeze from the southeast.

A man galloped his horse at full speed. He stopped and asked to come onboard the boat. He was Buffalo Medicine's son. The captains sent him to tell the nation that if they hoisted a red flag under a white one on a pole next to the river, this meant they wanted peace. If not, the corps would defend themselves.

They found the answer to the anchor problem. They substituted large stones.

To prevent problems with the Indians, they camped on a small sand bar in the middle of the river.

The following day, they set out early. After a couple of hours on the river, they saw one of the chiefs that they knew they couldn't trust along with two men and squaws on shore. The chief called out to Captain Lewis and asked to go up with the corps as far as the other part of their band.

The chief and his people walked on shore and followed the expedition. It was obvious that they planned to waylay the travelers where they intended to camp to offer them women. Captain Lewis objected and told them that they would not speak to another Teton except the one on board with them, who would be allowed to go on shore whenever he pleased. Those Indians proceeded on until later in the evening when the chief requested that the canoe put him across the river which the captains agreed to do. As they traveled, they saw huge numbers of elk and passed an old Aricara village at the mouth of a timberless creek. They spent the night on the side of a sand bar a quarter mile from the shore to avoid the Teton Sioux.

The following morning, the last day of September, they had not proceeded far before they saw an Indian running toward them. He requested the expedition take him to one of the Arikara villages. They refused. Captain Clark discovered a great distance away that many men, women, and children were descending a hill towards the river above which the chief with them told them was the other band.

A wind rose and rain fell hard that morning. They anchored on the opposite shore of the camps that band of Sioux. They sent each chief and senior warrior a carrot of tobacco. These Indians told the corps that it was good that they had not wasted time putting the river between them and the other band. The band that they had stayed with previously had been bad. These Indians appeared anxious for the expedition to eat with them.

The captains apologized, but they needed to continue upstream and proceeded under a reefed sail. Isaac understood why the sail was reefed, that is, folded or rolled, in two places. It was done to reduce the effect of the wind but allowed them to continue.

The Indians continued following the boat and the Chief on board threw small pieces of tobacco to them. The captains broke into a keg of whiskey that evening to refresh the men. The guard on duty said that he saw two Indians at a distance. These Indians seemed interested in knowing where they kept the whiskey kegs. Just before landing, the boat turned and rocked suddenly, nearly filling with water. This alarmed the Indian chief on board who ran and hid himself.

"What was that?" asked Captain Lewis.

"It's alright," Captain Clark told him. "It's just a sandbar. We have landed safely."

"I believe it is a sign that it is time for me to leave you," said the chief.

"Very well," said Captain Clark.

Captain Lewis gave him a blanket, a knife, and some tobacco and advised him to keep his men away. The expedition camped on a sand bar.

The following day, October first, the wind blew cold and hard from the southeast all last night. They set out early and passed a large Island in the middle of the river. Opposite this Island the Aricara Indians lived in two villages on the right side of the river about two miles above the upper point of that island the Cheyenne River came in on the left side and was about four hundred yards wide but little water flowed from the river's right side. The current was gentle and navigable all the way to the Black Hills. They had to haul the boat over a sand bar because the river was wide and shallow at that point. A boy called out to them in French and invited them to visit.

They had arrived at the trading house of Jean Vallé. He was from a prominent family who lived in Saint. Genevieve. Valle and two men had a few goods to trade with the Sioux. Mr. Vallie informed them he wintered the previous winter three hundred leagues up the Cheyenne River under the Black Hill. The channel of this river was coarse gravel. He said that the river was rapid and difficult to navigate where it forked one hundred leagues up. The north fork entered the Black Hills forty leagues above the forks. The country around that river was like the land along the Missouri but with less timber and more cedar. Some of the Coat Nur or Black retained snow all summer and was covered with mostly pine timber.

He told them that many goats and a kind of animal with horns about the size of a small elk lived there along with a white bear. The prairie hens in this area were booted, and the toes of their feet were constructed so that they could walk on snow. They had short tails with two long feathers in the middle. The mountains also had white-booted turkeys.

I have not seen any along the Cheyenne. However, many beavers can be found in the mountains."

"Sadly, we won't be exploring the mountains this trip," Captain Clark replied.

Jean Valle continued sharing his information. "The Cheyenne nation has about three hundred lodges. They hunted buffalo and regularly stole horses from the Spanish settlements. Like most Indians, they do their horse stealing in November."

The next day, Mr. Valle came onboard.

They observed some Indians on a hill on the south side. One Indian, a Yankton Sioux came to the river and fired off his gun and asked the men of the expedition to come to his camp nearby. They refused.

They passed a large island on the right side and expected that the Tetons would try to stop them, so they prepared their weapons for the potential confrontation. The wind was blowing hard from the northwest. The river here was cold and rapid and clearer than below the Cheyenne River. They camped on a sandbar in the middle of the river to keep some distance from the Indians and themselves.

The cold wind that continued to blow from the northwest reminded them that winter was coming. They set out early. It rained so they checked their supplies and found that some mice had gotten in and scattered some of their corn. They saw large flocks of bryant and white gulls flying south. Some Indians watched them from the north side that day, so they decided to make camp on the left side opposite where they saw them.

A cold drizzle fell the next day. While they were eating breakfast, an Indian swam across the river and begged them for gun powder. That night they camped on a sand bar at the site of the remains of an old fortified Aricara Village. This circular village had been deserted for several years. Seventeen houses remained, so the expedition took advantage of the accommodations. Isaac enjoyed sleeping under a roof that was more solid than a tent. The Island contained little timber, so they had to make do with driftwood for their cooking and warming fires.

The following morning, October fifth, frost was on the ground. Three Teton warriors on shore called out and begged for tobacco, but the expedition didn't stop. A large herd of antelope swam in the river and the men shot four of them. That evening the captains gave the men more whiskey to refresh themselves.

On Saturday the sixth they passed a picketed Arikara village of eighty lodges. Each lodge formed an octagonal shape twenty to sixty feet in diameter. They were spacious, covered with earth, and stood close together. Beside the lodges were several skin canoes, or "bullboats." These canoes had buffalo skins stretched over a hemispherical frame. Though hard to steer, they were handy for crossing the river and could be carried by one person. In the huts the corps found three different kinds of squashes. Shields killed an elk. They camped off the mouth of Otter creek on the right side which headed near the Jacque River. It had a lot of water for that time of year.

On the next frosty morning, they passed the Moreau River and an another fortified Arikara town that was partially burned and other than having been partially burned it was much like the village they had seen the day before. They passed another band of Indians who said they were Tetons. The Tetons asked for meat and the corps gave them some.

They passed the first inhabited large Arikara village they had seen. Captain Lewis went into the village while Captain Clark oversaw the setting up of the camp. Captain Lewis had taken the peace pipe with him. During the rainy afternoon, Isaac and Joseph Gravelines, an associate of Régis Loisel and Pierre-Antoine Tableau, accompanied Captain Lewis to the village. Gravelines had lived with the Arikara for several years and knew their language.

Isaac observed that the Arikara were not wandering plains Indians but were sedentary farmers in earth-lodge villages. Their social and political structure was distinctly hierarchical, with hereditary chiefs. Like the other village tribes of the upper Missouri, they were middlemen in intertribal trade. From Gravelines he learned that they had been in contact with traders for several years, and venereal disease was already a problem, so the men were warned not to have contact with their women.

That night a cold rain, and wind continued. They raised the flag, but they could not speak in council with the Indians, the captains gave them some tobacco and informed them they would speak with them the next day. All the grand chiefs visited them that day as did Mr. Tableau, a trader from St. Louis who George Drouillard had told Isaac about.

Pierre-Antoine Tableau was born in Lachine Parish, near Montreal, and received an unusually good education in Montreal and Quebec. By 1776, he went west as a fur trade agent. He lived several years in the Illinois country, took an oath of fidelity to the United States in 1785, and moved to Missouri some time before 1795, when he first went up the

Missouri River. He was an employee of Régis Loise and spent much of his time among the Arikara. That night he told the captains everything he knew about the Upper Missouri tribes which was substantial. He also served as interpreter and intermediary with the tribe.

Many canoes of their canoes were made in the form of a bowl with a single buffalo skin. These crafts carried three and sometimes as many as six men and could maneuver the highest waves.

The Indians were especially interested in York, Captain Clark's manservant. They called him "The Big Medicine" because they had never seen a man with skin so dark before.

Several times, three squaws in a single buffalo sink canoe loaded with meat crossed the river. At the time, the waves were as high as Captain Clark had ever seen them in Missouri.

They held council on the following day. The warm wind that morning that had been from the southeast shifted to a cold wind from the northwest as they prepared to speak with the Indians, Mr. Tableau, and Mr. Gravelines. The chiefs came from the lower town, and none from the upper towns which were the largest. The captains continued to delay and wait for them. At noon they dispatched Gravelines to invite them to come down. They believed that jealousy existed between the two villages. At one o'clock the chiefs all assembled and after some little ceremony the council commenced, the captains informed the Arikara of the American acquisition as they had told the Otto and Sioux nations. They gave presents to each of the three chiefs of each Village including an American flag. After the council was over Captain Lewis shot the air guns which no doubt intrigued them.

While council was going on, Gass, Isaac, and some of the other men went into the Arikara village. The houses were in a circle of a size suited to the dimensions of the intended lodge, they set up 16 forked posts five or six feet high and lay poles from one fork to another. Against these poles they leaned other poles, slanting from the ground, and extended above the cross poles. These poles received the ends of the upper poles, that support the roof. They then set up four large forks in the middle of the area. Poles or beams were between these. The roof poles are then laid on extending from the lower poles across the beams which rest on the middle forks, of such a length as to leave a hole at the top for a chimney. The whole then covered with willow branches, except in the middle where the chimney hole passed through. On the willow branches they lay grass and lastly clay. At the hole below they build a pen about four feet wide and projecting ten feet from the hut; and hang a buffalo skin, at the entrance of the hut for a door.

This labor like every other kind of labor was performed by the squaws. They also were the ones who raised the corn, beans, and tobacco crops. Their tobacco was different from any Isaac had before seen. It was passable for smoking, but not for chewing.

Chapter 11-Rebecca

The south branch of French Creek in early February was frozen solid. Rebecca sat spinning wool in the backroom of the house when her father came in the front door. Since the room she was in had no fireplace of its own, the door to the main room was open to help keep her room warm so she saw him when he came in. With him was a strong handsome young man.

Her father closed the door behind them and pulled the latchstring in.

"Look who I found wandering the road. He said he came up this way looking for work. He says he's a logger. Since I find myself in need of a man to help log, this young man is Godsent."

Rebecca's mother stopped washing the dishes she was doing, dried her hands on a dishtowel, and walked toward the young man.

"What's the young man's name," asked Rebecca's mother.

"My name's Cooper, ma'am, Stephen Cooper," the young man said.

Pleased to meet you, Mr. Cooper," Mrs. Miles replied.

Rebecca got up from the loom and went to the main room to greet this stranger named Stephen Cooper.

He saw her about the same time she saw him. His eyes lit up and she saw him clutch his hat tightly. His eyes met hers. "Well, who is this lovely one."

"This is Rebecca, my daughter," William Miles warned.

"I meant no disrespect," Stephen replied. "It's just that I didn't expect to see anyone so lovely hidden out here in the backwoods."

A pregnant silence followed, but Mrs. Miles broke it.

"We'll be having supper in a little bit, Stephen. There's a wash bucket out by the barn. William will show it to you so you both can freshen up. Before you go, I'll have Rebecca get you some blankets so you can sleep in the hay loft."

"Yes, Mother," Rebecca answered. She and her mother went into the master bedroom and Mrs. Miles closed the door after they were both in the room.

"He seems like a nice man," said Rebecca's mother.

"We don't know anything about him, Mother!" Rebecca snapped. Already her mother was matchmaking and Rebecca hadn't yet made up her mind if she liked him.

"Well, at your age, you can't be choosy. William Christian seems far too busy to settle down, and I doubt Isaac will ever come back. You know he's a Thorton and has always had a bit of wanderlust in him. You do know that, right?"

"Isaac is my friend, nothing more."

"I have seen too many times how a young man goes west and finds himself married to an Indian girl. Isaac's father was first married to a Lenape woman before he married Martha. You know the apple doesn't fall far from the tree."

"Isaac is not his father," Rebecca declared. "Besides, I'm not waiting for him, you know. I'm not concerned about whether Isaac comes back or not and this man, we don't know anything about him."

She liked William Christian, but recently their talks had become more formal, and he made it a point to never talk with her alone. Perhaps Stephen Cooper would be the one to sweep her off her feet, but she wasn't going to tell that to her mother.

"You're right, Rebecca. We don't know this young man. He seemed to come out of nowhere. He is handsome though. Don't you think?"

"Mother, you're incorrigible!"

Mrs. Miles said nothing and thrust the blankets and a down pillow into Rebecca's arms. "There, take those out to the barn."

Rebecca's father gave Stephen the room in the lean-to off the main barn. The room was small and had a fireplace. When Rebecca saw him in his room, he had already made up a bed to one side of the room and had his pack in the corner of the barn.

"Here's some clean blankets and a pillow," Rebecca said. "You'll be having meals with the family. We eat at six, noon, and six sharp."

Stephen nodded, "Thank you, Rebecca."

A thrilling chill went up her spine. She felt her pulse speed up and she could barely breathe.

Rebecca nodded back. "You're welcome."

Stephen Cooper sat in the row with Rebecca's family at a church service. That morning Reverend William Christian preached on good clean Christian living at the end. He stood silent for a moment and said.

"I have been trying to put this off as long as possible, but I am announcing today that I am quitting the circuit. I am marrying a young lady in a small settlement east of here. I feel the Lord is leading me to build up a congregation there as the community grows."

After the service ended, Stephen smiled at Rebecca. Oddly, Rebecca left the church day with an uneasy feeling, she didn't know why, but she felt an immediate distrust of Stephen Cooper.

Chapter 3-Isaac

Isaac had taken the trip to what was now Concord several years earlier, but he had never taken the trip downriver to Pittsburgh. The trip was easier than it had been to pole upriver and took less time than it had then too.

The trip downriver was uneventful.

"Well, here we are," Andrew said after they had left the boat in the hands of Andrew's boat hand, and they trekked up to the Mayford home.

There, Isaac met Captain Lewis who was staying at Andrew's father's home while he supervised the building of the boats that would take them on at least the first part of the journey west. Isaac was going with Andrew and his boatman down to Pittsburgh so that Isaac could determine whether he wanted to be part of the expedition.

After meeting the captain, Andrew and Isaac returned to the river to unload the flatboat.

"So, what do you think of Captain Lewis?" Andrew asked as they walked.

"I thought what he was talking about was very exciting," Isaac replied. "I think I'll go west with him. How about you?"

"Oh, I want to go west as far as the Mississippi, but I don't want to go further west. I heard that since the United States is purchasing New Orleans and all, I was thinking that I would try my hand at shipping raw materials down the Mississippi. I think I'll start with the coal we have here and sell it to towns all along that river. A new day is dawning in America, and I want to do part in expanding this growing country."

After they unloaded the supplies from the flatboat, Andrew and Isaac loaded the neighborhood furs into a cart and hauled them back to the trading post where Isaac settled the Concord account. As usual, they had more than enough pelts to pay for the supplies that the families had received from Pittsburgh.

"Are you certain that you don't want to go on the trek west, Andrew?"

"No way! I'm going down to New Orleans. I'm certain I can make money from the coal that we have in that part of Pennsylvania."

"Your father is fine with that?"

"Why wouldn't he be? He was fifteen just when he crewed on the American Elizabeth. I'm seventeen!"

Isaac had to agree. No one could argue with that.

The American Elizabeth had been a privateer ship for the patriots when Jonathan Mayford, Andrew's father crewed during the American Revolution. He had been a boy, even younger than Andrew. While at sea, he met Andrew's mother Lowry and they were married very young. Andrew's older sister Lacey was several years old before Andrew's father learned of her birth.

When they returned to Andrew's parents' house, a servant met them at the door and ushered them into a small room at the back of the house where they bathed in a tub. The servant took their buckskins and replaced them with the suits and the shiny black leather boots of wealthier members of Pittsburgh society.

After dressing, they were led into the dining room where Jonathan and Lowry Mayford were sitting along with Meriweather Lewis.

Isaac wasn't sure what he expected of Meriweather Lewis, but this man was not it. Meriweather Lewis was tall and thin and had dark brown short hair. His nose was hawkish, and his chin was pointed. His eyes were dark brown.

"Well, hello, boys! You certainly clean up well," he exclaimed. He stood up and shook the boys' hands. He spoke with the twang of a Virginia accent. "I understand that you're considering coming to explore the Louisiana Purchase with the Corps of Discovery."

"I can't say that I am," Andrew answered, "but I believe that my cousin Isaac here is."

"Is that what you are calling the expedition, Captain Lewis?" Isaac asked. "The Corps of Discovery?"

"Yes, that is what we'll be calling it. I am deeply concerned about the state of our future relations with the natives, and I believe that this expedition will forward our nation with compassion and idealism. I know this sounds rather utopian, but I want to spend the rest of my life making for a better world. As we discover more of what this country has to offer, we'll be able to extend our culture into the wilderness to the peoples who live there."

They sat down to dinner. Jonathan Mayford sat at the head of the table and his wife Lowry sat on the other end. On his right hand, Captain Lewis sat and to his right, Andrew sat and Isaac sat opposite Andrew. The Scottish housekeeper served roast beef, potatoes carrots, and onions smothered in rich brown gravy. With it, she served yeast rolls and butter. For dessert, she served baked apples with heavy caramel sauce and sweetened cream.

Isaac listened as Captain Lewis spoke. He was intrigued with the former personal secretary to the President of the United States.

"Let me tell you. There are so many things we're going to learn from this expedition. First, we're going to learn so much about the animals and plants that are different from the ones that we have here. Are you interested in animal and plant science, Isaac?"

"Somewhat, sir. My father has taught me a lot."

"I have heard of your father, Isaac. He and your Uncle Philip did a lot to open the Ohio and western Pennsylvania lands."

Isaac nodded. He had been a child when his father and his uncle were negotiating with the Indians. Sometimes it was hard for him to believe now that there had ever been tensions between the Indians and the people of this part of Pennsylvania.

"Do you know much about subsistence hunting and fishing?" Captain Lewis asked.

Andrew was the one who spoke up. "Does he? His father taught him everything that a boy could want to know. He's almost as good a hunter and fisherman as his father!"

"It makes me all the more desirous of you coming with us on this adventure of ours, Isaac."

"I'll be helping navigate Ohio," Andrew told Isaac. "I've done it numerous times, you know."

Isaac did know. He too had seen much of the Ohio River, but he wasn't going to brag. It had been a while since his last trip, and he imagined that the river had changed quite a bit since the last time.

The fact that he chose to be an explorer did not surprise Isaac and he felt inspired by him.

Isaac could see that Meriwether Lewis focused on his dreams. He could see that the man was not in harmony with his true nature, he could fall to moodiness, become aloof, or be withdrawn.

He imagined that Lewis was often disappointed by the realities of life, his shortcomings, and those of others, and was relentlessly driven to improve upon it all - striving for greater accomplishments. Lewis needed to accept the natural limitations of the world and its inhabitants to make it possible for him to enjoy life more fully. Isaac wondered if that was possible.

Isaac imagined that Meriwether Lewis' greatest chance at success was in tying his fortunes to an endeavor that made the world a better place for others. This Corps of Discovery might very well turn into a highly successful and lucrative enterprise and be just what Lewis needed. Fortunately, the current president, Thomas Jefferson was a Democratic-Republican.

The Federalist Party, on the other hand, held the ideas of general meaning. That said, the Congress or the President has the right to interpret the Constitution based on significance. Overall, this meant that if the Constitution doesn't say it can't do something then the Federalists believed they have a right to do it.

Lewis, like Jefferson was a staunch Democratic-Republican. Lewis believed in interpreting the Constitution exactly, that the Congress or the President should follow the Constitution word for word.

"I heard that you were President Jefferson's private secretary. When were you appointed?" Isaac asked.

"I was appointed on April first, 1801."

"How did you meet the President?"

"We both lived in Virginia and conversed with various prominent figures in politics, the arts, and other circles."

"How did he know that you would be interested in doing this expedition?"

"I compiled information on the personnel and politics of the United States Army, which had seen an influx of Federalist officers because of "midnight appointments" made by outgoing president John Adams in 1801. I then was elected a member of the American Philosophical Society in 1802. Jefferson saw some of my writings and knew my backwoods background and offered me the opportunity to lead this expedition across the continent."

"Are you planning on going with just the few men you can get here in Pittsburgh?"

"No, I am determined to recruit William Clark> I worked well with him in the past. At thirty-three, I believe that he is the perfect man to share command of this expedition. My first matter of business is to go to Kentucky to see Clark and convince him to join the expedition."

"I guess this Louisiana Purchase that everyone is talking about is a big deal."

"I'll say. The land purchase will double the size of our country! That's why President Jefferson wants to get an accurate sense of that new land and its resources."

"Double?"

"Yes, but there's more to it. The president also hopes to find a "direct and practicable water communication across this continent, for commerce with Asia".

"What about the natives of the area?" Isaac asked.

"Good question, Isaac. I am glad you asked. Jefferson placed special importance on declaring U.S. sovereignty over the Native Americans along the Missouri River so we're going to do everything possible to make peace with the tribes in the area."

Isaac fell into the routine for the next several weeks of every day going down to the docks and helping build the flatboat near where the three rivers met. They worked on the craft all through July and August to Lewis's specifications. Two young men helped build the craft and they would be part of the crew going west with Lewis.

Isaac learned a lot during his time in Pittsburgh, as did Captain Lewis. Several days in August, Andrew Ellicott and Robert Patterson taught Captain Lewis how to use surveying equipment to find latitude and longitude.

"Are you certain you don't want to go ahead and join the expedition now, Isaac? You certainly fit the qualifications to join this expedition, son. You're unmarried. You look stout and healthy enough and from what Jonathan here tells me, you are accustomed to the woods, and I am guessing, capable of bodily fatigue to a considerable degree. You don't have a girlfriend back home do you?"

Isaac's thoughts went immediately to Rebecca, but he shook his head. "No, I don't."

"Well then you'd make a perfect candidate," he said.

As the boat took shape, others joined the ranks of the members of the group who would go downriver to first to Kentucky and then down the Ohio River to the Mississippi and beyond.

Isaac met eighteen-year-old George Shannon who was just a few months older than Andrew and was a friend of his. George was always talking about his abilities in the woods. He was always talking about how great he was in the woods. Isaac had his doubts, Shannon was young and had a lot to learn.

Then there was twenty-eight-year-old John Colter. He was five foot ten and was a solitary person who kept to himself as much as possible but was likable and a hard worker. He liked his solitude but was much more sociable when he had a couple of drinks in him. Colter was very honest. If he told you he would do something, he would do it.

At last, the boat was ready. The boat was fifty-five feet long, with an eight-foot beam, a thirty-two-foot mast, a shallow draft, and a hold thirty-one feet long. At the stern was a cabin with a deck on top, and there was a ten-foot deck at the bow.

The boys spent several days loading supplies onto the boat including trinkets for the Indians, and specialized equipment for the expedition. Finally, the boat was built and loaded. They were ready to shove off.

They left Pittsburgh at 11 a.m. with a party of thirteen hands. Seven of them were soldiers, the pilot, and five young men, including Andrew and Isaac who were considering the possibility of going with Lewis up the Missouri. Lewis's dog Seaman was also with them. The dog immediately liked Isaac.

"Seaman is a good judge of character, Isaac," Captain Lewis patted his dog on the head.

They arrived at Bruno's Island, three miles below Pittsburgh, and went on shore.

"Why are we stopping?" Isaac asked as he threw his line to George Shannon who was already on the shore. George took the line and pulled the boat toward the shore.

"I don't know exactly. Captain Lewis said something about visiting Mr. Brunot."

Isaac looked toward Captain Lewis who had his air gun in his hand. Several gentlemen joined him, and they met, he raised the gun over his head. He planned to demonstrate his new gun to them.

The island was close enough to Pittsburgh that even Isaac knew that the island was named for Felix Brunot, a French physician who settled in

Pittsburgh about 1797. This island stood where Chartiers Creek emptied into the Ohio from the south. He knew from staying at Andrew's parents' home that Brunot was a friend of Lewis.

"I thought Mr. Lewis was in a hurry. If he stops every three miles, he'll never get to Kentucky this year not to mention the Mississippi," Isaac joined George Shannon on shore and helped him secure the boat to a tree.

While the boys were securing the boat, the local gentlemen were examining the air gun when suddenly it went off. The man holding the gun followed the projectile's trajectory.

A group of women about forty feet away screamed and Isaac watched as one of those women fell. The other women first backed away from her in horror. Isaac saw that the ball had passed through the woman's hat and grazed her temple. She had passed out and blood gushed from her temple.

A couple of the women leaned down and one of them said. "She's dead! You killed her!"

The other woman examined her more closely. "No, she's breathing!"

The woman who had been shot began to stir and after a moment she sat up and the other women helped her to her feet.

"Are you alright, Mabel?"

"I think so. Just a little dizzy, I think."

After a few moments of conferring between the men and the women, they determined that the wound was not life-threatening.

Captain Lewis directed the men to return to the boat, and the group proceeded toward a ripple at McKee's Rock.

At McKee's Rock, they had to get out and lift the boat over thirty yards because the river was extremely low in that location. After they passed two more areas where they had to lift the boat out, they halted for the night. They had supper and Lewis gave the men some whiskey.

They all retired at eight. Whether the early bedtime was due to exhaustion or due to the quality of the whiskey, Isaac didn't know. He went to sleep almost as soon as he laid down.

Chapter 10-Isaac

A howling bitter cold wind whipped the door of his hut open on the morning of the ninth. Isaac wrapped the scarf his mother made him tighter around his face and neck when he arose and stepped out the rawhide door to six inches of new snow on the ground. He reattached the door closed, warmed himself at the nearby campfire, and stared over the Mississippi. The river had risen, and large ice sheets bobbed on the massive river.

Rebecca always enjoyed the ice on the creek back home. It's funny that he should be thinking about her now, he thought. No doubt rereading her letter the evening before had everything to do with this.

After breakfast, Matthew Ramey's wagon returned. Several men came with him, and several barrels were loaded in the back of the wagon.

"I have more whiskey for you, boys," Ramey called out to the men who were huddled around one of the campfires. Knowing that there could be trouble, Isaac immediately went back to his hut to grab his firearm.

Sergeant Floyd immediately stepped forward and took control of the situation. "I'm sorry, Mr. Ramey. Captain Clark gave express orders that your whiskey is strictly off limits."

"What do you mean, you're not going to let us do any business with your men? Your men have a right to drink. Don't they? It's a free country! I want to talk to your captain."

"I'm sorry," Floyd replied. "We have explicit instructions not to allow you to sell the men any of your whiskey. Now if you'll kindly leave. . ."

One of the men went for his gun and immediately George Shannon, John Colter, and Isaac all had their weapons pointed at the man with the gun.

Ramey put his hand on the man's shoulder. "It's not worth the bother. I know of other camps who would love this whiskey."

He then said to Sergeant Floyd. "We won't be troubling you anymore, *sergeant*."

After Ramey left, Captain Clark was ready to escape camp and explore the area. However, Captain Clark called Isaac and Collins to his cabin before he did.

"I need to find out where you found that hog that was skinned and hung up."

The boys agreed to show him the location. When they got there, they found that crows had eaten what meat had been left.

"Well, we aren't getting any meat from that hog," Captain Clark said. "Let's go hunting so we can, at least, bring some kind of meat home."

On their way back, they killed several prairie chickens. They shouldered their birds and started back when they noticed what appeared to be an ancient Indian fortification on the other side of a small pond.

"Let's walk across. It looks solid enough and it will save us some time," Clark attempted to cross a pond, but the ice broke. He was unable to get his foot out of the pond before it got wet.

"I guess we should walk around this pond after all," he said.

The fortress on the opposite side of the pond had nine mounds forming a circle. Two of them were about seven feet above the plain. They found great quantities of earthenware and arrowheads in one of the two larger mounds.

They returned to their camp before sunset, and Captain Clark's feet were frozen to his shoes. He warmed his feet inside his boots by the fireplace well enough that he could take off his boot without damaging his foot. He continued warming his foot by placing it in warm water to prevent frostbite.

The following morning, Captain Clark was hobbling around camp when James Mackay came.

"I see you have an accent, sir," Isaac said. "Were you from Scotland?"

"Indeed, I was born in Scotland and came to America in 1776."

"Have you been in this area long?"

"I engaged in the fur trade in Canada and from there made a trip to the Mandan villages on the Missouri in 1787. I came to the Louisiana territory about 1794 and swore allegiance to the Spanish government. I then became manager of the then-Spanish-controlled Missouri Fur Company's affairs on the upper Missouri. I traveled up the Missouri River in 1795 and established a post. From there, I sent John Thomas Evans up the river hoping he would reach the Pacific."

"So did he?" Isaac asked.

'No, in fact, Evans got no farther than the Mandan villages. I personally explored the Niobrara, Loup, and Elkhorn rivers north and west of here and returned to St. Louis in 1797. Since then, I've been busy around here taking care of my estate, surveying, and doing official duties for the local Spanish government. The lands further west is a mystery to me, I'm afraid."

"I am looking forward to hearing your advice and whatever information you can give us about the Missouri River country. I am sure that whatever you can share will be of great value to me," Captain Clark said. "I am certain that you will also be an asset to the American government when she takes official title."

"I look forward to working with Americans again. I missed speaking my native tongue. Regarding information, I can furnish you copies of Evan's maps of the Upper Missouri," McKay told him.

Captain Clark's face had turned an unhealthy red hue. His eyes were glassy.

"You're not well," MacKay said in a matter-of-fact tone.

"I'm feeling a little feverish. I'm guessing that the fact I almost froze my feet last night is affecting me more than I thought it would.

"I will let you get some rest then. I'll look for those copies and get them back soon. Now, take care of yourself."

That night Captain Clark was sick, and Isaac helped him in whatever way he needed.

"You're a good man, Thorton." Captain Clark said as Isaac handed him a cup of hot herbal tea with a shot of whiskey. "Where did you get the whiskey?"

"Captain Lewis made sure we have some for medicinal purposes," Isaac replied. "He brought it with him from Pittsburgh. He showed me where it's kept in the provisions. I would count this as a medicinal purpose You'll sleep better."

"I guess I should thank Captain Lewis for letting you know where it's kept."

The next morning, the rivers continued to rise because of ice jams. The boat was still afloat. McNeal had wandered from his hunting party and the other men in the party went looking for him. He returned at dark that evening, but Sergeant Ordway remained out that night. He returned in the morning, none the worse for wear.

That day Clark's chimney caught on fire. The grass used in the chinking between the stones caught on fire. All the men joined together to make a fire brigade and soon had the fire out. The men helped Captain Clark repair the fire damage on the cabin.

At sunset, Major Rumsey from the commissary arrived with some provisions in the wagon of Mr. Todd. Nathan Rumsey was a contractor for army rations in the area. Seven or eight men came with Major Rumsey, and all were drunk from whiskey that Major Rumsey had on the wagon. The barrel had been meant for the party. Clark ordered a gill of the whiskey for each man.

The next morning, Monday, Major Rumsey brought two trunks of goods and asked if he could sell them to them as provisions for the party. Clark agreed if Captain Lewis also agreed. Clark paid the contractor for what had been furnished to this day and agreed to purchase thirty gills of whiskey, ammunition, rations, vinegar, soap, and candles.

The two groups had a shooting match against each other. This time, Robert Frazer was the best shot. Windsor came in second. Shields came in third, and Field came in fourth.

Colter and Gibson returned after dark that evening with a letter from Captain Lewis, one from Louisville, and three newspapers.

After the men from the commissary left, work continued for the group as it had been. The men hunted and kept the boats from being damaged by ice on the rivers. The weather was unpredictable. It was cold one day and sunny the next. Clark was sick off and on. Visitors and curiosity seekers both European and Native American visited often.

Seiken was discharged on February 4, 1804. He said that he didn't like the rules that the captains had for them and that he wanted to go down to New Orleans. Captain Clark told him to go and gave him his pay for his time there. He complained it wasn't as much as he was promised, and Captain Clark told him that he hadn't done anything to warrant what he had already been paid. Seikins left in a huff the next day.

"If I see your cousin, I'll be sure to say hello!" he exclaimed to Isaac as he slung his pack onto his back to begin the walk to St. Louis. Seiken was planning to stay in St. Louis until spring. He planned to crew a flatboat going south.

Chapter 7-Isaac

The following day Captain Clark marked the locations for their huts, and men began clearing and cutting logs for their dwellings. They had to be careful about how they felled the trees because the wind blew hard all day. One wrong move, and a tree felled wrong could fall on someone's head and kill him.

Isaac and George Shannon notching logs from the trees the men cut down so that they could be fitted together to create their shelters. While they were working some Shawnee men walked by. Isaac knew they were Shawnee by their dress. Their clothes and moccasins were made from deer skins. They wore long leggings with smaller leggings above the moccasins, long shirts over the leggings, and cloaks made of possum over their shirts. Most local tribes wore these clothes, but what gave them away as Shawnee was the unique bead designs on their armbands. In addition, these Shawnee had long hair that was not cut into a mohawk even though many of the tribe did wear their hair that way. They stopped for a few minutes to watch the men who were cutting the logs and at the man who was staring through a scope. The Indians did not stop to talk. They didn't even leave the trail.

After the Shawnee were further down the trail, Isaac spoke. "I remember the first time I met a Shawnee."

Isaac was aware that George Shannon had grown up with the Shawnee. He simply said. "Yes?"

Isaac stared out at the river as he continued to speak. "I remember my father took me and my older brother Matthew to a Shawnee town when we lived back at Fort Pitt."

That must have been a long time ago because the town has been Pittsburgh for a long time."

Isaac nodded. "It was. My father was raised by the Leni-Lenape who, along with the Shawnee, signed the first treaty with the new American government there at Fort Pitt. He went to see their chief to convince them not to attack the Americans at the fort. The Shawnee claimed that the Americans had broken their treaty, but since the Shawnee had a treaty with the Americans and the Leni-Lenape, my father didn't feel that there was any problem bringing us boys with him when he spoke to them."

"What did your father and the chiefs talk about?"

"I don't know. All I remember is playing with a rawhide ball with some Shawnee boys that day. What I remember most about that time was that we were all competitive little boys who wanted to win a game."

"Yes, it's too bad we don't all realize that all men are more alike than different," George replied. He looked over at York who was pulling a large log toward them.

Sergeant Charles Floyd interrupted them, "Get back to work, boys. We need those logs notched before the end of the day, and more are coming."

The boys looked at the logs that were piling up around them. Yes, they did need to pick up the pace if they wanted their next meal because they wouldn't be able to have their evening meal until they made a major dent in that pile.

On Friday, Captain Clark sent Charles Floyd to Cahokia with letters from Captain Lewis and others to take to the post office. Isaac's letters to his family were among them.

That day Isaac and Shannon finished notching the logs and started helping build the log walls in one of the cabins when they saw a canoe with two men dressed in buckskin breeches and gray-green woolen shirts paddling up the river. The two men landed their canoe at the camp's landing and pulled their canoe onto the shore.

Captains Lewis and Clark left the work party and went to greet the men. "Hello there!"

The man who seemed to be the leader reached out his hand to Lewis's outstretched hand. Hello, I'm Samuel Griffith. I have a sizable farm nine miles up the Missouri. This is Martin Gilbert, a salt trader."

Captain Lewis told him about the mission of the Corps of Discovery.

"Welcome to this vast country!" Griffin said. "I warn you. You'll never want to leave! I came here from New York in 1795 and decided to stay."

"Where are you all heading?" Captain Lewis asked.

"We're just on our way home from trading for goods that we'll need this winter once we get upriver."

The two men spent the night there and the next day they pushed off and continued their journey up the Missouri. The men told the young men about the beauties and dangers that they encountered as they traveled on the Missouri.

On Monday evening, Charles Floyd returned with wagons filled with provisions as well as letters from families.

As they passed out letters from the post that Floyd brought back from Cahokia, Lewis and Clark sat down with the men of the expedition and explained their winter plans. The plan was simple. They would spend the winter preparing as much as they could for the journey ahead.

The men moved into their huts the following evening.

December twenty-first was a cloudy day. A waggoner brought supplies and charged Captain Clark three dollars for his services, but at least the job was done. Captain Clark sent Shields and Floyd out to hunt, and they killed seven very fat turkeys. While Shields and Floyd were out hunting, Clark instructed the rest of the men, including Isaac, in erecting the captain's cabin.

The next morning sleet fell heavily, and ice cracked the limbs of trees. The river fell fast. The boat went aground in the creek. The sleet became a miserable cold mist. Clark had the men remove the valuables from the boat and put them under guard on the bank. The weather prevented the men from continuing their building projects.

Isaac chopped wood outside Captain Clark's cabin when George Drouillard arrived with seven men along with several horses on the afternoon of December 22,

As George and the other men rode into camp, Captain Clark came out of his cabin. "What is going on here? I thought I sent you to bring horses."

"I did, sir. Captain John Campbell has sent you a detail from his company of the Second Infantry Regiment. These men were stationed at Southwest Point."

"I was unaware that these men were coming," Captain Clark replied.

Just by how they wore their uniforms, Isaac could see that Campbell had sent four of them back to Tennessee. He kept Corporal Richard Warfington and Privates Hugh Hall, Thomas P. Howard, and John Potts. The other four were immediately rejected and sent back to Southwest Point.

On that day, officially Captain Lewis hired George Droullard in the public service as an Indian Interpreter. Droullard brought Clark a letter from Charles Gratiot. Gratiot was born in Switzerland. He arrived in Montreal in 1769 to engage in the fur trade and established a store at Cahokia in 1777.

Captain Clark told the men that during the Revolution Gratiot was of assistance to Clark's brother, George Rogers Clark. In 1781, Gratiot moved to St. Louis, married into the prominent Chouteau family, and became a leading fur trader and citizen.

Rain fell again the next day. A local man rolled into the camp with a wagon load of turnips. Shortly after the man left, George Drouillard returned from hunting with three deer so that night the expedition dined on venison and turnips. The new arrivals that George Drouillard had brought started building their huts while the original group of men set to caring for their dwellings. John Shields, who was finished with his hut, went to get butter.

Chapter 8-Rebecca

Rebecca was washing dishes, and her mother was sewing a patch on a pair of Rebecca's father's pants when they heard the bells on the reins of a horse and rider in front of their cabin.

Rebecca's mother looked out the tiny window beside the front door. Rebecca followed her gaze and saw the thick lake-effect snowflakes falling into drifts. The snow covered the horse and rider making them look like snow creations like the Thorton boys always seemed to like to build during these wet snowstorms.

"It looks like the circuit preacher has returned. I imagine we'll have service this week."

"Yes," Rebecca dried her hands on her apron and tossed the drying towel onto the dishes she had washed. The dishes could air-dry.

"I guess he's not stopping here," her mother said. "I guess he'll be staying with either the Thorton or the McCray families."

She sounded rather disappointed. Rebecca wasn't blind to her parents' attempts at matchmaking.

"I would imagine it would be rather cold for him to sleep in our barn," Rebecca replied.

Sunday, after the service, William Christian and Mr. Miles walked their horses to the Miles barn because Mr. Miles invited him to have the noon meal with them. When William dismounted, he followed Mr. Miles and his horse to their stable.

Like most other Methodist circuit riders, he was equipped for the itinerancy. A good horse was of paramount importance to him as a preacher. He had named his horse "Saint". Saint was the minister's constant companion and was always treated like one. After the long ride, he always gave Saint a feed bag, brushed him down, and cleaned his hooves.

"So, what do you think of the new preacher?" Rebecca's mother asked her as they worked together to put the serving flatware on the table.

"I like him. He seems to know his Bible."

He certainly seems to talk to you a lot. What do you talk about?"

"We talk about the impressions he makes of the different towns he visits."

"You need to encourage him to discuss more personal things like what he wants to do in the future."

"You mean like if he plans to get married? You're predictable, mother."

The conversation ended because the two men came in from outdoors.

At dinner, the preacher talked about his religious beliefs with the Miles family even though Rebecca's mother tried to divert the conversation to more personal matters.

The closest he came to being personal was talking about his horse.

"Saint needs new shoes. Do you know where I can find a blacksmith?"

"You could visit Robert McCray, our local blacksmith, tomorrow morning. I'm sure that he would be happy to offer his services"

"His help would be greatly appreciated. I must spare Saint's shoes."

'Do you have problems finding feed for him?" Rebecca asked.

"Yes, unfortunately, Saint suffers when provisions are scarce, but, of course, this was only a problem during the winter months. During the spring, summer, and into the fall, I allow Saint to rest and graze in an open field by the trail. I always buy grain for him even though fodder is expensive."

"Why did you name your horse Saint?" Rebecca placed the basket of hot bread on the table while her mother placed the bowl of butter next to it.

"I named him Saint because he's the best horse I ever had. Besides, the way he puts up with me, he has to be a Saint, right?" William grinned at Rebecca. Her heart gave a jump in her chest. Could he be "the one"?

A few weeks later, Reverend Christiansen returned with Rebecca's father who had gone to Waterford for supplies.

"You'll never believe the excitement we had in town," Mr. Miles told his wife and daughter as he handed his wife the small packages he carried.

Preacher Christiansen continued. "When I was preaching in a town south of here, I had just finished preaching when a couple of local drunks came out of the local tavern and threatened to dunk me in the pond."

"Yes, fortunately, I heard them. They told him that they didn't like his preaching and didn't want him in town anymore because their wives were getting onto them for drinking so much."

"So did you get dunked?"

William laughed. "No, your father here stopped them before they could do me any harm."

"After I saved him, he told the two men that he hoped to see them and their wives the next time he was in Waterford." Mr. Miles slapped the reverend on the back. He gave a wink at Rebecca. William had not made any romantic gestures toward her, but she knew that if he had, her father would be all for it.

The next day it was pouring rain, and William Christiansen told the Miles family that he needed to be in Warren the following day. He wouldn't let Rain stop him. Like other itinerants, he journeyed in every conceivable type of weather to reach his Methodist gatherings on time.

That rain had been the last rain they had until Reverend Christiansen returned a month later.

The man, horse, and saddlebags were covered with sweat and dirt, creating a dry, flakey mud. The odor was almost more than Rebecca could bear and William Christensen must have seen her reaction because he said. "I'd be much obliged if you could manage some water to give Saint here a bath. We rode over fifteen miles on this uncommonly warm day."

"Of course," Rebecca replied and went behind the house to get a bucket of water from the well. "I'll heat up some more water for you so you can get a good washing too."

"Thank you."

At that moment, Rebecca's mother came from the garden where she had been weeding carrots.

"I thought I heard Reverend Christiansen's voice," she put down the basket where she carried her weeding tools and went to shake his hand.

"I'm sorry for the odor, ma'am,"

"Well, we'll get you some water right away so you can get a good wash up," she replied.

"As I told Rebecca here, I need to take care of Saint," he said.

"I did tell him that we would heat up some water for his bath though," Rebecca said.

"Yes, Rebecca and I can heat water for a deep bath in our tub. I'm sure that it will feel good to be clean after such a long hot ride."

"Indeed, ma'am."

While he bathed, watered, and fed Saint, Rebecca and her mother heated the water and took one of Mr. Miles' nightshirts and a pair of his leather pants and put them aside for William to wear while they washed and dried his smelly, muddy clothes.

By the time Reverend Christensen finished his bath, Mr. Miles came home to find William dressed in his clothes but barefooted because he didn't have any clean stockings. He also saw the clothes drying on the bushes outside the cabin.

"I see that the women have shown our hospitality to you, Reverend. Must have had a mighty dusty trip," Mr. Miles said as he sat down in the kitchen chair across from the itinerant.

"Yes, sir," William replied.

"Have you ever seen weather this hot and dry before?" Mr. Miles asked.

"Yes, we had similar weather last summer. I had traveled more than eight hundred miles and did not encounter a single storm. However, one day a violent thunderstorm came up and I was wetted to the skin to reach an appointment even though I had an umbrella."

In October, it rained especially hard. Travel was unusually difficult on wet roads and mud was a constant source of trouble for them.

On one of these especially rainy days, Rebecca wondered what the weather was like where Isaac was. How was he doing? Had he made up the Mississippi River and started traveling across the newly purchased land?

She laughed. Funny that she should be thinking of Isaac now when she was interested in another young man. She wondered what he would have thought of William. She wondered if he would be jealous.

The winter snow came early. In November, William encountered early winter sleet. Cakes of ice formed on his coat to nearly half an inch thick. His umbrella became much too heavy to carry and too frozen to close. He dismounted, started a fire, and warmed at his campfire before he continued down the trail. The storm became a blizzard.

He traveled over thirty miles during a severe blizzard to reach the scheduled meeting in Union Township. But, when he arrived, no one was there. He traveled on to the Concord settlement and the warmth of the Miles' home.

With the snow covering the ground Preacher Christian had difficulty distinguishing the road. The severe snowstorm had obliterated the landscape. He felt so chilled that he became certain his feet were frozen. The water froze as it ran from Saint's nostrils.

He had to cross French Creek which had grown to the size of a river. There were no bridges, so river crossings were hazardous.

He preached to the small congregation the following day, and one person was saved. All the trouble that he had was worth all the effort he made because one more person was going to be able to enter the pearly gates.

Just before Christmas, William Christiansen brought mail from Waterford for the families. There was a letter from back east from Lacey and Matthew for the McCrays and the Thortons. Rebecca received a letter from Isaac.

Dear Rebecca,

We arrived in Kentucky today and met up with Captain Clark and a few more of the men and boys who could be going with us up the Missouri. Captain Lewis told us that he wants to be certain that each of us is ready and willing to do be a part of this exciting but dangerous adventure.

Captain Clark recommended a fellow named George Droullard to go with us as an interpreter to the Indians. Droullard is remarkable. He reminds me a lot of Pierre Lamere. I am sure that my father would love him.

Andrew left us to go down the Mississippi. He took a couple of other Kentuckians with him. One of them says he's been down the Mississippi before. They say that there's potential danger from the Indians and River Pirates. I'm not sure who is more adventurous, him or me. I guess we'll find out. I'm guessing Andrew will win in that department, though. He's so much like his father who had been a privateer.

We're going to winter here at Wood River near the mouth of the Missouri River. I will be able to send you more letters during the next few months, but beyond that, I doubt I'll be able to send any.. We are here to gather more supplies and get to know more about the natives in the nearer areas and Captain Lewis has some diplomatic details to complete before we head up the Missouri River. I hope all is well with you. While we're here, I'll say I'd probably be able to get more letters from you if you want to send them, that is.

Rebecca's mother threw up her hands. Rebecca knew that her mother wanted to get her married and she was willing to let any eligible bachelor do. The fact that William Christian appeared to be an honorable Christian leader made him seem the best prospect a mother could hope to have.

Chapter 9-Isaac

Isaac awoke to a series of gunshots. He woke with a start.

"Was that gunfire? Are we being attacked?"

"You silly boy, that's just gunshots because it's Christmas." George Shannon said and pulled Isaac's blanket from him.

Isaac laughed. "I guess it is just a celebration. Merry Christmas, George."

"Merry Christmas, Isaac."

That afternoon, Shields returned with a head of cheese and four pounds of butter. It wasn't much of a Christmas, but it was nice not to have any type of duty that day so Isaac could relax, He sat on a log and scribbled with a quill onto the paper as he wrote a letter to Rebecca. The ink that he used was from the berries still clinging to a sumac near the river.

As he was writing, he saw a shadow fall over the water in front of him and he looked back and saw that there stood three Shawnee Indians. "We would like to speak to your captain," said the taller one.

Isaac nodded and took them to Captain Clark's tent. "Captain Clark, these men would like to speak with you, sir.

"Very well," Captain Clark stood up and shook the Shawnees' hands. "How can I help you men?"

"We came to tell you that the nations are planning to go against the Osage soon."

They told him the details.

"I see," said Captain Clark. "Thank you for the information. I will be sure to let Captain Lewis know. If you discover anything more, you'll let us know, won't you?"

The Shawnee grunted in acknowledgment. As soon as they left and before Isaac was dismissed, George Drouillard came into the tent.

"You look like you have made a decision, George," Captain Clark said.

"Yes, sir, I have decided to go west with the expedition."

"See, Isaac, that's how it's done. You simply decide."

"I'm still not sure, sir. I would like to go up to the Mandan camp with you though. I'm just not sure that I want to go all the way west with you."

"You are welcome to come with us, but we also need people who can come back and share what they learn this year too. Well, go on, with you then, go back to writing your letters. George and I have some business to attend to."

George Drouillard proved himself valuable immediately and went hunting. Two days later he returned with a large buck. He had also seen three bears.

The following day, Captain Clark sent Drouillard, and Sergeant Ordway went to Cahokia to inform Captain Lewis of a new plan. Captain Clark sent Sergeant Ordway to Cahokia, He arranged the guards on a new security plan and wrote to Captain Lewis.

On New Year's Eve, Mr. Matthew Ramey came by that morning with a couple of jugs of whiskey.

"Well, everybody! I brought you a little cheer to bring in the New Year!" Ramey exclaimed. "Nothing like a jug of whiskey to wet your whistle."

Willard, Seikins, Hall, and Collins immediately started chugging from the jugs. They soon became drunk and belligerent.

Willard said, "Let me have some more of that jug you got there, mates!"

He grabbed the jug out of Hall's hands.

"Hey, what did you do that for? It's my turn to drink."

Selkins stood there and began to defecate right there into the campfire.

"Hey!" exclaimed Sergeant Floyd. "You men are confined to quarters until you sober up."

"We was just having some fun!" Collins said slurring his words. "We're having a New Year's party."

Captain Clark came out of his cabin. "What's going on here?"

Seikins answered, "We're just having a New Year's party and sergeant here is busting up our fun!"

"This is no party! You men are dead drunk! To your quarters now. Move it or I'll have the lot of you in irons."

The next morning, New Year's Day, Captain Clark issued an order that Matthew Ramey could no longer sell alcohol to his men because Willard, Seiken, Hall, and Collins had all been stumbling drunk.

The New Year brought an inch of snow to the camp and clouds blocked out the sun. Despite the dreariness of the day, visitors came and went. Isaac helped Collins nurse his hangover when a woman came into camp. She went to the officers' tent to speak with Captain Clark. A few minutes later, Captain Clark came out of his tent with the woman. He then spoke to the men sitting around the campfire.

He said, "Mrs. Dupree here has offered to wash clothes for the detachment. I would like you all to get together any of your clothes that need to be washed and bring them to the tent area. Isaac and Collins, I would like you to carry the laundry for her."

Isaac looked over at Collins. The boy had not been able to keep food down and his face was extremely pale. However, to refuse would have not looked good for the young man.

Collins nodded. "Yes, sir."

As the men were getting their laundry together, several traders came with bags of sugar. Captain Clark bought six pounds.

"We hear that some of your boys are good shots." One of the traders said.

"That we are," Gibson said. "If a shooting match you want, a shooting match you'll get!"

These men wanted a shooting contest. Clark put up a dollar for the two best shots to win. Gibson was the best and won their dollar.

A couple of the men from the country people, Reed, and Windsor, had brought a jug and were drunk. They loaded the canoe with salt and dry goods and offered the contractor beef at four dollars a pound in trade or three for fifty cents in cash. Three men with Mr. Lisbet, a blacksmith, offered to sell them pork. He had also offered to reshoed their horses for them, but Captain Clark said that they already had one. Mr. Lisbet told them that he had gone up north and visited the Mandan tribe. They lived a six-day journey from the Assiniboine River, a tributary of the Red River of the North. There were British fur-trading posts on both rivers, from which traders sometimes traveled to the Mandan villages.

Early January saw the ice begin to cover parts of the Mississippi and covered most of the Missouri River.

On the night of the fourth, Warner caused Potts to drop his food on the ground.

"What did you bump into me for?" Potts turned and looked Warner straight in the eyes.

"What do you mean? I didn't touch you." Warner turned away and rolled his eyes.

How would you know, you pig? Your corner of our room smells like you took a dump and then slept in it!"

Warner turned around and stared right back at Potts. They were nose to nose.

Potts pushed Warner out of his space, and Warner pushed back. Potts then punched Warner in the mouth and Warner punched him in the gut.

Corporal John Robertson was the head of the mess that day. He ran out of the mess and threw up his hands!

"Fight it out if you have to! Suffer you to bruise yourselves a lot!" He returned to the mess.

Even Isaac who was a civilian knew that Corporal Robertson had no authority to allow the two men to continue to fight.

The following day, Corporal John Robertson was called out for his lack of leadership in the situation and was reduced in rank to private.

The next day at quarters, Captain Clark called out for some men to help Higgins raise his hut. Several men volunteered. He then asked Shannon and Isaac to hunt grouse. The hunters returned with a part of a hog which they found hung up in the woods and brought some bear meat too.

Isaac was on duty that night when the banks of the riverbank started falling in. Isaac had to grab the post that was holding the boat on shore. He shoved it deeper into the sandy earth.

"I can't control this thing!" Isaac exclaimed. "You'll need to awaken Captain Clark!"

Shannon ran to the captain's hut.

Captain Clark returned with Shannon. He took one look at Isaac's situation and called for John Colter to stand duty with Isaac so that he would help readjust the boat and its moorings.

In the early morning, Captain Clark ordered the men fix the moorings when large pieces of the bank slipped into the river. All hands were called to go down and make all the men help secure the boat and canoes.

He ordered Warner and Potts who neglected their duty to go build a hut for the woman who agreed to wash and sew for them.

Some of the men found another hog on the prairie. They skinned it. Clark sent out Shields into the neighborhood to find out whose hog it was.

The banks continued to cave in, which forced them to do whatever they could to keep the boats from being damaged.

Whitehouse and Reed were better with practice on the cross saw than they had been the previous week.

During the next couple of days, it rained causing the bank to fall faster than ever into the boats.

People who lived locally regularly came to trade and offer information about the Native Americans who lived in the country that The Corps of Discovery would explore.

On the last day of January 1804, Isaac was sitting by the fire when George Shannon threw three letters into Isaac's lap.

"Looks like one of them is from your lady friend back home," Shannon said.

"Hey, who gave you permission to snoop on my mail?" Isaac unsealed the letter from Rebecca.

"Ah, no need to get upset," Shannon replied. "It's not as if I unsealed the letter."

"It's good that you didn't," Isaac replied. "You're my best friend here, and I'd hate to have to whip the tar out of you."

"You couldn't whip the cream in a butter churn," Shannon replied.

"Well, go annoy someone else for a while. I have letters to read."

Shannon went to talk to Sargeant Floyd and Isaac unfolded the letter from Rebecca.

Dear Isaac,

I received your letter that you sent in November, at the end of December. I hope to get this letter sent so that you can get it sometime in January.

Mother has had me spinning wool into yarn so that she can sell it in Erie. I think she's doing this to remind me that I'm not getting any younger and that if I'm not careful, I will have to develop this as my trade!

Your mother tells me that I should pay her no mind and that she spun for your Aunt Elizabeth for several years before she met your father. She says that I just need to make up my mind and not let anyone tell me what is right for me. I like your mother. She always seems to make sense.

One of the other letters was from his mother and the third was from his brother Matthew who lived in Boston.

In the letter he got from his mother, she warned him that there was a new itinerate preacher in the area. She said that he was tall and dark and very handsome. He was the kind that would make any girl swoon. She said that she also saw Rebecca talking with him after service one day and that she knew for a fact that when he was in the area, the Miles family had him taking Sunday dinner with them.

Isaac could tell what she was doing. She was trying to warn him that there were other men around who might see her as available, which she was. Rebecca could be with anyone she wanted. He noticed that as he was thinking this, he clenched his fist so hard that his hand turned red.

From his brother Matthew, a lawyer in Boston, he learned that Matthew's wife Lacey had given birth to another son they named Jerrod.

Chapter 4-Isaac

The next morning Isaac awoke with a start. At first, he didn't recognize the canvas walls of the tent where he slept. A snoring Andrew sprawled on the cloth pallet beside him. Then it all came back to him. He was on his way down the Ohio River.

Because of the loudness of Andrew's snoring, Isaac knew he wasn't going to be able to go back to sleep so he got up and flipped back the tent flap.

Water was dripping from the trees and at first, he thought it was raining but then realized it just was heavy dew.

George Shannon and John Colter were already up, and George was in the process of adding a log to the fire as Isaac approached them.

"Did you have a good night?" John asked.

Isaac shrugged. "I guess so. It might have been better if that cousin of mine weren't snoring all night."

"I'm sure you'll have to get used to it. George Shannon said. "It's a long way to the Mississippi."

One of the soldiers, who had been detached by Lieutenant William A. Murray from Pittsburgh told Isaac. "Captain Lewis is paying Mr. Moore seventy dollars to conduct him to the Falls of the Ohio. Can you believe it! I wish I was being paid that much! I'd be able to marry Betsy Winger if I were getting that kind of money.

Isaac shrugged. It was none of his business what Captain Lewis was paying anyone.

The air was thick and humid, and it dampened his clothes. Isaac held his damp backside up to the fire. So much of the thick white haze covered the water of the Ohio that he couldn't see the opposite shore.

He then heard the thud of footsteps and voices coming from upriver. At first, he couldn't see who was coming because of the fog, and then he recognized the voices as those of Captain Lewis and Mr. Moore.

As they came closer to camp, Isaac heard Captain Lewis explaining his theory of his to the river pilot. It was a theory Captain Lewis had explained at the Mayford table earlier in the season, "The fog appears to owe its origin to the difference of temperature between the air and water the latter at this season being much warmer than the former. The water heated by the summer's sun does not undergo so rapid a change from the absence of the sun as the air does consistently when the air becomes coolest which is about sunrise the fog is thickest and appears to rise from the face of the water like the steam from boiling water."

"You might be right." The two men were now coming out of the mist and Isaac saw Mr. Moore looking at the captain and nodding.

At that moment, Andrew came out of the tent he shared with Isaac, his red hair sticking out in every direction.

"I slept like a baby!" He exclaimed. "How about you, Isaac?"

"He says you kept him awake all night," George replied. "He says you snore like a bear in hibernation!"

"You don't say," Andrew scratched his head and reached for a tin cup and the coffee pot.

"Perhaps you and George wouldn't mind sharing a tent," John Colter said, and John nodded at him. Isaac looked over at John and realized that John was insinuating that George snored as loudly as Andrew did. Isaac would be doing the older young man a favor as well.

"I don't mind if you don't mind, George."

"I don't mind if Andy doesn't mind."

"Nah, I don't mind," Andrew replied. "Just don't call me Andy. My name is Andrew."

"Then it's settled," John said. "Tonight, we exchange tent mates."

For the next several days, the group fell into patterns of getting out and maneuvering through low areas in the river and waking up to thick foggy mornings. At one point on the second day, they hired a team to drag the boat into deeper water. The local people were so used to strangers getting caught needing someone to pull them that they charged extreme prices for their assistance.

At the beginning and end of each day, Lewis wrote down the temperature of the air and water using one of his mahogany thermometers that he had purchased in Philadelphia before coming west. He examined the leaves of the trees and wrote down their names. They were names of trees that Isaac was already familiar with like Ohio buckeye, horse chestnut, black gum, sour gum, black tupelo, and sassafras. He was certain, however, that as he went west, the flora would change, and Captain Lewis would record all of it.

On September 4, Isaac was manning his oar on the boat when the bottom of the boat scraped along rocks on the river and water began pouring into the boat through a dislodged knothole.

"There's a leak," Isaac shouted and George and John who had been taking a break at the bow of the boat got up and picked up wooden buckets that were on the deck of the boat and began bailing.

"It's coming in too fast!" John exclaimed.

"Get to the shore!" Captain Lewis yelled, and he joined the men who were bailing and poured water overboard as the oarsmen directed the boat toward the shore. As they came toward the shore, they all jumped out and pulled the boat up on the sandy beach as far as they could.

By the time they reached the shore, the boat was nearly filled will water.

"Quick, unload the hardware and the gifts for the Indians. We need to dry them out and see if any of them are damaged."

Fortunately, the wares weren't damaged. They repaired the knothole with cork and pitch. Once repaired, they reloaded the boat and continued downstream.

At Georgetown, they purchased a canoe complete with paddles and poles, but this canoe also leaked and was unsafe. About three miles downriver, the men pulled the trucks and barrels from the boat and emptied their contents of them onto the rocks above the river. They dried out the items in the sun, put them in oilcloth bags, and put the bags in casks to keep them from getting further damaged. Lewis also hired another hand to take them as far as Wheeling in Virginia.

They passed the line that divided western Virginia, Pennsylvania, and eastern Ohio. The water in the river was so clear and low that they could see different types of fish. The boys all took their knives and whittled spears to gig some of the fish for dinner.

That night they enjoyed a fish dinner complete with cornbread from cornmeal they had obtained in Georgetown.

They passed Steubenville, Ohio, and Charleston in Virginia, finally arriving in Wheeling on the seventh. There Captain Lewis went on shore where he waited for Mr. Caldwell, a merchant, who Lewis had consigned some supplies which he had sent by land from Pittsburgh. Captain Lewis found the articles in good order and there he also met with Colonel Rodney who was one of the commissioners appointed by the government to adjust the landed claims in the Mississippi Territory. Colonel Thomas Rodney was from Delaware and was a Revolutionary War soldier. He was also appointed judge for the Mississippi Territory by President Jefferson. His brother was the Revolutionary patriot Caesar Rodney. With him was Major Richard Claiborne of Virginia who was to accompany Rodney to Mississippi to serve as clerk of the board of commissioners to settle land claims in the territory, a board headed by Rodney.

On the eighth, all the men were tired from all the portage that they had to conduct so Captain Lewis gave them the day off. Not that they would be able to rest, they just didn't have to man the oars and poles for the day. There was still trading and laundry to do.

"I'll do your laundry if you go into town to trade flour for bread," Isaac told his cousin.

"It's a deal," Andrew replied and threw his laundry bag at his cousin.

"Your laundry smells like something died in it!" Isaac complained. He threw his cousin's clothes into a pile.

"You talk as if your clothes smell like roses! They don't smell any better than mine do!" Andrew exclaimed.

"I'll go with Andrew if you do my laundry too," George replied.

"What do I look like? A washerwoman?" Isaac asked.

"Ahh, let Mayford and Shannon go. I'll help you with the laundry, Thorton," John replied.

So, Isaac and John Colter did the laundry Andrew and George Shannon's laundry while the other two went into town to trade flour for bread.

Captain Lewis and the crew had dinner with Dr. Patterson that evening.

"So, you're planning to commission William Clark to accompany you on this expedition?" Dr. Peterson asked.

Captain Lewis nodded. "I sent a courier ahead several weeks ago to ask him if he would be able to get some men together to go with us."

"Lucky man," Dr. Patterson replied. "I would do anything for an opportunity to see this new land of ours."

"Well, I'll tell you what, Dr. Patterson. If you're serious about what you're saying, I would be willing to the rank of Second Lieutenant if you would accept the appointment in his stead. "

"Would it be appropriate for me to go west with you?" Dr. Patterson

Captain Lewis replied, "Oh no, that would not be necessary. The group will be wintering in Illinois anyway, so if Clark decides not to come, and I need you, I will send for you."

It rained the night of the ninth and the clothes that Isaac and John Colter had carefully washed were rinsed again this time with rainwater. The next afternoon, Andrew and George picked up the bread they had traded flour for, and the expedition continued downstream.

Squirrel appeared to be on the menu that night because Captain Lewis had trained Seaman, his dog, to chase squirrels and bring them to him so they could cook them for their meals. They continued downstream eating what they could catch and what they could purchase or trade for as they traveled. They started seeing birds, first pigeons heading south. It appeared that already winter was not far off.

On the eighteenth, they came to Letart's Falls. Though they were called falls, they were more like rapids than falls, but they were the most considerable course of water that Isaac had seen on the Ohio so far. The descent at Letart's Falls as far as Isaac could see was a little more than 4 four feet in two hundred fifty yards. He had been downriver much further and knew that they were nothing like the Falls of the Ohio would be.

Chapter 22-Isaac

By the first of February, hunting was becoming scarce. A young war chief of the Menetarras named Seeing Snake and his woman Shea-hokeah came with some corn and asked the blacksmith to make a war hatchet for him. He also asked the captains to allow them to go to war against the Sioux and the Arikara who killed a Mandan in the past. When they got a negative response from Captain Lewis, they left that same day.

The following day was milder. Jessomme was still unwell. One his squaws had taken sick too. Mr. La Roche, the clerk for the Northwest Company, wanted to go with the expedition as they continued their journey in the spring. The captains said that they would talk it over.

The blacksmiths fired up their forge on the third because it was another cold but sunny day. Only a few natives visited the fort that day to employ the blacksmiths. Their boat and canoes were now firmly enclosed in the ice and almost entirely covered with snow. The ice that enclosed them, lay in several strata of thicknesses and were separated by streams of water. The ice could easily crush the boats if they didn't get the boats out of it. They cut through the first strata of ice, but water rushed up and rose as high as the upper surface of the ice. The water was so deep that it made it impractical to cut away the lower strata which were firmly attached. The vessels' bottoms wouldn't come loose from the ice. The men weren't certain how to alleviate the situation.

They first tried to break the boats free using axes. They made several unsuccessful attempts. Next, they tried heating stones to drop into the boats to melt the ice, but this didn't work either because every stone they were able to acquire burst into small particles when exposed to the heat of the fire.

Isaac realized that these stones, like some of the stones back where his family lived contained calcium carbonate thereby making them porous. When they heated these rocks, the trapped moisture turned to steam which caused rocks to break. They finally determined to fix iron spikes at the end of small poles as the means of them to free the vessels from the ice. They prepared a large rope of elk skin and a windless which they without doubt would be able to draw the boat on the bank provided they could free the boats from the ice.

The next day, Captain Clark set out with a hunting party consisting of sixteen of the expedition. Gass and Joseph Fields were also among these men. The stock of meat that they procured during November and December was nearly exhausted. A supply of this meat was important to obtain not just for immediate consumption, but they needed meat to take with them when they continued their expedition in the spring into the unknown lands. No buffalo had been found near the fort in several weeks.

Captain Clark decided they would go down the river to find the game. The men transported their baggage on a couple of small wooden sleds that they pulled themselves and took with them three pack horses which they had agreed would be returned with a load of meat to Fort Mandan as soon as possible. The local Indians also were short of meat that time of year.

Near the fort, Shields killed two deer that evening, but both were very lean. One was a large buck, that had shed his horns.

The next day, many natives brought more corn in exchange for the work that the blacksmith had done for them. They liked a type of battle ax that many of the expedition's soldiers, including Captain Lewis, found inconvenient.

The iron blade was made of extremely thin iron seven to nine inches long and from four and three-quarters to 6 Inches on its edge, from whence the sides proceeded nearly in a straight line to the eye where its width was not more than an inch. The eye of the ax was round and about one inch in diameter. The handle weighed about a pound and was no more than fourteen inches long. The great length of the blade of this ax added to the small size of the handle. It rendered an uncertain stroke and easily avoided, while the shortness of the handle rendered a blow much less forceful if well-directed, and still more inconvenient as they primarily used this instrument in action on horseback. An older version of the ax was even more inconvenient, it is somewhat in the form of the blade of a spontoon but was attached to half of the dimensions of the newer style ax. The blade was ornamented with perforations of three small circular holes.

Mr. McKensey left that morning and shortly after that Charbonneau returned.

When the hunters returned, they told Isaac that they came upon some Indian camps where they killed three deer. The next day they came upon more Indian hunting camps and killed even more deer. They killed ten elk and eighteen deer the following day and remained there all night. On the ninth, they built a pen to secure their meat from the many wolves in the area.

Charbonneau informed Captain Lewis that he had left the three horses and two men with the meat that Captain Clark had sent. He told Captain Lewis that the horses were heavily loaded and that not being shod horses couldn't travel on the ice. Captain Lewis sent some men down with two small sleds for the meat and instructed them to set out early the next morning. The two men left to lead the horses from the plains.

The rest of the hunting party returned on the twelfth. They had set out on their return towards the fort and killed some elk and deer in their way. On the thirteenth, the blacksmiths shod three horses so they could bring their meat home.

About five o'clock that evening, Sacajawea, one of the wives of Charbonneau, went into labor.

Isaac was there to help.

"Hold my hand, Isaac," she said in English.

Isaac took her hand and she squeezed it as each contraction came in waves. As the labor continued, her grip became more intense to the point that Isaac felt pain himself.

The young woman's labor pains were tedious and the pain violent. Isaac had never seen anything like it. He had always been sent from the house whenever his mother or other women in his family had delivered a child.

Captain Lewis's brow furrowed as the young woman's labor continued into the night. Isaac knew Captain Lewis favored this wife of Charbonneau to go with them west. The other woman avoided spending time with the expedition whereas Sacajawea was trying to pick up English words to communicate directly with the soldiers. If Sacajawea died in childbirth, it would be a blow to the entire expedition.

Mr. Jessomme came into the hut where the young woman labored.

"You know, I frequently administer a small portion of the rattle of the rattlesnake." He removed a snake rattle from the pouch he carried.

"That sounds like an old superstition," Captain Lewis said.

"I have tried it many times and the practice has never failed to produce the desired effect of hastening the birth."

"At this point, I'll try anything," Captain Lewis said.

Captain Lewis took the rattle from Mr. Jessomme and administered two rings of it. He broke the rings into pieces having the rattle of a snake by Captain Clark gave it to him and he administered two rings of it to the woman Sacajawea and added it to a small quantity of water. Whether this medicine was truly the cause or not, she had not taken it more than ten minutes before she brought forth her son. Perhaps this remedy was worthy of future experiments, but Captain Lewis was convinced of its efficacy.

"Congratulations, Sacajawea delivered a first child, a fine boy." Captain Lewis said as he put the child to the young woman's breast while the captain went to get Charbonneau.

Charbonneau came into the tent.

"Boy?" he asked.

Sacajawea smiled wearily and nodded.

"What shall we name him," he asked.

"Since he is your first son, I believe we should name him Jean Baptiste Charbonneau after you."

"Yes," he said.

With that, Isaac and Captain Lewis left the family to their privacy and went to their respective huts.

The following morning was cold but fair. The thermometer stood at fourteen below zero and a wind howled from the southeast. Captain Lewis ordered the blacksmith to shoe the horses and some others to prepare some gears to send them down with three sleds to join the hunting party and transport the meat to the fort.

Captain Lewis's men with the horses sent for the meat did not return until four o'clock that evening. The horses were exhausted.

Captain Lewis directed Isaac to give the horses some meal bran that was moistened with a little water, but he found that they would not eat it but preferred the bark of the cotton wood which forms the principal diet offered by the Indians during the winter months. Their women felled their trees and fed the boughs to the horses as well as the bark of their tender branches. The Arikara, the Sioux and the Assiniboine frequently pilfered horses of the other neighboring tribes. Therefore, the Mandan had a rule to put their horses in their lodges at night. In this situation, the only food of the horse consists of a few sticks of cottonwood from the size of a man's finger to that of his arm.

The Indians frequently pushed their horses all day long for many days when they pursued the buffalo or transported meat to their villages during which time the horses seldom ate during the day. At night the horses were placed in a stall where food was a scant allowance of cottonwood. One would think that the Mandan horses could not exist for long or at least could not retain their flesh and strength, but the contrary was the fact. This valuable animal under these conditions was seldom under-nourished or unfit for service.

A little after dark, Captain Clark arrived with the hunting party. On this expedition, they had killed forty deer, three buffalo bulls, and sixteen elk, most of them were so meager that they were unfit to use, particularly the buffalo and male elk. Wolves, which were numerous in the area, helped themselves to a considerable proportion of the hunt. If an animal was killed and lay exposed to the elements for only one night, the wolves invariably devoured them. They had to put their meat in pens so that wolves could not access them.

On the fourteenth, Captain Clark dispatched Drouillard, Frazer, Goodrich, and Newman with two sleds drawn by three horses for the meat.

They set out on the Ice and proceeded on about twenty-five miles.

When they halted to water their horses where the river opened near a piece of timbered land, about one hundred and twenty warriors of the Sioux Nation hid and waited to plunder and murder anyone who passed by them. The Sioux rushed out of woods towards the four men whooping and shouting as they came.

The Sioux took away the three horses but offered no violence to them. One of these Sioux returned one of the horses to the men.

The man to whom the Indian returned the horse, gave that Indian some corn bread, and divided another loaf of corn bread, among them, giving their chief that was with them a large share. These Sioux took the two other horses, and two knives from them, they then formed a half-circle around them. At the end of their discussion, they decided not to murder these men. The Indians would have killed them, but two of the warriors opposed this idea. and would not agree to participate. The Indians then allowed the men to return to the fort.

Gravelines, who lived among the Pawnee, arrived at the fort with a group from that tribe. He told Captain Lewis that the Sioux were the ones who had robbed the party that went down the river. The Sioux warriors told the Arikara nation what they had done. One of the Arikara warriors told it to the Pawnee who told Gravelines about the incident.

The party robbed by the Sioux returned to the fort at nearly midnight after Gravelines had arrived. They were exhausted. Upon arrival, they reported what happened to the officers. The Officers immediately called on the party for twenty volunteers, to set off early in the morning, in pursuit of those robbers. Twenty of them volunteered immediately and were prepared by the time the sun rose in the east These men included Isaac.

"You know you're not obligated to help with this Isaac," Captain Clark told him.

"I know, but I want to."

Several Mandan warriors set out with them but only three or four remained with them the whole day. They walked about eighteen miles and halted. They got some of the meat that the hunters had left hanging upon a tree and boiled and ate it. Some proceeded on to the place where the horses were taken. They found a sled the Indians had cut the horse from. They found many pairs of moccasins at their camp.

One chief of the Mandan was sent back to the fort from Captain Lewis's Party because the sun blinded him. This complaint was common that time of year and was caused by the sun's reflection on the ice and snow. It was cured by "gently sweating the affected part by throwing snow on a hot stone.

The party with their sled proceeded on down the trail until late in the evening. They arrived at two old Indian lodges where they expected to find the Indians. They sent Isaac to spy out the area, but he found no one so they went to the lodges and slept all night. Isaac's feet were sore from walking on ice for thirty-odd miles that day.

February sixteenth dawned clear and cold. One of the Indians sprained his ankle when he tripped on the ice. When that happened, the rest of the Indians also decided to leave. The party proceeded about six miles to where some lodges were where some Mandan had robbed Graveline's men in the fall. When they came to the site, they saw smoke where they expected Indians waiting for another opportunity to steal more horses or to attack them.

The party went up the riverbank about a mile above the lodge, laying low in the bushes so as not to be seen. They left the horse, sled, and baggage including their blankets. Captain Lewis sent Sergeant Ordway with a part of the men, the horse, and the sled back from the river with orders to advance immediately if they heard a horn blow signaling for them to fire in the event of an attack. Captain Lewis went with the rest of the party down the bank of the river until they came to the lodges, where they found that the Indians no longer there. The largest lodges were on fire, hence the smoke. Captain Lewis then sounded the horn. The rest of the party came up.

The Indians had torn down the hunting party's meat pen where they had stored two elk. The Sioux had stolen all the meat, except a few small pieces of buffalo meat which they left in the small lodge which they broiled and consumed. The Sioux had left the river, had gone up a steep bluff into the prairies, and escaped across the open prairies. Captain Lewis decided not to follow them any further, but to continue hunting for more game.

Four men went down to the river bottom to hunt. The rest of the party hiked about ten miles and camped at the upper end of the river bottom on the southern shore. One of the hunters killed a deer. Two or three other hunters returned in the evening. Isaac killed a deer and a wolf.

On the seventeenth, all hands who were still able to walk went out to hunt in different directions. They aimed to drive the game from the woods into the open so that the best hunters who were in the bottom could kill them. They all returned in the evening and had killed ten deer and four elk. They packed some of them in the sled and hung up the remainder on trees to keep the wolves from devouring it.

The next day, they loaded the meat onto the two sleds. One of the sleds was drawn by sixteen men, and the other by the horse which the Sioux had returned, when they robbed them. They brought the sleds loaded with the meat up the river on the ice. The Missouri was still frozen, and the ice was very thick.

Once they were back at the fort, the weather turned spring like. The men decided to take advantage of this by washing their clothes and drying them in the sun.

The chiefs Big White and Big Man took advantage of the weather and visited Captain Clark that morning. These two Indians informed him that several men of their nation had gone to consult their medicine stone about a three-day march to the southwest to learn that year's prophecy.

They had great confidence in this stone and said that it told them about everything that was to happen during the year when they visited it every spring and sometimes in the summer.

Once they arrived at the stone, they had a smoke ceremony and then went into the woods some distance away to sleep. The next morning, they returned to the stone and found white marks raised on the stone representing the peace or war they were to meet with and other changes they must meet. The stone was level, smooth, and about twenty feet in circumference, thick and with pores. Some of the mineral quality was affected by the sun. Big White told him that Hidatsa would go there as well.

Captain Lewis returned with two sleds loaded with meat, after finding that they could not overtake the Sioux war party. They hunted the next two days and killed thirty-six deer and fourteen elk. Several of them were so meager that they were unfit for use, but the meat they brought up on the two horse-drawn sleds weighed three thousand pounds. Another was drawn by sixteen men and carried about twenty-four hundred pounds.

The mild weather ended. At noon on the twenty-second of February, rain began to fall, and turned to snow. Two hunters went south and returned with two elk and hung them out of reach of the wolves.

Now that they had a good store of meat laid up, the next morning, all hands worked to cut the canoes loose from the ice, which was nearly even with the top of the vessels. They had great difficulty because of the different divisions of Ice and water. After cutting as much as they could with axes, they had all the iron they could get, and some axes were put on long poles and picked through the ice and under the first water which was more than six inches deep. They disengaged one canoe and nearly disengaged the second that same day.

The Corps of Discover members started early in the morning to cut the boat loose, which was more difficult than the canoes to remove from the ice. They loosened the second canoe from the ice and were ready to draw it out and were loosening the boat from ice when some of the corking drew out which caused her to leak for a few minutes until they discovered where the leak was located and replaced the cork.

The next day, they set up a windlass and drew up the two canoes onto the upper bank, and attempted to do the same with the boat, but the rope which they made of elk skins was too weak and broke several times. Night was coming and they left the boat without successfully removing it from the river Black Moccasin, chief of the little village of Big Hidatsa and several others, gave them some meat which they packed on their wives. Black Moccasin asked for the blacksmiths to create an ax for his son.

Mr. Bunch, one of the under traders for the Hudson Bay Company asked permission for him and his two wives to stay all night. The request was granted. Two Indian boys also stayed all night. One was the son of the Black Cat.

The next day, the men of the expedition doubled up the rope, pulled the boat out of the ice, and pulled the canoes further up onto the bank. They also began working on dugout canoes that the expedition would use to continue their journey to the north.

The next day, they prepared the tools to make dugout canoes because the boat and canoes they had could go no further than these Mandan villages. While the men worked on the dugout canoes, Captain Clark started drawing the map of the country along the Missouri, its tributaries, and the surrounding landscape. Richard Warfington and Isaac would take these maps south with them when they returned to St. Louis.

On the last day of February, Mr. Gravelines, two Frenchmen, and two Arikara arrived from the Arikara with letters from Mr. Tableau and informed the captains that the Arikara were determined to follow the Americans' counsel. They told them that the Sioux threatened to kill the Americans whenever they again met up with them. Several bands of Sioux were forming to attack the Mandan.

The captains informed the Mandan and others of this information and requested that they allow the Arikara to live near them so that together they could fight the Sioux and anyone who fought with them.

Isaac helped make the dugout canoes. Begin by selecting a large log that is large enough to fit a few people. Some of the men brought in logs that were big enough to make a canoe that would hold a few people. It couldn't be just any log. It had to be free of knotholes. Once they had the log, Isaac helped remove the bark and hollowed it out using an adze. He helped shape the canoe and covered it with pitch to make it waterproof. They would have to wait until the river was clear of ice to test the canoes, however.

All these preparations reminded Isaac that he was going to be returning to civilization soon and he sighed.

"What's wrong, Isaac?" Richard Warfington asked.

"Do you think that you and I are doing the right thing? Sometimes I wonder if returning is the best idea. Perhaps I should be going with them after all."

"I think you're making the best decision for you."

"But what if she doesn't want me back? What if she's already married to someone else," Isaac said. "What if she's not as anxious to see me as I am to see her again?"

"You'll never know if you don't go back. There will be other expeditions into the west."

"Yes, but there won't be another first expedition into the west."

"I'm guessing there will never be another girl for you either," Richard replied.

"True. Very true," Isaac murmured.

Chapter 17-Rebecca

The leaves wore their fall colors. Gone were the greens of summer and replaced with autumn colors. Maple red, oak orange, and birch yellow lined the path that led to French Creek. Rebecca carried her full bucket from the creek when she met Joseph McCray on the trail.

Rebecca set the bucket of water on a nearby stump.

"What is it, Joseph? Did a letter come?" Joseph never ventured down to the Miles homestead unless he had a reason and usually he brought the mail.

"No, a man is coming up the road with a load of goods by pack-horse."

"I'll tell Mama." Rebecca picked the bucket and hurried home."

"Mama, someone is coming down the road with supplies!" Rebecca exclaimed.

"Thank goodness! I was getting tired of making do," Her mother turned the metal arm that held the stew pot so that the stew would keep warm but not cook.

Since Andrew Mayford had gone downriver to New Orleans, the men had to go to Waterford to trade furs for supplies. The fact that someone was coming to them with supplies was a heaven-sent surprise.

Rebecca's mother put her shawl over her shoulders and followed Joseph to the road. On the way, they told Rebecca's father who was working in the field that they were going to the settlement. He put his hoe against the nearest tree and headed with them.

When they arrived at the settlement of Concord, Rebecca saw that the young man who brought the supplies had dark hair, dark eyes, and a muscular build. She glanced at her mother. She could almost see the wheels turning in the older woman's mind. Her mother smiled one of her biggest smiles and turned toward Rebecca. She raised her eyebrows.

Rebecca rolled her eyes. She could imagine her mother thinking that Rebecca wasn't getting any younger and that another perfect prospect had arrived.

The young man immediately went over to William Miles and shook his hand. "I was just telling Mr. Thorton here that my name is John Brown."

Rebecca noticed that even though he was talking with her father, his attention was drawn toward her, the only single young woman in the group. She noticed that her mother was smiling ear to ear as usual whenever another suitable prospective male entered the area.

"This is my wife and my daughter Rebecca."

"I'm charmed to meet your lovely family," John Brown replied. "As I was telling the Thortons and McCrays, Jonathan Mayford hired me to bring these supplies here by horse. He said to tell you that he wanted to be sure you received these before fall, but the creek levels had dropped and his son Andrew has not returned from his trip south. Jonathan also wanted to let you know that Andrew sent word to him that he was doing well down in Mississippi. He hopes to return by the spring."

"You must spend the night with us," William Mills insisted. "We have a room where you can stay."

"I much appreciate that, Mr. Miles," John said. "It has been a long trip."

"I plan to buy land nearby," John said. "There's a piece of land just east of Waterford that I have my eye on that I would love to purchase. I figure that I can put up a house, not a cabin mind you, but a real house, and perhaps raise some dairy cattle. I believe the soil is perfect for raising and selling dairy cows. Plus, I could sell milk here locally as well. I foresee these towns will grow once the Erie Canal is built."

"I have heard about that canal, John. Do you think that it will be built soon?"

"Yes, I do. And now with all that land opening up out west, pioneers and immigrants will need milk cows and I hope to have a number ready to sell. I think dairy cows may even be more lucrative than selling whiskey ever was."

Rebecca's mother smiled the whole time. He would be a good catch for some girl, but Rebecca now knew in her heart that it would not be Rebecca. This young man was not for her.

She could only think about Isaac.

She felt her heart racing, she felt anxious for change. She wanted nothing more than to escape the confines of this part of the country. She hoped to find the young man she had grown up with, but perhaps he had changed since going west.

Unfortunately, Rebecca couldn't leave yet. Winter was coming. John Brown would not be going west or even south so she wouldn't be able to go south with him. There was no way to take a canoe now either. The creeks were down. Besides her mother needed her here to prepare for the upcoming cold months. She would have to wait. She would have to wait for spring and Isaac's return.

Chapter 18-Isaac

The two upper villages of the Arikara tribe were near each other and built nearly alike. No trees grew near these two villages, so they had to cross the river to the timbered bottomland for most of the wood they used for fuel and construction. Captains Lewis and Clark visited the village, brought several party members, and returned that evening. The two upper villages were near each other and built nearly alike. There was no wood near these two villages. They had to cross the river to timbered bottomland for most of their wood.

The expedition cooks took their best ax on shore to cut some wood. While they cooked the evening meal, some Indians stole that axe therefore the cooks slept on onshore to guard their tools and fuel while the other members of the expedition slept onboard the boat. The cooks stood guard over what wood was left. In Kentucky, firewood was so plentiful that they burned much of it to get rid of it, but wood was a valuable commodity along this part of the Missouri River.

The captains sat at counsel with the Indians. One of the chiefs said he wished to visit his great father President Jefferson but doubted that it would be safe to go through Sioux territory. Captain Lewis offered to send their chief along with the chiefs of other nations upstream on the Missouri River.

As they spoke to the Arikara chiefs, the captains diplomatically explained the United States government's power over them. The chiefs accompanied them on board the boat. Captain Lewis gave each chief some sugar, a little salt, and a sunglass and set two onshore. The third went with them to visit the Mandan tribe.

The Arikara nation, consisting of five hundred men, appeared peaceful. These people were dirty, kind, poor, but proud of their tribe. Their men were tall and their women small and industrious. These women raised a lot of corn, beans, and squash. They also raised the tobacco that their men smoked. The women collect all the wood and do the drudge work as was common among the Indians.

The men wore moccasins. Their leggings had a flap in the front and the men wore a buffalo robe over their decorated shirts. The women wore moccasins, fringed leggings, and a shirt of goat skins with sleeves. This garment was long, white, fringed, and tied at the waist with a robe during summer.

Conversing with the Arikara through sign language, Isaac discovered that this nation consists of nine Pawnee tribes. Feuds and wars with their neighbors had reduced their numbers so the factions came together for protection. Their language was so diverse that not every tribe could understand all the words of others. They did not beg. They lived in warm large houses built in an octagon. A cone formed at the top and left open for smoke to pass. These houses were made of poles and willows covered with earth and grass.

He learned that they desired to be at peace with all nations, but the Sioux were a problem for them. The Sioux who traded goods with British traders for their corn had great influence over the Arikara. They poisoned their minds and kept the Arikara in perpetual fear. As a token of goodwill, like the other tribes they had encountered on the plains, the Arikara tried to get the corps to accept some of their most beautiful women, but the captains refused.

One afternoon, John Newton pulled George Shannon aside.

"I'm ready to quit this blasted expedition. I came to see the wilderness, not to work my butt off so that the captains could sit and gab with the old chiefs around here! Do you realize how rich we could be if we could trap furs this winter? One of these nights, I'm going to head out on my own! Want to come with me?"

Isaac overheard the conversation and immediately after John Newton left, he approached George. "What are you going to do?" he asked.

"I have to report him, of course," George replied. "I've had enough problems without taking part in a mutiny."

"I'll come with you, George. I heard the whole thing."

Later that day, Captain Clark confined John Newton for mutinous expression.

At the next camp, the Sioux would not talk to the captains. Therefore, the expedition moved on.

That afternoon, when they stopped because it rained. The captains formed a court martial of seven of their party and tried Newton. He was sentenced to seventy-five lashes and was banished from the permanent party. Moses B. Reed, the deserter, was also confined.

Here, the river was narrow and gentle. Plenty of cottonwoods grew in the river bottoms. The land was open, diverse, rich, and level.

That night the captains began whipping Newman and the Arikara chief with them cried.

"Why do you punish him like that?" He asked.

"He threatened to get others to leave camp in mutiny."

"We never punish men like that. If we must, we put the offender to death, but we never whip our people."

"What about children?" Isaac asked.

"Not even our children!"

The rain continued through the night. The morning was still cloudy when they set out. At seven they saw an Arikara hunting party who were on their way downstream to their villages. They had twelve buffalo-skin canoes laden with meat and skins. On shore, some young men were herding along the riverbank. These men, women, and children shared their meat with the expedition.

They passed an old Cheyenne village that was surrounded by an earthen wall. The Cheyenne had retreated to this place. Here they had taken their first stand against the Sioux who had attacked their villages. From here, the Sioux drove them even further from the headwaters of the Red River where they cultivated lands for many seasons.

The wind direction changed and blew hard from the northwest.

From shore, Isaac watched several Indian boys swimming with goats in the river. At first, he thought they were just swimming with them, but then he realized they were killing them with sticks and hauling them to the shore. The boys on shore kept the goats in the reddening water. He saw fifty-eight killed in that way. Captain Lewis shot three goats. Several Indians visited them that night and brought meat with them. They merrily sang all night.

More herds of antelope flocked to the northeast side of the river. The chief told Isaac that the antelope wintered in the Black Hills. In the fall, they returned to the hills. In the spring, these animals dispersed on the plains. Since winter was approaching, the massive herds were now on their way up the mountains where they would feed on the tree bark. In the spring, they would be as numerous on their return.

The next day the expedition continued upriver. After traveling six miles, they passed the mouth of Cannon Ball River which headed toward the Black Hills. Above this river, at the foot of a bluff, they saw several small round stones in the water. The stones resembled shells and cannon balls of different sizes. They were of excellent grit for grindstones. The bluff continued for about a mile. The bottom lands were fertile and partially timbered with mostly cottonwood, green ash, and American elm.

As Isaac paddled in the lead canoe, he saw what appeared to be a stick floating on the water. As the canoe drew closer to the object, he saw that the object was a canoe with some poor-quality furs.

"Hello!" Isaac called out to the men paddling the boat.

"*Bonjour!*" the man in the front of the boat called out. He was dressed like the other French traders he had met along the Missouri River.

Isaac continued his part of the conversation with the men in their native tongue. "Are you heading to St Louis?"

"*Oui!*"

"Wasn't the trapping good where you were?"

"It was, but we were robbed! They took four traps and half of our skins."

Suspecting that the thieves were probably the Sioux, Isaac asked. "Do you know which tribe?"

"Near as I could tell, they were Mandan. Their signs were everywhere."

I'm sorry to hear that." Isaac pursed his lips tight together. He felt his head furrow. *Could the reports about the friendly Mandan be false? Could it be this tribe was even worse than the Sioux?*

They set out early the next day under a gentle breeze from the southeast. There was more timber than usual in the bottoms. Captain Clark, the interpreter, and the Arikara Indian chief walked out onto the high plain. While they were gone, Isaac counted fifty-two herds of buffalo and three herds of elk along with deer and antelope. All the streams from nearby high ground were so salty that he couldn't drink the water.

Later that afternoon, Isaac went hunting with Peter Cruzatte.

They walked through the high grass and saw something white ambling toward them.

"What is that?" Peter asked.

"A bear?" Isaac asked.

"I never saw a white bear before," Isaac said.

Peter raised his gun. "I have a bead on him."

The bear roared and fell back with the projectile's impact.

"You hit him," Isaac exclaimed.

The bear got up and ran back from where he came.

"Blast it!" Peter exclaimed. Peter dropped his tomahawk and gun and ran after the bear. He then turned around to grab his weapons, but it was too late. The bear had run off into the underbrush.

"What bad luck," Isaac exclaimed.

"Well, feeling sorry for myself isn't going to bring us our supper tonight," Peter exclaimed. He shouldered his musket and the two of them continued following the Indian trail.

About half an hour later, they heard a snort in front of them. It was a buffalo cow. Peter took this shot too. The cow fell over onto her side. The two of them ran toward the animal. Isaac was the first one to see the movement of the huge young animal.

She's not dead!" Isaac yelled. "Run!"

The buffalo chased them, and they had to hide in a small ravine. This time Isaac, who still had a ball in his musket, aimed his gun and took his shot at the buffalo cow. This time, the cow went down and did not get up. They took the choicest meat from the animal, put huge chunks into their packs, and headed toward camp.

The next day some rain fell during the night and in the morning turned to snow. They came to the mouth of the Heart River.

"We need to look for a location to set up camp for the winter," Captain Clark told the men.

The next morning, Captain Clark had a stiff neck and Captain Lewis treated him with a hot stone wrapped in flannel. They passed a small Teton Sioux war party heading toward the Mandan camps. They passed a former Mandan village that had been devastated by smallpox.

Snow fell again the next day. They passed five fortified lodges which was where the Frenchmen they had met on the river a few days earlier had been robbed. There were signs that the Mandan had recently left the area.

Captain Clark's rheumatism was not as bad as during the past two days, so they continued downriver. They came to an island where a Mandan chief visited the Arikara chief who traveled with the expedition. They smoked the peace pipe together.

They passed a Hidatsa village. This tribe appeared to have similar customs to the Arikara, their dress was the same, but spoke more softly and milder. Their gestures were not as abrupt as the other tribe either.

The Arikara chief went onshore with some Mandan and many of them were on each side of the river watching every move the white men were making. The captains invited two chiefs they called Coal and Big Man to visit their camp.

To their surprise, they met a trader named Hugh McCracken who had been on the Assiniboine River. He had arrived nine days earlier with goods to trade for horses and buffalo robes. He had another man with him.

McCracken introduced himself to the captains. "I work for the Northwest Company> I mean, I should say the Hudson Bay Company. The truth is, I am a free trader working for neither firm. I have traded with the Mandan and lived with them several times before I guided David Thompson of the Northwest Company back in 1797.

The following day, they arrived in Mandan country. Many people from the Mandan village flocked to see them. Captain Lewis walked to the village with the Arikara chief and the interpreters. Captain Clark didn't attend the meeting because he suffered severe pain from rheumatism. That wasn't the only reason, however. They also decided that it was best if both captains did not leave the boat at the same time until they knew if the natives would be hostile or not.

Some chiefs came on board the ship and visited Captain Clark. He smoked with them. He delighted them by having York demonstrate how to use the steel corn mill. Lewis had purchased three hand-operated mills for grinding corn while gathering equipment in Philadelphia in 1803. These could easily become great items for the Indians to trade pelts to obtain.

As they got to know the Mandan, the men of the expedition learned that in addition to their farming and hunting, the Mandan were important as middlemen in intertribal trade. They were peaceful and accommodating with whites and were less aggressive in their relations with other Indians than their allies the Hidatsa. Prominent men of Cheyenne and Arikara birth dwelled with the Mandan suggesting a relatively low degree of ethnocentrism. They had a rich ceremonial and religious life.

The tribe had suffered in the smallpox epidemic of the 1780s. These people did not bury their dead, but placed the body on a scaffold, wrapped in a buffalo robe, where it lies exposed for the scavenger birds to consume.

On the twenty-seventh, they set out early and came to the village called Matootonha d where they stopped for a few minutes. Captain Clark was feeling better so he walked to a chief's lodge and smoked with them, but could not eat, which did displease them a little.

Here, Captain Clark met with Mr. Jessomme. Jessomme had lived with this nation for eighteen years. Clark got him to interpret, and he proceeded on with them. They came to a central point opposite the Knife River and formed a camp on the right above the second Mandan village on the opposite shore. They raised the flag. Captain Lewis and the interpreters walked down to the second Mandan village and returned in about an hour. The captains sent three carrots of tobacco to the other villages and invited them to come down and counsel with them the next day. The captains learned from the main chiefs had some knowledge of other Indian nations.

Jessomme seemed to be a cunning and insincere man. He told them that he was once employed by George Rogers Clark in Illinois and as he described himself, Captain Clark believed that Jessomme had never served with his brother. Clark believed he must have been a British spy for the British of Michilimackinac and St. Joseph. However, Clark did think he might be made useful as an interpreter, and he told all of this to Isaac.

Jessomme went to talk with some of the Mandan when Isaac heard Captain Clark say under his breath. "I don't trust that man."

"But you're going to keep him as an interpreter?"

"Yes, as my brother taught me, it's best to keep your enemies close."

Jessomme had now moved out of earshot.

"Why is that?" Isaac asked.

"Jessomme is a free trader who has been living with the Mandan for about fifteen years. He draws his goods on credit from the Northwest Company."

That doesn't make him an enemy, does it?"

"Well, what he told me having been a spy for George Rogers Clark in the Illinois country during the Revolutionary War couldn't have been true. I learned from Mr. Evans that he has acted as the Mandan interpreter for many different groups and individuals but was not a reputably good one."

"So why use him?"

"He seems to have participated fully in the social and ceremonial life of the Mandan, which may account for the low opinion some whites expressed of him. Evans told him that Jessomme planned his murder in 1796 when Evans tried to exclude him from the Indian trade. David Thompson, whom he accompanied to the Mandan in 1797, was not impressed with his character either. Alexander Henry the Younger called him "that old sneaking cheat."

"So, you're letting him be your interpreter anyway?"

William Clark shrugged. "Until I find a better option, he's the best we've got right now If you could keep your eyes on him, I would appreciate it."

Isaac nodded and went to the campfire where Jessomme was stoking the fire.

John Colter brought a pile of firewood and laid it by the fire.

"So, I hear you know about the Indians in these parts. What do you know about the Hidatsa?"

"Hidatsa? Oh, you mean the Big Bellies."

"Big Bellies? Why do they call them Big Bellies?"

Jessomme laughed. "Well, it's not because their stomachs are any bigger than others. It's just what we traders call them."

He went on to explain what he knew about the Hidatsa. The Hidatsa were of Siouan language family and lived in sedentary farming villages of earth lodges north of the Mandan A long association and close cultural connections existed between the Hidatsa and the Mandan, despite their distinctiveness. All these groups suffered from the great smallpox epidemic of the 1780s as well as Sioux attacks. The reduced population and the need for a defensive alliance were no doubt responsible, at least in part, because the five Mandan and Hidatsa villages drew closer late in the 1700s.

All these groups were sedentary farmers in permanent earth lodge villages who hunted to supplement their agricultural products. However, the Hidatsa tribe is said to have learned corn growing from the Mandan after they reached the Missouri River and were semi-nomadic. The Hidatsa seemed to have had a stronger military tradition than the Mandan.

The next day, many of the Hidatsa came downriver to see them and hear the council. The wind was so violent from the southwest that it prevented them from going into council because the chiefs from the lower village could not cross the river. The corps entertained several curious chiefs and offered them gifts. Like other tribes the men of the Corps of Discovery had met, Mandan and Hidatsa also believed that Clark's servant York had great medicine because his skin was so dark.

The Black Cat Grand Chief of the Mandan, Captains Lewis and Clark, and Jessomme walked up the river about one and a half miles. The captains observed that the location was good for a fort, but the timber was scarce and the timber there was small.

They talked with the grand chief about the other chiefs of different villages. He gave the names of twelve of them.

The Mandan women brought several gifts of boiled corn and in appreciation, Captain Clark presented the chief's wife with a in glazed earthen jar. They sent for the Hidatsa chiefs to smoke the peace pipe with the grand chief of the Mandan in their village and told them they would meet them in council the next day.

On October 29, Isaac was warming himself by the fire when Captain Clark told him to get his things and accompany him to visit an old Hidatsa chief in the council.

The chief had given his authority to his son on a war party against the Snake Indians who lived in the Rockies. The chief met them in council under an awning made from the boat's sail stretched on poles. Captain Lewis gave a long speech. Isaac saw that the old chief grew restless Captain Lewis continued speaking. The old chief interrupted Lewis and said that he was concerned that he wanted to make peace with Arikara and smoke out of the Sacred Stem with their chief.

Captain Lewis then introduced the Arikara chief to the Hidatsa chief and gave the peace pipe to the Arikara chief who smoked and then to the Hidatsa chief who also smoked and then to the rest of the chiefs who were present.

Captain Lewis approached the Arikara chief. "There were two Frenchmen robbed downstream and we would appreciate it if you could find out who robbed them. We would especially like to know that information by tomorrow.

Captain Lewis then gave small gifts to each chief and more gifts to the people of each village. As part of the end of the ceremony, Captain Lewis instructed Werner to fire off the cannon. The great noise of the cannon frightened the Hidatsa, and they left soon afterward.

The Arikara chief told Captain Clark that he wished to return to his nation the following day. Captain Clark put him off saying that they would talk to him after the other chiefs had spoken to them.

Captain Clark gave a steel corn mill to the Mandan who were very pleased to get the grinder that would make corn grinding easier.

The chiefs each had medals and they strutted and puffed out their chests with pride. One of the chiefs from the grand village of the Minatare was Chief One Eye, but he was out with a hunting party, so the captains sent a messenger with his medal and all the goods intended for his village. Some of the medals had portraits of President Jefferson on them which were called the President medals. Others were Washington season medals designed by the artist John Trumbull during Washington's administration but not completed until John Adam's term of office. These medals were struck in both silver and copper and portrayed domestic scenes that represented the civilization the government wished to convey to the Indians. One coin showed a woman weaving on a loom, another pictured cattle and sheep, and another of a man sowing wheat.

While the chiefs were in council, a fire broke out on the prairie and grew rapidly and violently out of control. It caught a man and a woman on fire and burned them to death. Several escaped among them was a small boy who was saved by getting under an untanned buffalo skin. The boy was half white and the Indians said that all white flesh is medicine. They said that the grass was not burnt where the boy sat, and this fire passed the expedition's camp at eight at night and looked extremely dangerous.

The next day, two chiefs came to talk with the captains. One of these men was a Cheyenne. They were grateful that the captains had given Big White Man a medal, clothes, and the flag. However, these two men had not returned from hunting in time to join the council and wanted medals too.

Captain Clark took eight men and one of the canoes upriver as far as the first island which was seven miles from their camp to see if they could locate a good location for their winter quarters. They found cedar on an island at this point which was some distance from the water. Captain Clark dismissed this location to set up their winter quarters because he did not think that they could get a good wintering ground there. He decided to drop back down river a few miles instead where he knew there was wood and game.

The Mandan chief spoke with Captain Lewis.

"I am grateful for what you have given us, and we want to share our corn with you and your men," he said through the interpreter. I will do as you suggest. I am leaving with the Arikara Chief to smoke the pipe of peace with that nation."

Captain Lewis patted the Indian on the shoulder. "Thank you. We are grateful for your cooperation. It will not be forgotten."

While the party was out searching for their winter quarters, many Indian chiefs visited the camp.

When the men returned, Captain Lewis gave the expedition a dram of whiskey and they danced during the evening which pleased the Indians.

The last day of October was a beautiful sunny morning. The Mandan chief sent his secondary chief to invite the men to his lodge to receive some corn. Captain Clark was seated on a robe beside the chief and the chief threw a handsome robe over him and after the peace pipe was passed around, the chief spoke.

He said, "I believe what you told me and that you are looking for peace among all nations. This gives me great satisfaction because now all my people can hunt without fear and our women can work in the fields without looking over their shoulders every moment for the enemy. They can now take off their moccasins at night because they don't need to run at a moment's notice. To the Arikara, we will demonstrate that we intend to be at peace and will not make war without any cause."

The chief then pointed to the warriors at his side. "Some brave men will accompany the Arikara Chief now with you to his village and nation to smoke with that group of people. When you came up the Indians in the neighboring villages and those hunting upon hearing of you had great expectations of receiving gifts from you and returned to the village. All were disappointed and some were dissatisfied with the lack of gifts for his village. He wanted to see his Great White Father."

He then brought to Captain Clark two steel traps that had been stolen from the French a short time earlier. He also motioned for the women of the village to set twelve bushels of corn in front of the captain. After the chief finished speaking and smoking the peace pipe in a great ceremony, Captain Clark spoke kindly to them using great gestures of kindness and this satisfied the chiefs very much. The captain returned to the boat.

Upon returning to the boat, Captain Clark met the principal chief of the third village and Little Crow. He invited both to the boat's cabin where they talked for about an hour. Not long after these chiefs left, the Great Mandan Chief came dressed in the clothes that the captains had given him. He had his two sons with him. He requested that the men dance again for them because they enjoyed it a lot when they did.

That day, Captain Lewis wrote to the Northwest Company's agent who had a fort on the Assiniboine River which was about nine days march from there to the north. The agent, Charles Chaboillez was born in Montreal. He entered the service of the Northwest Company in 1793, and at this time was in charge of the company's operations on the Assiniboine River, as bourgeois of Fort Assiniboine.

The river's water was seasonally low.. Captain Lewis was concerned about how late it was into the winter season. He was concerned about the ice shutting off the flow of the river so he determined that they must spend the winter in the area.

The chiefs gave them ten bushels of corn and two buffalo robes.

Isaac went with Captain Clark to the village and found corn, beans, squash, and all kinds of garden vegetables among the Indians at this village. The Mandan and the Arikara were the only Indians that they saw that cultivated the earth and these tribes resided on the Missouri River.

The village was located on a large high plain and they grew their crops in the bottom land below it. The village consisted of about two hundred lodges containing fifteen hundred people and was built the same way the Arikara built their lodges. Their main chief was Black Cat. These people were extremely friendly with the expedition. 0On November 1, Mr. McCracken set out at 7 o'clock to the fort on the Assiniboine and. took a letter with him from Captain Lewis concerning the British Minister's protection. The commander there, Edward Thornton, entered the British diplomatic service in 1791. He served in various posts in the United States from then until 1804, being chargé d'affaires and acting minister in Washington since 1800. In February 1803, he issued a passport to Lewis and requested that all subjects of His Majesty permit Lewis to pass and render all aid and protection possible, on a mission to which he insisted was purely scientific.

The chiefs of the lower village came and asked the captains to visit their village and take some corn. They wanted to make peace with the

Arikara. They had never made war against them but after the Arikara Killed their chiefs, they killed the Arikara like birds, and now they were tired of killing them. They wanted to send a chief and some brave men to the Arikara to smoke the pipe of peace with them.

In the evening, they set out and fell to the lower village where Captain Lewis got out and continued at the Village until after nightfall. Captain Clark took the boat and proceeded on. He landed on the right side at the upper point of the first woods on the right side after landing and continuing. Captain Lewis sent a message down after nightfall to inform Captain Clark that he intended to return the next morning at the chiefs' request.

The next morning, at daybreak, Captain Clark went down the river with four men to look for a proper place to winter. They proceeded down the river three miles and found a place well supplied with wood. They returned satisfied that they had found the location of their winter quarters.

Captain Lewis went to the village to hear what they had to say. Captain Clark took the boat further downriver and formed a camp near where a small camp of Indians used for hunting. Clark and the four men wasted no time and began cutting down the trees around their camp. They pitched their tents and laid out the foundations for their huts.

In the evening Captain Lewis returned from the Arikara with a gift of eleven bushels of corn. He called for some small articles which the captains had promised. The wind came from the southeast that day so the weather was fair. Many Indians came to watch them work. Captain Lewis dubbed the camp Fort Mandan.

They found the cottonwood timber relatively easy to split, and as there is no other building timber in this bottom, they determined they would split this wood into puncheon to cover their huts.

One of the French hands was discharged, and he took off walking down the river.

On November 3, Sergeant Gass, the carpenter of the expedition, directed the men to build the fort. Fort Mandan's outer walls created a triangular stockade that was eighteen feet high. The plan was to build two converging rows of huts and a bastion at the angle opposite the gate.

The huts were placed in two rows, containing four rooms each, and joined at one end forming an angle. When raised about seven feet high a floor of puncheons or split plank was laid, and covered with grass and clay, creating a warm loft. The upper part projected a foot over and the roofs were made shed-fashion, rising from the inner side, and making the outer wall about 18 feet high. Between the huts, they picketed the walls. In the angle under the bastion created by the two rows of huts, they built two rooms, for holding their provisions and stores.

The rest of the Frenchmen and Isaac were all officially discharged on November 3. Some of the discharged French and Isaac wintered with the permanent party at Fort Mandan. Others spent the winter at the Mandan, Hidatsa, and Arikara villages. Those men wished to stay on their own among the Indians, trading and trapping after receiving their pay in cash. The six men who would return to St. Louis in the spring would receive their pay from Lewis's agent in St. Louis in 1805. Baptiste Deschamps, Jean Baptiste La Jeunesse, Etienne Malboeuf, Charles Peter Pinault, Isaac, and François Rivet stayed among those who wintered at Fort Mandan. They would return with the keelboat sent down the Missouri in the spring.

Jean Baptiste Lepage replaced the discharged John Newman and would go with the permanent party to the Pacific. He had already been to the Black Hills, on the Little Missouri River, and in the country which few other whites had seen.

The wind blew hard from the west. The men continued building their cabins. They sent six hunters in a canoe down the river to hunt. Mr. Jessomme, his squaw, and his child moved to camp. Little Crow loaded his squaw with meat for the captains as well as a buffalo robe. The captains gave her an ax.

A Frenchman dressed in Hidatsa dress came to Captain Lewis' tent.

"How can I help you?" Captain Lewis looked up from writing in his journal.

The man spoke in French. "Bonjour, I am Toussaint Charbonneau. I hope that it is I who can help you. I would like to interpret for you as you head west."

"Interpret what language?"

"I know Hidatsa."

"Well, that can help us for a while, but that knowledge will help us little as we go further west."

"I can help you there as well. You see, I have two wives of the Snake tribe. They speak Hidatsa as well as their native tongue."

"Alright, but we can only accommodate one of your wives on our trip."

"Alright," Charbonneau replied.

While talking with the Frenchman, Isaac learned that Toussaint Charbonneau was a French Canadian, born about 1758, who had worked for the Northwest Company and had lived among the Hidatsa as an independent trader for several years. Rumors from some of the other traders nearby said he was a coward, a bungler, and a wife-beater. However, he had also heard that he was a good interpreter and a considerable cook. He seemed worth any risk.

November 5 began clear and pleasant. All hands rose early to stake out the second line of huts and split out puncheons to lay the loft which they intend to cover over with earth to make the huts warmer and more comfortable. Isaac was put on the task of digging a latrine to keep the place healthy.

During the night, the Sergeant of the Guard woke them to see northern lights that did not appear red but were darkened and sometimes nearly obscured. These lights appeared in light multicolored streaks, and at other times great spans of light containing floating columns that appeared opposite each other and retreated leaving the lighter space at no time of the same appearance.

"Like ghost lightning," Isaac said with awe in his voice.

In the morning Captain Clark rose at daybreak. Thick dark clouds appeared in the north. By eight o'clock, the wind began to blow hard from the northwest and was cold.

Mr. Graveline, the Arikara Interpreter, two of the French hands, and two boys set out in a canoe to spend the winter with the Arikara. Mr. Graveline was to accompany the Arikara chiefs to Washington in the spring.

A great number of geese were flying south, evidence that ice was soon to come.

On the seventh, they built the captains' room. The men stuffed some old tarpaulin and grass and mortar in the cracks and then covered the lot with a thick coat of earth to make it draft-free. Once the huts were built, they started building the chimneys.

They found that the cottonwood easily split and they had hoped to get enough to cover their buildings, but that was an impossible task.

The Mandan grazed their horses in the day on grass, and at night give them an armload of boughs to eat. Horses, dogs, and people all slept in the same lodge or roundhouse. This round house was covered with earth, and a firepit was built in the center of the room. The Indians' horses and dogs lived in their lodge with them.

Numerous flocks of wild geese passed to the South. They flew high, a sign that heavy snow would soon arrive.

The next day, the men continued to build their fort. Numerous Indians came to see them. The Arikara chief, The Coal, came and brought a side of buffalo. In return, they gave him a few things to share with his family. They crossed the river on a buffalo skin canoe and the squaw took the boat and went on to the town three miles upriver. The day was cold and raw. More geese and other birds, flying higher this time, continued their journey south.

They finished raising one line of their huts and began hewing and guttering the puncheon to use to cover the huts.

On November 11 they started dobbing their huts and covering them with whatever they could find that would keep the wet and cold weather out.

The interpreter Charbonneau's pregnant wife came to the camp with buffalo robes for the officers. Isaac motioned using Indian sign language and told her that his name was Isaac Thorton and asked her name. She said that she was called Sacagawea. The officers passed out the buffalo robes to the party. Ordway got one fine one and Shields got one that he said that he was going to give to his wife. It wasn't the last buffalo robe that anyone in the expedition would get. They prepared many of their robes and Isaac appreciated the day when he had his own to cuddle under to stay warm as winter set in.

Early the next morning Big White, the main chief of the Mandan lower village came to visit the captains. He had his wife with him, and he carried about a hundred pounds of fine meat for the corps. Captain Lewis gave his wife and children some small gifts. They gave her a small ax which she was pleased to get.

Three men were suffering from the symptoms of fever, swollen lymph nodes and small sores on various parts of their bodies.

Captain Lewis went with the hunters down river had not yet returned and the remaining men were assigned to unload the canoe so they could bring stone into camp with which to build their chimneys.

Isaac and Charbonneau were both warming themselves by the fire that night when Isaac asked.. "I wonder how this Mandan originated. The Mandan speak a language that was different from their neighboring nations."

Charbonneau tossed a stick into the fire.

"Good observation. I'm told that the Mandan nation originated when old men came out of a small subterranean village and lake where they had gardens but that's just folklore. What I know for fact is that they lived in several villages lower on the Missouri River, but smallpox destroyed most of their nation which reduced them to one large village and several small ones."

"I have heard that said about many of the tribes along the Missouri," Isaac replied.

"It was even worse for the Mandan than other tribes. Before this epidemic, the other nations were afraid of them, but after their numbers were reduced, the Sioux and other nations took advantage of it and killed many of the Mandan, so they moved further upriver. Those other Indians continued to wage war, so they moved even higher until they entered Pawnee country. They lived in friendship for many years and lived in the same area until those people waged war on them. They moved near the Watersoon and Winataree where they now live in peace with those nations."

Isaac already knew that based on what they had seen and heard from the traders and trappers they met, The Mandan numbered about three hundred and fifty men, the Minatare have about six or seven hundred, the Watersoon or Maharha have about eighty, and the Hidatsa have about six hundred men. The Hidatsa, the Minatare and Crow Indians spoke nearly the same language and may have been from the same nation.

Charbonneau continued.

"The Crow, Hidatsa, Minatare, and the Crow may have once been the same nation. Their enemies drove these people west from the hills of South Dakota and were centered in the Yellowstone basin, including the valleys of the Powder, Tongue, and Bighorn Rivers. The Crow tribe was at war with the Sioux and Snake Indians. The Crow had four hundred lodges and about twelve hundred men and followed the buffalo and hunted for their subsistence on the plains, in the Rocky Mountains. The French had given the Crow their name, but the tribe called themselves Absaroke which translated as crow, sparrowhawk, bird people, or anything that flies." They separated from the Hidatsa proper in the 1700s, hence the similarity in language. Their tongue was of the Siouan family."

"There's just so much we could learn from these people," Isaac held his hands out to warm in the fire.

"The Hidatsa and the Watersoon were at war with the Snake Indians and the Sioux and had been at war with the Arikara until they made peace a few days earlier. The Mandan were at war with anyone who make war with them. Currently, they are at war only with the Sioux and just want to be at peace with all nations. If you notice, they are seldom the aggressors in any fight."

By November 12, ice began to run in the river and snow fell all day. Captain Lewis spent the day at the Mandan village. The captains moved into their hut that day and the Grand Chief of the Mandan and Checharklagru, chief of the Assiniboine, and seven men visited them. Captain Clark smoked the pipe of peace with them and gave the chief a cord and a carrot of tobacco. The Assiniboine nation roved the plains in the area above the Mandan and traded with the British companies on the Assiniboine River. They comprised several bands of descendants of the Sioux and spoke their language. A bad group conducted raids. They traded horses and corn with the nations.

The hunting party led by Captain Lewis returned towards evening and they were exhausted. They had been stuck on a sand bar and were stuck for about two hours. The ice ran against their legs. Their clothes froze on them. One of them got frostbite on one of his feet. Captain Clark gave them some whiskey to revive their spirits.

Chapter 19-Rebecca

After John Brown went back to Waterford to purchase the property he was looking to buy, a frost hit a second and a third time and the trees of many colors dropped their leaves and blanketed the ground with the brown dead remnants of those leaves.

Rebecca sat near the road watching the cattle grazing in the nearby meadow. It would still be a few more weeks before the heavy snow fell, and cows would have to stay in the barn. She sat on the bank of the small creek.

The water from this creek would flow into French Creek. From French Creek, this water would flow into the Allegheny which went into the Ohio which went west into the Mississippi. From there, as she learned in Isaac's last letter, he had written that he was going up the Mississippi to a river called the Missouri.

It had been nearly a year since she received that letter from Isaac. She wondered what he was doing now. Heck, sometimes, she wondered if he was even still alive.

She sighed. She had to stop herself from this train of thought. Nah, he was still alive. She would know if he were not among the living. Wouldn't she? Why did she even care? Why did it matter so much?

The sound of crunching leaves and a horse whinny interrupted her thoughts. She turned around and saw the black pained hooves, the perfectly formed legs with smooth glossy brown legs. Her eyes continued up the horse's forelocks on the horse's head. His head bobbed as the rider pulled back on the reins. His dark chestnut mane flowed back in the morning breeze. His eyes appeared weary from traveling that day and probably even more.

Her eyes went to the saddle a well-designed English saddle. The rider's pant legs were brown wool rather than buckskin. He was not from here.

She looked up above the saddle and focused on a man's face.

His long golden locks were held back by a light blue ribbon. His face was chiseled. His eyebrows were light, but not too light, his lips full and kissable. The face of an Adonis.

She looked into his brown eyes and felt as though she could have gotten lost in those eyes. She stood up. Her mouth fell open.

If she had been impressed with the horse's majesty, she was even more impressed with this man's elegance. Neither could have been more perfect.

She snapped her mouth closed. It wasn't proper to gape at anyone.

He smiled. He seemed amused. "Hello, my name is Paul Peterson. I'm from Erie."

"I. . .I. . ." Rebecca felt the blush rise in her cheeks.

He was the most handsome man that Rebecca had ever seen, no probably to it. He had a charismatic aura that drew her to him. Was he the one?

Was he real? Could she be dreaming?

"I hear that your father is looking to sell some land," Paul said.

"I don't think so," Rebecca murmured. "Um, he's in the barn shucking corn."

"Wonderful. If you could steer me toward the barn," he said.

Rebecca's mind was so foggy that she couldn't think how to tell him where to go.

"I'll take you there."

Paul threw one leg over the saddle and slid down to the ground. His body was firm and well-defined.

Rebecca shook her head enough that Paul noticed.

"Are you alright?" he asked.

"I'm just a little chilled." She answered.

"Perhaps it's time we walked toward your father's barn," Paul took the lead on his horse and walked with Rebecca to her father's barn.

They found her father almost immediately in the breezeway where he was removing the husks from the corn. He dropped the husks in one pile and the corn in another.

"Father," she said. "This is Paul Peterson from Erie. He's here because he says he heard that you have land for sale?"

Mr. Miles picked up the pile of husks and carried them over to the nearby manger. During the early morning hours, the cows would eat these still-green husks and convert them into milk.

Mr. Miles shook his head. "No, I don't know where you might have heard that. I'm hoping to get more land, not sell what I have."

"Is that so," Paul replied. "Well, I'm in the business of not just buying property around here, but I also sell it. I have some land up by Erie you might be interested in."

Rebecca's father shook his head. "Not interested in buying near Erie either."

"It would be a great investment," Paul replied. "The town of Erie is growing in leaps and bounds. You'll easily make your money back if you invest in land now."

"I'm not interested," he said. "Now, if you had something closer to here, I might consider it."

"Well, I can let you know what I can find," Paul replied.

"I appreciate that," Mr. Miles replied.

Paul had supper with them that night.

Rebecca couldn't help thinking that there was something off about him now that she was over her initial shock of meeting him. She couldn't shake the distinct feeling that he was too good to be true.

"You have the prettiest daughter, Mr. Miles," Paul said and smiled across the table at Rebecca.

He flirted with Rebecca the entire time he was at their home.

"She's becoming a fair cook too." Mr. Miles smiled at his daughter as well.

"Is that so?" Paul said. "Did you make these biscuits?"

"No, Mother made them," Rebecca replied. "She made the entire meal."

"Well, this meal is excellent. I'm sure the apple doesn't fall far from the tree."

Since Paul was there for supper, he would spend the night in the room in the barn. Paul had taken his horse to the stable and was brushing him and Rebecca's mother asked her to take blankets and pillows out to the shed for Paul.

While Rebecca delivered the bedding, Paul arrived in the room.

Rebecca set the bedding on the straw mattress.

"You'll probably need to tighten the bed ropes," she said.

Paul took her hand. Rebecca felt the electricity as he lifted her hands and held it to his lips.

"Thank you very much for your hospitality, Miss Rebecca," he said. He held her hand longer than she was comfortable, and she pulled her hand away.

"I have to go," she said and left the room.

As she hurried away, she made it a point never to be alone with him.

A few days later, he left with Philip McCray and his young son Joseph McCray to Erie to trade for some supplies before winter set in. He did not return when they returned. He had decided to stay in Erie even though Philip and Joseph had returned home.

The day after they returned, Rebecca went to Judith McCray's house to see Judith's new baby named Robert after his father.

"Oh, he's so sweet," Rebecca said when Judith placed the babe in her arms. For a moment, little Robert began to fuss almost immediately.

"I don't think he likes me," Rebecca looked down at the squalling baby.

"It's alright. He's ready for a meal," Judith said. "I'll just have to take care of that."

"A lot of times, people name their children after one of the parents, but the child doesn't look anything like either one," Judith said as she repositioned herself and put the baby on her breast. "I think he looks like his father though. Don't you agree?"

"Yes, I think so too," Rebecca said. "I can see the resemblance."

"I hear that Paul Peterson stayed at your place the other day," Judith said as she sat in her willow rocking chair. She put a light blanket over the baby's face.

"Yes," Rebecca replied. "He's certainly a good-looking man, isn't he?"

"Yes, he is. I don't know if you know this story, but before we moved here, my husband Robert was infatuated with a woman he said was beautiful and he asked her to marry him. She led him on for a long time and then threw his love back in his face."

"That's terrible. I'm glad he found you," Rebecca said. "What does this have to do with me?"

"I have to tell you something about your friend Paul."

"What's that?"

"As you know, Joseph and his father went with Paul Peterson to Erie. Joseph told me that Paul was courting several girls at different times during the day while Joseph and his father were in town. He's probably still seeing them, which is why he did not return with them. Joseph learned that he offered to purchase the properties of these girls' fathers."

"I see," Rebecca thought she should have felt angry and used, but she didn't. What did she feel? She wondered," What was that she was feeling? Was she feeling 'relief'?

Judith leaned toward Rebecca. 'You don't seem all that upset."

"I don't know what I feel," Rebecca replied. "I guess I just feel relieved."

"Relieved? What do you mean, relieved? How is that?"

Rebecca shrugged. "I don't know. I guess, I felt in my belly that he was too good to be true. It's relief because I wouldn't want to hear from Mother that I let another good one get away.'""

"I'm sure there's someone out there for you."

Rebecca shrugged again. "Perhaps I am beginning to understand."

"Understand what?"

"I'm beginning to understand that everyone has been right all along."

"About what?"

"Isaac and me. Every time I think maybe this one is the one, my mind comes back to Isaac. I wake up every day, thinking about him, wondering about him, hoping he'll show up and tell me that he's returned."

Rebecca sighed. She didn't even know if he was alive or dead. He was in the wilderness and there was no way to contact him. The letters from him had stopped coming months ago.

What would she say to him if she did come walking up the road from Pittsburgh? She had heard that he might be returning this fall to St. Louis, but she didn't know that for certain. Unfortunately, autumn wasl here, and still he had not returned. Winter would soon make the roads almost impossible to navigate.

Even if she wanted to, she wouldn't be able to find anyone to take her there.

Rebecca suddenly realized that what she had been thinking, she must have been verbalizing her thoughts.

Judith said, "You're right. You have no choice. You'll have to wait until he returns."

"Yes, perhaps in the spring," Rebecca murmured.

Chapter 20-Isaac

On November 11, the council with the Mandan continued. The Indians brought more corn, beans, and squash to the men of the expedition. It was the same as previous councils where the Indians promised peace with the United States government and with neighboring tribes.

After the council ended, the ice began to run thick, and the river rose half an inch during the night. Heavy snow fell. Only two Indians visited them that day because of a dance at the village the night before which included a ceremony of adoption and the interchange of property, between the Assiniboine and the nations of this neighborhood. This adoption ensured good treatment for any visiting traders.

Twilight fell, and the hunters had not returned.

"I'm worried about the hunters. They were supposed to return tonight," Captain Clark said when Isaac brought firewood into the captain's cabin.

"Isaac, would you be willing to take a horse and travel overland to find out why they are delayed?"

"Now? No, wait until daylight," Captain Lewis replied.

Before he left, the man on duty ushered two Frenchmen in to see the captain.

They had been trapping downriver and brought twenty beavers.

"We had hunters down that direction. Did you happen to see them?"

The Frenchmen shook their heads. They had not seen anyone hunting.

The camp had to ration their pork because they were afraid that they wouldn't be able to get enough meat to last until George Drouillard's hunting team returned. To make matters worse, the Indians warned of bad weather.

Charbonneau came to the camp with information that three bands of Assiniboine and some Cree were at the Mandan Village. He told Captain Lewis that he learned that Cree numbered about two hundred and forty men. They spoke the Chippewa language. The Plains Cree were buffalo-hunting nomads whose range was almost entirely in Canada, north of the Assiniboine and the Sioux. Their tribe lived near Fort Des Prairies.

Before Isaac was to leave on the horse, George Drouillard arrived with one of the Frenchmen. He Informed the captains that the canoe was about eighteen miles in the river downstream loaded with meat and was stuck in the ice.

Isaac returned with George Drouillard by canoe instead of by horse. A while later he arrived at the other boat and handed the pot to the men still with the canoe. They put the pot in the boat's bow, filled the pot with driftwood, and lit the wood. Soon the heat from the pot melted the ice around the canoe and set the canoe free.

After they returned with the meat, the next day turned extremely cold. Freezing rain had fallen overnight and covered all the trees with ice. They looked like crystal chandeliers in the morning sun.

All the men moved into the huts even though they were not finished. The unfinished huts offered more protection from the elements than their tents ever would.

Several visiting Indians reported to Captain Lewis that several Assiniboine were at the Hidatsa camp. The Hidatsa accused the Assiniboine of refusing to trade their horses for corn with them. One old Indian claimed to have come with four buffalo robes and corn to trade for a pistol. They refused the trade. Captain Lewis said that they weren't to judge in Indian matters, but a government representative would soon be available who would settle trade disputes.

The men worked until late dobbing their huts. They coated the walls with clay and grass to close the chinks between the logs

Some horses were sent down to stay in the woods near the fort, to prevent the Assiniboine from stealing them. The Indians found white man's customs interesting, and the men of the expedition were equally as interested in the Indian customs.

The men had raised the roof of the food storage area and smokehouse using timbers. They didn't have enough timber so they filled in as best as they could with chinking and dobbing covered with earth, grasses, and ashes. They stored their food in the storage building under the blockhouse and smoked their meat in another part of the same building.

On the nineteenth, the hunters returned with thirty-two deer, twelve elk, and a buffalo. Some men including Isaac were assigned to prepare the meat for the smokehouse.

Some Indians came by and told stories. One of them was about the Buffalo woman.

Long, long ago, their band chose two young and handsome men to find out where the buffalo were. While the men were riding in the buffalo country, they saw someone in the distance walking toward them.

As always, they were cautious because this could be an enemy. They hid in some bushes and waited. At last, the figure came up the slope. To their surprise, the figure walking toward them was a beautiful woman with long straight shiny black hair. When she came closer, she stopped and looked at them. Although they were hiding, they knew she could see them. On her left arm, she carried what looked like a stick in a brush bundle.

One of the men said, "She is more beautiful than anyone I have ever seen. I want her for my wife."

But, the other man replied, "How dare you have such a thought? She is wondrously beautiful and holy, far above ordinary people."

Though still at a distance, the woman heard them talking. She laid down her bundle and spoke to them. "Come. What is it you wish?"

The man who had spoken first went up to her and laid his hands on her as if to claim her. At once, from somewhere above, there came a whirlwind. Then, there came a mist, which hid the man and the woman. When the mist cleared, the other man saw the woman with the bundle again on her arm, but his friend was a pile of bones at her feet.

The man stood silent in wonder and awe. Then, the beautiful woman spoke to him. "I am on a journey to your people. I am coming to see a good man whose name is Bull Walking Upright."

"Go on ahead of me and tell your people I am on my way. Ask them to move camp and to pitch their tents in a circle. Ask them to leave an opening in the circle, facing north. In the center of the circle, make a large tipi, also facing the north. There I will meet Bull Walking Upright and your people."

The man saw to it that all her directions were followed. When she reached the camp, she removed the sagebrush from the gift she was carrying. The gift was a small pipe made of red stone. On it was carved the tiny outline of a buffalo calf.

They gave the pipe to Bull Walking Upright, and then she taught him the prayers he should pray to the Strong One Above. "When you pray to the Strong One Above, you must use this pipe in the ceremony. When you are hungry, unwrap the pipe and lay it bare in the air. Then, the buffalo will come where the men can easily hunt and kill them so the children, the men and the women will have food and be happy."

The beautiful woman also told him how their people should behave to live peacefully together. She taught them the prayers they should say when praying to Mother Earth. She told him how they should decorate themselves for ceremonies.

"The earth," she said, "is your mother. So, for special ceremonies, you will decorate yourselves as your mother does, in black and red, in brown and white. These are also the colors of the Buffalo."

"Above all else, remember this is a peace pipe I have given you. You will smoke it before all ceremonies. You will smoke it before making treaties. It will bring peaceful thoughts into your mind. If you use it when you pray to the Strong One Above and Mother Earth below, you will receive the blessings you ask."

When the woman had completed her message, she turned and slowly walked away. All the people watched her in awe. Outside the opening of the circle, she stopped for an instant and then lay down on the ground. She rose again in the form of a black buffalo cow. Again, she lay down and then arose in the form of a red buffalo cow. A third time she lay down and arose as a brown buffalo cow. The fourth and last time, she had the form of a spotlessly white buffalo cow. Then she walked toward the north into the distance and finally disappeared over a far-off hill.

Bull Walking Upright kept the peace pipe carefully wrapped most of the time. He called all his people together every little while, untied the bundle, and repeated the lessons the beautiful woman had taught him. And he used it in prayers and other ceremonies until he was more than 100 years old.

When he became feeble, he held a great feast. There he gave the pipe and the lessons to Sunrise, a worthy man. Similarly, the pipe was passed down from generation to generation. "As long as the pipe is used," the beautiful woman had said, "your people will live and be happy. As soon as it is forgotten, the people will perish."

For years after that, Isaac thought about this story and wondered if this was what had happened with this tribe.

The Indian's storytelling had been a nice break from the boring task of dobbing the smokehouse, but they were back at it the next morning. As soon as the last of the dobbing was put on the smokehouse, they put the meat in the shed's rafters to smoke.

The next day was warmer than the previous days had been. Several Indians came down to eat fresh meat. The three chiefs from the second Mandan village stayed all day. They were curious about the white man's technology and enjoyed looking at Captain Lewis' contraptions. They told Captain Lewis that the Sioux who had settled on the Missouri River above Cheyenne River, threatened to attack them that winter. They mistreated the two Arikara who carried the pipe of peace to them.

They whipped them and stole their horses. The Sioux were angry that the Arikara made peace with the Mandan through the Americans. The captains said that the Americans would deal with the Sioux.

The next day they took one of the canoes to collect stone for the chimneys. They wasted no time getting the chimneys built with four started that same day. While working on the chimneys a rock fell on Geroge Douillard's hand. Fortunately, it wasn't broken.

The next day, the captains set out a canoe with four men under Sergeant Pryor's command to the second Mandan village for one hundred bushels of ears of dry corn which Mr. Jessomme gave them, but they only received eighty bushels.

At ten o'clock, the sentinel rushed into Captain Clark's cabin.

"Quick, help! An Indian is about to kill his wife in the interpreter's hut!"

"I'll take care of it," Captain Clark said.

He went down to the hut.

The man had his club raised over his wife and was about to hit her with it."

"You need to stop right now!" Captain Clark replied. "I forbid rash acts like that of any kind near the fort."

"According to Mandan law, I have every right. She ran away after an argument with me and has been hiding here with the interpreter's squaws, but since you don't allow it. I will take her home."

That evening she returned to the interpreter's hut. He had beaten and stabbed her in three places. The captains directed that no man of this party was to have any intercourse with this woman under the penalty of punishment.

The husband came with her things and threw them at the feet of Captain Lewis. "One of your sergeants slept with my wife and if he wants her, he can have her."

Captain Lewis directed Sergeant Ordway to give the man some gifts in trade for the woman's life. "I don't believe that anyone in this party has touched your wife except the one he had given to use her for a night in his bed. Going forward, no man in this camp will ever touch your squaw or any wife of any Indian. Write down that as a direct order, Sergeant Ordway."

"Yes sir."

'Now, take your wife and live in peace with her."

The Indian grunted his acknowledgment.

At that moment, Grand Chief Black Cat arrived and lectured the man in his language. The man and wife left, and both seemed unhappy.

The morning was warm, and the afternoon was fair. Black Cat spent the day with them. He had a lot of stories to tell. He and his family spent the night at the fort.

Some men went after more stone for the chimneys, and others were making a large rope to draw the barge up on the bank to avoid getting damaged and crushed in the river ice.

The men put more cover on the huts with puncheon or logs hewn on one side and finished making the cording. By the twenty-third, things were becoming routine. The guard was reduced to one sergeant and three men.

On the twenty-fifth, Captain Lewis, two Interpreters, and six men went to visit the Indians in the different towns and camps in this neighborhood while the rest of the men continued to work on their huts. Two Hidatsa chiefs came to see Captain Clark, the first of that nation to visit them at Fort Mandan. Captain Clark gave them each a handkerchief, paint, a saw band, and a few other articles. They were pleased with the gifts.

The men had finally finished their huts. On the twenty-sixth, it was cold and snowy, and they didn't wander away from the fires much except to get wood and get meals. Several men had bad colds. Shields had rheumatism.

Captain Lewis visited the Menetarras on the twenty-fifth and returned on November twenty-seventh with two chiefs and told Captain Clark that two clerks and five men of the Northwest Company and several of the Hudson Bay Company had arrived with goods to trade with the Indians. The clerks were Mr. La Roche and Mr. McKinsey.

The twenty-seventh dawned cold and cloudy. Ice chunks floated in the river. The wind blew from the northwest. They finished dobbing that day. Captain Lewis returned to camp with two chiefs and a considerable party with them. The Hidatsa had told the Mandan that the white man intended to join the Sioux to cut them off during the winter.

Captain Lewis had told them that was not true and said it with such conviction that the Indians realized that these accusations were false. After that, the Indians in all the towns and camps nearby treated Captain Lewis and the party with great respect except for chief Horned Weasel who did not choose to see the captain and left word and told to Captain Lewis by his wife that he was not at home.

On this same day, seven traders arrived from the fort on the Assiniboine from the Northwest Company. They told them that LaFrance was causing problems. After La France deserted the Americans, he had gone to the British and reported unfavorably to them about the American intentions. Captain Lewis sent word to Mr. La Roche and Mr. McKensey that they would face serious consequences if they did not stop LaFrance's libelous accusations.

That next morning several inches of snow fell during the night and continued to fall throughout the day. More slabs of ice bobbed in the river.

Black Cat came to see them. Captain Lewis showed those chiefs many things that were curiosities to them and gave them a few presents like handkerchiefs, arm bands, paint, and twists of tobacco. The Indians left just after the noon meal and seemed very pleased. After they left, they had a talk with Mr. Le Roche to remind the Native Americans that these were symbols of friendship from the Great American Father.

Because of the snow, no work was done that day. Miserable and cold, the men huddled by their fires and stoked it from their woodpile.

The following day was equally cold and blustery. Mr. La Roche and one of his men came to visit the corps. They informed La Roche that they forbid them from giving medals or flags to the Indians. He denied having done so. They captains agreed that one of the interpreters would speak to him on condition that he did not say anything more than what was necessary to make trade agreements with the Indians.

That evening Sergeant Pryor was taking down the mast on the boat when he dislocated his shoulder.

"I've seen a few of these in my life," Captain Lewis said. "Isaac can you hold Sergeant Pryor while I reposition the joint.

Captain Lewis jerked Pryor's arm. The shoulder joint was not as it should be.

He tried it again. Still the arm remained in an awkward position.

He tried a third and then a fourth when the arm finally returned to its normal shape.

"Now I want you to take it easy. No heavy lifting for the next few days! Captain's orders!" Captain Lewis exclaimed.

On the morning of the last day of November, an Indian called from the opposite side of the river from Fort Mandan and asked to be brought over. He said that he had a message his chief wanted him to convey. The captains sent a canoe to bring him to their side of the river. After he had smoked, he said hoped that the river was completely iced over across this part of the river and expected to be able to cross on the ice.

He told the captains, "Eight Mandan were out hunting southwest of the fort. After they finished hunting, they were on their way back when they were attacked by a large party of Sioux. One of the parties, a young chief, was killed, two men were killed, and nine horses were taken. The men who made their escape said that half of the party who attacked them were Pawnee."

"Come by our fire, tell us more," Captain Clark said.

The man continued speaking.

"One of these men who was wounded said. 'This day I shall die like a man before my enemies. Tell my father that I died bravely and do not grieve for me.'

Captain Lewis turned toward Isaac. "You know what you need to do."

Isaac nodded. A few days earlier two Pawnee had come and were staying in the fort. Isaac knew that Captain Lewis wanted him to help those Pawnee warriors escape back home, for fear of their being put to death.

On December 1, all members of the expedition cut and hauled pickets for the fort walls. At ten o'clock the half-brother of the dead man came and informed them that after Captain Clark's departure the night before, six Cheyenne had arrived with the pipe of peace and said that their nation was one day's march away and intended to come and trade.

Three Pawnee accompanied them and said that their leaders were three days march and were also coming to trade with them. The Mandan believed the Cheyenne were dangerous because they were at peace with the Sioux and the Sioux wished to kill the Mandan. The chiefs, however, had informed the nation that it was their wish not to hurt them and forbade them from killing any Mandan. The corps gave them a little tobacco. The half-brother of the dead man was satisfied with the councils and departed.

In the evening Mr. George Henderson came to the Mandan camp. He was an agent of the Hudson Bay Company. He had been sent to trade with Hidatsa villages. He oversaw a party of Hudson's Bay Company men who had come from the Assiniboine River to compete with the Northwest Company traders.

The snow continued to thaw until morning when the wind shifted back to the north. The chiefs and many of their young men of the lower village of the Mandan along with four Cheyenne who had come to smoke with the peace pipe with the Mandan came to visit Fort Mandan.

The next day, the father of the Mandan who was killed gave Captain Lewis some dried pumpkins and a little pemmican. Captain Lewis in turn gave him a few small gifts. The Black Cat and two young chiefs visited them and as was the custom, stayed all day.

While the captains visited with the visiting Indians, the men finished building the main bastion that day.

The next day snow fell throughout the day and evening. Two of the Northwest Company came to see the captains. They informed them that the company was establishing an outpost on the Assiniboine River in two days. Their party consisted of five men.

On December 7, Big White, Grand Chief of the first village rode in on his horse and woke up the whole camp.

"There's a large herd of buffalo nearby. My people are waiting for your men to join us in the chase."

"We'd be honored to join you in the hunt," Captain Lewis answered. He then called fifteen men together including Isaac to join the Indians.

They watched with amazement at the skill the Indians displayed as they killed buffaloes with arrows as they rode on horseback. That day, the members of the expedition killed fourteen buffalo, five of which they got to the fort by placing them on a horse. They carried the remains of the other buffalo on their backs into camp. One buffalo cow was killed on the ice after drawing her out of a hole in the ice in which she had fallen. They butchered her at the fort. The Indians took the buffalo that they did not bring in under a custom which is established amongst them that any person seeing a buffalo lying without an arrow sticking in him, or some mark can take possession of that carcass. A hunter who kills many buffalo in a chase could only carry off part of one buffalo and any meat left out all night would fall to the wolves, which were in great numbers. When buffalo were around, it made sense that someone lay claim to carcasses that were not taken.

The temperature was one below zero the next morning, and three men were badly frostbitten and needed tending. Isaac, who had not gone that day, helped with their injuries.

The next day, Captain Clark took another fifteen men who joined the Indians who were on horseback. The corps killed eight buffalo and one deer. Captain Clark left two of the men behind to skin and keep wolves off the buffalo and brought in some of the meat. Great herds came the evening of Clark's return to the fort. Isaac saw great numbers of buffalo coming into the bottoms on both sides of the river. Several of the men including York were frostbitten that day. Another man had his feet badly frostbit. Two men injured their hips when they slipped on the icy ground. The Indians killed a great number of buffalo that day.

That day, the sun dog or parhelion occurred when the sun's rays reflected off ice crystals in the very high atmosphere. It was commonly associated with advancing storm systems. Natives recognized it as a harbinger of an approaching storm.

The next day, Captain Lewis took eighteen men and five horses to get the meat killed the day before and to kill more. The sun shone clear, both interpreters went to the villages that day.

Three days later the weather began to moderate. Joseph Fields and Isaac shot a cow and a calf. They sent the horses to bring back the meat. The next day was sunny and cold. They went hunting again but didn't kill any buffalo, just some scrawny deer. Isaac and seven other men camped in the river bottom eight to ten miles from the fort.

The next day, a couple of the party went down to the Mandan villages to trade for corn. The Mandan stored their corn along with squash and pots of dried beans in pits in the ground close to the front of their lodges.

Although the day was cold and stormy several chiefs and warriors went outdoors to play the Mandan hoop and pole game. In this game, they had flattish rings made from clay stone and two men had sticks about four feet long with two short pieces across the front end of it, and underneath on the other end, they would slide some distance. They had a place fixed across their green from the head chief's house across about fifty yards to the second chief's lodge, which was smooth as a house flower petal. They had a battery fixed for the rings to stop the rings against. Two men would run at a time each with a stick. Each with a stick and one carried a ring. They ran about halfway and then slid their sticks after the ring. They had marks made for the game, but the men of the corps could not understand how they scored the game. They gave the men different kinds of food which the men of the corps ate in every lodge that we went in. They were very friendly.

When they returned to the fort, Captain Clark had returned with the hunters. The hunters had not killed any more buffalo because the buffalo had returned to the prairies.

Hugh Heney, François-Antoine Larocque, and George Budge from the Northwest Company, who had been staying with the Mandan, came from the village to trade for the robes and furs that the expedition was accumulating. Isaac helped load the furs onto the sleds that George Budge brought.

While loading the sled, Isaac learned that The Northwest Company was first formed in 1783 by Canadian merchants engaged in the fur trade. The concern was divided into sixteen shares, without any capital being deposited. Each party furnished his proportion of the articles necessary for carrying on the trade. After a severe struggle and rival competition with others engaged in the trade, in the year 1787 more partners were admitted. The shares extended to twenty and the establishment, which was no more than an association of commercial men agreeing among themselves to carry on the fur trade and founded on a more solid basis.

Both the Northwest Company and Hudson's Bay Company engrossed and carried on almost the whole of the fur trade in that extensive country, situated between Hudson's Bay, the Rocky Mountains, and that high tract of country, west of Lake Superior, which separated the southern from the northern waters and have factories, forts and trading establishments on the Winnipeg, Assiniboine, Sturgeon, Saskatchewan, Elk, and most of the other great lakes and rivers, which communicate with or discharge themselves into Hudson's Bay, and the North sea. Some of the expedition's men traded for tobacco from them.

The next day, Mr. Henry shared with them some of his sketches of the country between the Mississippi and the Missouri River and some sketches he had put together from descriptions from Indians who had been further west.

One of the Indians came to let the men know that they were going buffalo hunting again and that they were welcome to join them. Gass made a sled for the Northwest traders to go home in. They paid him in trade goods for the expedition. Mr. Henry and La Roche also left them for the Hidaka camp.

Captain Clark sent out seven men to hunt for the buffalo. The weather was too cold, so they returned to camp. Captain Clark was working on a small map of what Mr. Henry had told him and sent Jessomme to Chief Black Cat to know the cause of his detaining or taking a horse of Charbonneau the interpreter, which they found was the rascal Lafrance, a trader from the Northwest Company, who told this Chief that Charbonneau owed him a horse to go and take him. He did so as was the Indian custom. He gave up the horse.

On the nineteenth, the men returned to erecting the fort walls with half working and half warming by the cabin fires.

They continued erecting pickets for the next four days. These days were warm and pleasant. A woman came with a child with an abscess and Captain Lewis lanced it. She gave him as much corn as she could carry.

On the twenty-second, several women and berdache or men dressed as squaws came with corn to sell to the men for little things. Male transvestites were to be found among several plains tribes.

The men of the corps obtained two horns from the animal that the French called the rock mountain sheep or what the men of the expedition called big horn sheep. The Mandan call this Sheeparsarta. This animal was about the size of a large deer, or small elk. Its horns came out and wound around the head like the horn of a ram and the texture was not unlike it but much larger and thicker particularly the part used to butt.

The next day, Indians of all descriptions came to the fort with corn to trade. Little Crow loaded his wife and son with corn for the trip. Captain Lewis gave them a few gifts. Little Crow's wife then made a kettle of boiled pumpkin, beans, corn, and choke cherries. This dish was considered a treat among the Mandan.

Some Indians visited the fort to trade and others came to just gawk at the strangers with the light skin and hair and the man with the extremely dark skin and big lips, huge white teeth, and bright whites of his eyes.

The men finished the pickets and started erecting a blacksmith shop. In the evening the officers distributed flour, dried apples, pepper, and salt among the party to celebrate Christmas.

Christmas fell on a Tuesday in 1804. That morning, in unison, three men discharged a single round from their weapons. Immediately after, Sergeant Ordway discharged the swivel gun.

At noon, Captain Clark presented a glass of brandy to each man under his command. They drank to President Jefferson and immediately Shannon hoisted the American flag, and each man had another glass of brandy.

At 10 o'clock they each had another glass of brandy. At one, another gun was fired as a signal for dinner. After downing the brandy, the men removed their cots from one of the rooms.

The musicians gathered and prepared to play their instruments while the rest of the men danced. At half past two, another gun was fired to assemble at the dance, and so they kept happily dancing until eight o'clock that evening without the company of females except the three wives of the interpreters, the wife of Rene Jessomme and Toussaint Charbonneau's two wives, including the younger one named Sacajawea. These women took no part in the festivities but watched as the men danced. The officers requested that the natives stay away from the fort during the festivities in respect for the white man's holiday. They obliged.

The next day still no Indians came to camp. One of the men took out a backgammon board. Captain Clark played the game with the boys.

A man from the Northwest Company came down from the Hidaka to get one of the interpreters to assist them in making a trade with the Hidaka.

The man entered Captain Lewis's office and told the captains. "The Hidaka who persuaded the Assiniboine that stole their horses, have all returned. The last of the party brought eight horses which they stole from an Assiniboine camp found on Souris River."

The Corps had a small forge, complete with bellows, and fueled by charcoal, so that Shields and Willard, the blacksmiths, could work iron and other metals. Besides repairing expedition equipment, now that the cabins were up, they started making tomahawk heads and other articles to trade with the Indians for food. Several Indians came down to the fort and were intrigued by blacksmith tools, especially the bellows. The men set to work putting in the floor of the interpreter's cabin and the blacksmith shop.

On the twenty-eighth, frost fell like snow and the wind blew very hard and icy cold. The next day was cold too.

The thirtieth was cold and clear. Many Mandan came to trade with them. They brought corn, beans, and squash as well as some bread. This bread was made of parched corn and beans mashed, mixed, and made into round balls. They also offered sweet corn which they boiled when it was in the milk and dried to keep the corn sweet through the winter.

From that day until the Corps of Discovery left the Mandan camp, many Indians came. The blacksmiths spent the days mending axes and hoes. In exchange, the squaws brought corn to trade for the work the blacksmiths did for them.

Chapter 21-Isaac

They ushered in 1805 by discharging their two cannons. Sixteen men took their musical instruments to visit the first Mandan village to dance. Captain Lewis, Charbonneau, and half of the men went to the dance. The Mandan enjoyed the men's music and their dancing. They were especially delighted with York as he danced in his personalized style. François Rivet, one of the Frenchmen, danced on his head. Isaac kept time with a jug. Pierre Cruzatte played his fiddle. One guy played his flute and another kept time with his drum. Snow fell again during the evening night and They returned that evening. Snow continued to fall all day and into the evening. Some men and squaws brought corn to exchange for blacksmith work.

The weather remained frigid for the first two weeks of January, but the cold didn't stop the hunters from hunting.

When Isaac entered the Mandan dwelling the old Mandan men sat in a circle. The men passed a pipe from one elder to another. Each man would take a drag and then pass the pipe to the next man in the circle. They then handed the pipe to young men who dressed up for the event. The young men then walked to the women who sat around the inside walls of the dwelling and brought their wives to the circle.

The younger man asked the old man to take his wife who wore nothing but a robe. He asked him for the honor of allowing his wife to sleep with the honored elder. The first girl led the old man who had difficulty walking, to another lodge to lie with him. Later, the girl and the older Mandan returned to the lodge.

After the women visited with the elder Mandan of the village, they approached the expedition members. One of them was George Gibson.

Gibson smiled at Isaac who sat beside him and left with the young Mandan woman.

Another Indian wife reached out her hand to Isaac. "You come?"

Isaac shook his head. "I'm not interested."

Gibson turned back toward Isaac. "You're not married or anything. Your girl back home doesn't have to know anything about it."

Reluctantly, Isaac stood up and followed the young woman back to her dwelling. She motioned for him to sit down on a pile of furs which he did.

She then removed her robe.

Rebecca's smiling face came to Isaac's mind. Guilt stabbed Isaac's heart. He couldn't. He wouldn't do this.

"No, I'm sorry. I can't." Isaac stood up and headed for the door.

"I don't please you."

"No, that's not it. You are very beautiful. I just can't."

Isaac stood up and headed back to the lodge. The woman followed him.

Isaac sat back down with the other expedition members who remained or had already returned from their liaison.

A few minutes later the woman's husband approached Isaac.

"She said you're not satisfied with her?"

Isaac shook his head. "No, I just can't."

The husband threw a beautiful buffalo robe over Isaac. "Please sir, do not despise me and my wife. Take this robe as a gift."

Isaac picked up the robe and handed it back to the man. He shook his head. "No, I can't take this. The problem is not with you or your wife."

Isaac stood up and looked at John Colter who was sitting beside him. "Tell the others that I am going back to the fort."

Colter nodded and Isaac left.

Back at the fort, Isaac sat down on his makeshift bed. It was quiet at the fort. The only other people around were either on guard duty or sleeping because they would replace the men on watch.

Isaac undressed and lay down. It wasn't long before he was asleep.

The next thing he knew, he floated in a canoe on the river, but it wasn't the Missouri River. The river was wider than the Missouri so he immediately knew he was back on the Mississippi River. On the dock ahead of him, Isaac saw what he thought was an aberration. The ghost was all white and flowy. The ghost wore a woven bonnet like Rebecca always wore to church. The aberration turned slowly toward Isaac. Isaac was horrified to see the aberration was Rebecca.

Isaac awoke beads of sweat glistened on his forehead. He sighed. He was back in his cot in the fort. The room was cold and he started to shiver. He wiped the sweat from his face with a linen rag. Wrapped in his buffalo robes, he wondered what his dream meant.

Could it be that Rebecca would not be there for him when he returned? Could she have died in the interim since he left? He shook his head. That wasn't as likely she was already married to the other man.

He suddenly felt the urgency to return from this trip. He just hoped he would not be too late.

The next day, Jean Baptiste Trudeau came to visit the fort. Captain Clark and some of the men were in the common area when Jean Baptiste began to tell them a wild tale.

"There's this place west of here that a man named Menard told me about in one of the areas where you may be traveling. He was on what he called the Roche Jaune River. He told me that the area is amazing. There are big brown bears that are bigger than the black bears you saw back east. There are geysers that shoot up into the air and pools of water so hot you can boil your food in."

"When was he there?" John Colter asked.

"He said he was there sometime before 1795."

"Yeah, I don't see it. I must wonder if your friend wasn't telling a wild tale."

The French traders of St. Louis had received enough information from Indians before Lewis and Clark's time to have given it a name, perhaps derived from the yellow rocks in the river's upper canyon. The Indians shared that the Great Falls of the Missouri, as the Indians told him, were roughly due west of the Mandan villages.

Three of the hunters went down the river and killed nothing for two days except a wolf, which they were obliged to eat. They said they relished it but found the meat was tough.

Several of the natives had been out on a very cold day, one of them gave out on his return in the evening. He was left in the prairie covered with a buffalo robe. He recovered and moved to the woods, where he broke a few branches to lie on, and to keep his body off the snow. In the morning, he arrived at the fort, with his feet badly frozen. Captain Lewis gave him laudanum and treated his feet with warm baths.

Isaac went with Captain Lewis to check on Charbonneau's wives. The oldest wife was ill, and his other wife, Sacagawea, was about eight months pregnant, but she cared for the older woman.

At mid-month, a great number of Indians moved down the river to hunt below the Mandan villages. Those people had killed many buffalo near their villages and had saved a great proportion of the meat. They stored a large portion of meat because they were left more than half of the year without meat. They kept corn and beans during the summer and as a reserve in case of an attack from the Sioux, which they are always feared. They seldom went far to hunt except in large parties. About half of the Mandan nation passed the fort that day to hunt. Mr. Charbonneau, the interpreter, and another visited some Menetarres lodges near Turtle Hill and had returned, both with frosted faces.

Charbonneau informed the captains that the Clerk of the Hudson Bay Company who lodged with the Menetarres had been bad-mouthing the expedition's white explorers. Rumors were flying that the Northwest Company intended to build a fort at the Menetarres. He saw the Grand Chief of the Hidatsa who spoke slightly of the Americans and said that if the white man would give their great flag to him, he would come to see them.

The next day, the captains sent Sergeant Pryor and five men with the Indians to hunt. Several of the men had infections that Captain Lewis treated with mercury.

"You were smart not to partake in the Mandan wife-swapping custom," Captain Lewis told Isaac after he assisted him with the procedure.

"Tell me something I don't know," Isaac answered.

That evening George Shannon returned from hunting and informed Captain Clark that Whitehouse had frostbite and couldn't walk home.

That night they watched the moon as it eclipsed and turned red.

The following morning George Shannon gained permission to take two horses to carry Whitehouse back to the fort. His frostbite was not as bad as they thought it would be. His feet were painful, but he kept all of his toes.

On the sixteenth, about thirty Mandan came to the fort including six chiefs. The Menetarres had told them they were liars and that if they came to the fort the white men would kill them. They had been with them all night, smoked the peace pipe, and were treated well.

One of the first war Hidatsa chiefs came to see them that day. He brought with him a man and his beautiful squaw to wait on him. He wanted to share his wife with the officers. The officers declined the generous offer.

Captain Lewis treated them to the chance to shoot the air gun. He then ordered Ordway to shoot the cannon. This pleased them. Little Crow, second chief of the lower village, came and brought the Menetarres some corn.

The war chief gave Captain Lewis a deerskin pelt containing his war chart of the Missouri.

"We intend to go to war this spring against the Snake people," he told Captain Lewis.

"I don't think this would be a wise decision," Captain Lewis told him. "Look at all of the nations who have been destroyed by war. I believe you should reconsider what you intend to do. I prefer that you have peace with all and trade with one another. I have seen that there is plenty for everyone. You will have plenty of horses as well. But if you displease the Great Father in Washington, you will not receive his protection as the other nations who listened to his words have.

This Chief was a young man of twenty-six years. He replied. "Are you suggesting that if my tribe goes to war against the Snake Indians the white man will be displeased, and he will keep my people from having enough horses?"

Isaac knew that both Captains Lewis and Clark were concerned that if this tribe went to war with the Snake it would be detrimental to the Corps of Discovery expedition. Isaac also knew that the captains worried most about the Sioux because they knew that the Sioux would take advantage of the situation if they could. They wanted nothing more than to get a friendly reception from the Snake people.

On the nineteenth, two men went up to the villages. The Indians were friendly and shared a meal with them. After they were done eating the Indians presented the men with a bowlful of buffalo head, saying, "eat that." Their superstitious credulity was so great, that they believed by using the head well, the living buffalo would come and that they would be supplied with a plentiful meat supply.

The next day, one of the men was very sick with a disease Captain Lewis said was syphilis. He said it came from sleeping with the Mandan women. The captain gave him mercury to relieve his symptoms.

On the twenty second, they tried to cut the boats out of the ice but were unable to dislodge them. The water gushed over where they had cut through the ice with an ax, so they quit. The next day they returned to try again to cut the boats from the ice, but it snowed three inches making the work difficult.

The twenty-fourth was a cold day, and the hunters went out to get more meat. They returned empty-handed. The interpreters seemed to understand each other better every day. They were now joking with one another.

On the twenty-fifth, a band of Assiniboine arrived at the villages with the Grand Chief of that tribe to trade. His name was Fils de Petit Veau. One of the interpreters and another man set out to the Hidatsa camp on the opposite island.

The men worked to cut the boat from the ice. They also collected wood to make charcoal.

The next day, all the men were put to work making charcoal for the blacksmith fire. The blacksmiths made ax heads in exchange for corn which they needed to continue their journey.

On the twenty-seventh, Isaac was assigned to help Captain Lewis in the sick room where the captain bled one of the men because he had pleurisy. He also greased him to draw out the sickness. He then started a fire to make the man sweat to draw out the sickness. Next, he removed the blackened toes of the Indian boy who had been frost-bitten several days earlier.

While Captain Lewis was working, Charbonneau returned and came into the sick tent and informed him that the Assiniboine had returned to their camps. He brought three of Mr. La Roche's horses to remain there because he feared the Assiniboine, who are expert thieves, would steal them.

The weather on the following two days was above freezing, so the following day, they attempted to cut through the ice to get the boat and canoe loose, but without success. The man who had been sick the day before was getting better, but now Mr. Jessomme was unwell. Captain Lewis gave Jessomme a dose of mercuric salts.

Captain Clark sent men to collect stones and put them on a large log heap to heat them. He intended to warm some water in the boat and by that means, separate the boat from the ice. The attempt was to no avail when all the stones broke and flew into pieces in the fire. The men were burning a large coal pit, to produce charcoal for the blacksmith fire so the blacksmiths could mend the Indians' hatchets, and make war axes, the only means by which the corps could procure corn from them without diminishing their trade goods that they wanted to share with other Indian tribes.

January 30 dawned to another fine morning. It clouded up at 9 o'clock, when Mr. La Roche visited the captains, and the captains gave him an answer respecting the request he made when he was their last. They refused his request. The captains had no intention of helping Larocque to acquire, at United States government expense, geographical knowledge that would be of advantage to the Northwest Company and the British government.

Sergeant Gass went upriver to find another type of stone with which to heat the water in the boats so they could remove them from the ice.

The January thaw ended. The wind was high from the northwest, and it snowed during the night. Isaac helped Captain Lewis remove more of a boy's toes. with two horses. Jessomme was somewhat better., George Drouillard had fallen ill with the pleurisy the evening before. Captain Lewis bled him and gave him some sage tea. He was better the next day.

Isaac became irritable. The cold weather was disheartening and had been so warm the past few days. He had hoped for an early spring, and the warm weather had been promising, but obviously, this was not the precursor to spring.

The cold dark dismal return of winter depressed Isaac. He was weary of the cold weather and was anxiously waiting for spring so he could return home.

Chapter 27-Isaac

By the autumn of 1806, Isaac and Rebecca had moved into their small cabin near the Boone plantation. Their home was within a mile of the cabin where the Shield family lived, and they waited for word from the Corps of Discovery. They hadn't heard a word from the expedition since Isaac and the rest of the crew brought back the large boat with the souvenirs from upriver.

"There was another rumor at the market today. They said that everyone on the Lewis and Clark Expedition was killed." Rebecca took the pot of coffee off the fire, poured Isaac another cup, and took his empty dinner plate from him.

"And I heard that the Spaniards have them as prisoners and have them working in the mines. If I had a penny for every time I heard that they were dead or prisoner, I'd be a rich man," Isaac replied. He picked up the pitcher of cream on the table and poured some into his coffee.

"You are a rich man," Rebecca smiled. He knew what that gleam in her eye meant.

Isaac smiled back. "Indeed I am."

On September 23, 1806, James Shields, John Shields's eldest son came running up the path toward Isaac and Rebecca who were sitting enjoying their morning coffee before their chores.

"He's back! Papa's back! They'll be moorings at the plantation!"

The two on the porch smiled at one another.

Rebecca waved Isaac away. "Go! I know you want to see them. I'll take care of the chores here."

Isaac kissed her on her cheek and followed the Shields boy down to the river.

It was good to see everyone again. The boys are now seasoned frontiersmen. Returning with them was Chief Big White, who was notably obese.

Three of the party have their eyes inflamed and swelled in such a manner as to render them extremely painful, particularly when exposed to the light. Their eyeballs were inflamed, and their lips appeared burnt with the sun. This condition was caused by the reflection of the sun on the water.

"Well, well, if it isn't Isaac Thorton. Did you miss us?"

"Somewhat, yes, but I found a way to keep busy." Isaac gave a sheepish grin. "Rebecca met me at the dock when I arrived here a year and a half ago. We've been married over a year now."

The men, for no one could call any of these leather-faced men boys now, slapped him on the back congratulating him on all his nuptials.

"There's going to be a ball in our honor in St. Louis," Captain Clark told Isaac. "I would consider it a personal honor if you and your bride would join us for the event."

"It would be an honor, sir."

The ball was held at William Christy's tavern on September 25, 1806. Isaac and Rebecca arrived just as the festivities were getting started.

Eighteen toasts were drunk, Captain Lewis began the toasts. "To President Jefferson. The friend of science, the polar star of discovery, the philosopher, and the patriot."

William Christy offered the final toast. "Captains Lewis and Clark—Their perilous services now endear them to every American heart."

"Hear, hear!" the guests and travelers clanged their mugs together.

After the toasts, Captain Lewis introduced himself to Rebecca.

"So you're the young lady who stole our young Isaac from us." Captain Lewis said to Rebecca.

"It was you who stole him from me, sir." She retorted and then said. 'But I forgive you. I don't think that he would have been happy with himself if he hadn't gone on the adventure."

"I beg your pardon, my lady," Captain Lewis replied. "I hope we didn't inconvenience you too much."

Rebecca laughed. "I think that it was one of the best things that could happen to us. We wouldn't have realized how much we valued each other if he hadn't gone."

Isaac who had been talking to George Douillard, returned and put his hand into Rebecca's.

Captain Lewis commented on Rebecca's baby bump. "I see that you are going to have an addition to your family soon."

Isaac replied to this one. "Yes, another member of the Thorton family. My parents back east are thrilled with the prospect."

"Congratulations to you both," said the captain.

Isaac said. "I noticed that John Colter isn't here. He didn't survive?"

"No, no, he's alive and well as far as I know. It's an interesting story. After traveling thousands of miles, and after the expedition returned to the Mandan villages, we met two men named Forest Hancock and Joseph Dickson. These two frontiersmen were heading into the upper Missouri River country to trap beavers. Colter asked to be honorably discharged two months early so that he could lead the trappers back to the region we had just explored. We, of course, obliged."

As Captain Clark moved on to speak to others, Rebecca looked at her husband and saw the admiration that he felt for the captain. "Do you regret not going with them to the ocean?"

"Not at all," he replied. "I want nothing more than to build a life here with you by my side."

After Captains Lewis and Clark would return to Washington with Chief Big White. Other members of the Corps of Discovery, Potts, George Drouillard, Jean-Baptiste Lepage, Peter Weiser, and Richard Windsor were planning an expedition to join John Colter in 1807.

They had asked Isaac to join them, but he declined. His wife and he had a son and wanted to remain to raise his son. "I am happy to stay here where the two rivers meet."

"I think you might want to reconsider. A great fortune to be made in the fur trade, Isaac," Captain Clark told him. "Your father would be impressed with the pelts up that way. The fur trade may be carried on from the heads of the Missouri River to the mouth of Columbia much more cheaply than any route conveyed to the East Indies. You could form an establishment on the Rochejhone River for the reception of the furs of that river and south or you could put one at Marias River below the great falls of Missouri. The Shoshones within the Rocky Mountains the Tushepaws on Clarks River and many nations west of the Rocky Mountains would visit those establishments from whom horses might be obtained on the most reasonable terms."

Isaac shook his head. "My father is a little old to be traveling like that."

"Are you certain that you don't want to come, Isaac?"

He shook his head again. "No, I found my place."

Captain Lewis became the governor of Louisiana Territory in the southern part of the territory. He died just a few years later in what appeared to be suicide. Some, however, speculated that he had been murdered.

Meanwhile, Captain Clark became the governor of Missouri Territory which included most of the rest of the Louisiana Purchase.

Isaac's wanderlust had been sated. He and Rebecca built their home in this newly organized Missouri Territory. He knew he was where he needed to be with the woman he loved at the junction of the Mississippi and the Missouri Rivers.

Preview of Moonrise on the Mississippi

"Well, if it isn't my friend, Andrew Mayford."

The year was 1809. Dirt streets, rutted and rocklike during the dry season and muddy during the rainy season, wound between the red brick buildings of Natchez Under the Hill. Andrew walked up to the storekeeper Daniel Moses. Daniel was sweeping the dust from the front step of his store on Silver Street.

Saloons, hotels, warehouses, grocery stores, a coal yard, an icehouse, a quarter-mile race track, a ten-pin alley, and even a few private residences lined Silver Street. Many of the businesses existed primarily to service the flatboats, keelboats, and steamboats that docked at Natchez.

Natchez was a city with a dual personality. Natchez Under-the-Hill was "Natchez improper" and "Natchez above the hill was Natchez proper."

"Natchez Improper" had gambling dens, saloons, and houses of prostitution that were popular with the rough boatmen and travelers at the waterfront. Known as Natchez Under-the-Hill, part of Natchez was one of the rowdiest ports on the Mississippi River. Here docked the keelboats and the flatboats.

Andrew was on Silver Street at the Moses Mercantile. His friend Daniel Moses owned the business. Daniel was sweeping the dust from the store's front step.

"Hello, Daniel! How's Natchez under the Hill been treating you?"

"Fair to middlin'. I see you made another successful trip down the Mississippi."

"It's not a lot of money, but it's a living," Andrew answered.

"What's your plans?"

"I just finished my business at the warehouse and am looking for a long soak and bite to eat before heading down to the boarding house. After that? I haven't got a clue."

The Spanish built Silver Street about 1790 to connect the town above to the riverfront below. In the 1800s, Natchez Under-the-Hill was already a major port on the Mississippi River. Natchez exported and imported agricultural goods, with cotton being the primary export. As the city became richer, the imported goods grew more luxurious. Natchez is one of the oldest European settlements in the Mississippi River Valley. It was the center of economic activity for the young state. Its strategic location on the high bluffs on the eastern bank of the Mississippi River enabled it to develop into a bustling port. At Natchez, many local plantation owners had their cotton loaded onto steamboats at the landing known as Natchez Under-the-Hill to be transported downriver to New Orleans or, sometimes, upriver to St. Louis or Cincinnati. The cotton was sold and shipped to New England, New York, and European spinning and textile mills.

'Natchez under the Hill is the most licentious spot on the Mississippi River." Daniel Moses said. "However, sometimes I want to leave it all. I'd be somewhere else if it weren't for the money."

Taverns, gambling halls, and brothels lined the principal street. Here, rumor has it, the only thing cheaper than the body of a woman was the life of a man.

Enslaved people were also sold at the landing at Natchez-Under-the-Hill, as well as on the city streets and at the Forks of the Road, and Natchez Under the Hill was the second largest slave market in the South.

"Where would you go, Daniel if you weren't here?"

Daniel shrugged. "I don't know. Maybe New Orleans or maybe just move up the hill."

More genteel of Natchez lived on the top of the hill, but they also liked a little vice. The men from on the hill came down where they could gamble their cotton earnings at the racetracks.

"So, will you be heading up the trace?"

Both men knew that Andrew would make the long trek back north to their homes overland on the Natchez Trace in a few days.

"Yep, I'm sure that my father has another load of grain heading down this way in a few weeks and he's counting on me to deliver them."

"The trace is dangerous. Two men were found murdered on the trail just last week. Neither of them had a coin on them."

Andrew shrugged. "I'm not worried. I have a well-armed and loyal crew."

Daniel nodded. "See you later, Kaintuck."

Both men laughed. It was a standing joke between them. Many of the men who made this trip were locally called "Kaintucks" because they were usually from Kentucky, although the entire Ohio River Valley was well-represented among their numbers.

Andrew was not, of course, from Kentucky. He was from Pennsylvania and his parents lived in Pittsburgh.

For years, the trace had been an Indian trail and where even earlier animals including buffalo used it for migration. Natchez was the starting point of the Natchez Trace overland route. This trail ran from Natchez to Nashville. Keelboat men maneuvered flatboats and barges transported all kinds of goods down the Mississippi River. Like the others, Andrew sold his wares and the lumber he used to construct his boat at Natchez and took the overland route to Nashville.

Natchez had been part of the United States territories since before Andrew's cousin Isaac went west with the Lewis and Clark Expedition. On October 27, 1795, the U.S. and Spanish signed the Treaty of San Lorenzo, settling their decade-long boundary dispute. On that date, all

Spanish claims to Natchez were formally surrendered to the United States.

A week later, Natchez had become the first capital of the new Mississippi Territory, created by the Adams administration. On March 10, 1803, the territorial assembly incorporated the town. After it served for several years as the territorial capital, in 1802, the territory built a new capital, named Washington, six miles to the east., but this didn't diminish Natchez' growth.

"Word has it that up north they are building steamboats that can sail upstream! Have you ever seen one?"

"I sure have," Andrew replied.

"Can you imagine how much a boat like that can move upstream on its own power could change everything here on the Mississippi."

"What I wouldn't do to be part of that experience," Andrew stated. "It sure would be better than dodging cutthroats and thieves on the trace."

"That it would. That it would," Daniel replied.

Chapter 25-Isaac

Water lapped on the side of the barge, and Isaac stood at the front of the boat as it drifted along the current toward the docks at the village of St. Charles. They weren't going to stay there long, but Isaac had a promise to keep for John Shields.

John Shield's wife was kin to Daniel Boone and his family, so they let her stay there in a small cabin to await Shield's return.

Isaac climbed off the boat and went to a man who was fishing at the dock. "Do you know where Mary Shields and her family are staying? "

The man spit on the ground. "No, I can't say for sure. I just came from downriver this week. I'd say that the shopkeeper at the trading post would probably know."

"Thank you," Isaac said. "Can you tell me where the trading post is then?"

"Not a problem. Just go up the road there and it's on the right. You can't miss it."

The trading post was about a half mile inland from the river. The trading post was a log building with a porch. At a puncheon log table, two men dressed in homespun played checkers.

Isaac would have asked them if they knew where Mary Shields lived with her children, but he didn't want to break their concentration.

As Isaac entered the store, the bell over the door rang to signal to the shopkeeper that someone had entered the store.

"Welcome, young man," said the proprietor. "How can I help you? I see you've been out in the wilds. Have you got furs to trade?"

"No, sir," Isaac replied. "I have a question to ask, is all."

"Well ask away then."

"I was wondering if you could tell me where Mary Shields and her family are staying."

"Mary? Oh, yes, she's staying in a small house on the Boone plantation. She's related to them, you know."

"Yes, sir," Isaac said.

"Well, let me tell you the easiest way to get there."

The house where the proprietor of the trading post directed him was a simple log cabin that was only a few years old. Old weeds poked through the new growth of the spring season. Several barefooted children and a dog played in the yard.

When the children saw Isaac coming down the road with a package, they flocked around him like chickens waiting for scratch. They followed him to the door.

"Whatcha got there, mister?" one of the little girls asked.

An older girl poked her in the ribs. "You know that Mama always says not to ask people questions like that!"

"Is Mary Shields your mother?"

"Yes, she is," the elder daughter said.

The biggest boy yelled. "Ma! There's a man here to see you!"

The door opened before Isaac had a chance to knock.

A tiny woman answered the door. Isaac didn't know what he expected, but he had not expected to see such a small woman compared to tall burly John Shields.

"Can I help you?" she asked.

"Afternoon, ma'am, my name is Isaac Thorton. Are you Mary Shields?"

"Yes, I am. Can I help you?" she asked again. She looked him up and down. He became conscious of the fact of how he might have looked. His buckskins were old and stained. He knew she must have guessed that he had been in the wilderness for some time.

"I am here as a favor to your husband."

Her suspiciousness turned to interest. "You know my husband?"

"Yes, I was on the expedition with him."

"John? Is he?" Her interested look changed to a look of concern.

"No, no, he's fine. He just wanted me to bring this to you," Isaac handed her the buffalo robe wrapped in a buckskin.

She unwrapped the buffalo skin, picked up the furry pelt, and held it up caress her face with it. "This is so warm."

"He wanted to you have it. He said he thought that you would appreciate it."

"I do. I do," she said. "Would you like to come in."

"No, I'm sorry. I can't." Isaac replied. "The rest of the men are waiting for me at our boat. We intend to arrive in St. Louis later today so we need to press on. We promised Captain Lewis that we would be in St. Louis and not dottle on our return. I just stopped here to give the buffalo robe to you and to let you know that your husband is thinking about you."

"Thank you, Isaac. You have been most kind," Mary said.

"No problem," Isaac tipped his hat and headed back to the pier.

As he got on the boat, Richard Warfington took his hand to help him onboard. "Did you find her alright?"

"Yes, it wasn't that difficult once I asked the right person."

"Alright then. Next stop, St. Louis!"

The man who had been fishing at the bank unhooked the rope from the mooring and then threw it to Isaac as the rest of the men used their poles to push away from the pier.

The next few hours seemed the longest few hours of the trip. Isaac thought about all that he had been through with the Corps of Discovery.

The doubts returned. Had he made a mistake coming back? Should he have gone ahead to see the Pacific Ocean with the Corps of Discovery? He then thought about Rebecca. He wondered what she was now doing. He dreaded all the time that it would take him to get all the way back up the Ohio to find out how she was doing. He feared that he would get all the way home only to discover that she hadn't waited for him at all and that she was already married to someone else. He worried that he had given up this chance of a lifetime for nothing.

The docks at St. Louis were even busier than he remembered with riverboats, canoes, and flatboats moored nearby. Now instead of a French flag flying from the flagpole on the docks, it was an American flag waving above the river port.

As they approached the dock, Isaac saw something white and flowing at the end of the pier. He blinked. It didn't go away. It just fluttered there in the breeze. He suddenly felt as though he was still dreaming could it be that every peaceful minute of the past few weeks had just been a dream and he would wake up back at Fort Mandan?

Isaac closed his eyes and opened them again. The white aberration continued flapping in the breeze.

Isaac squinted. The white fluttering object was not a ghost. A girl was standing on the end of the peer watching upriver. He couldn't quite make out her face, she was still too far away. She was dressed in a gown in a style that he had not seen before, but he would later learn that it was the prevailing fashion across the Western world.

"The first girl I've seen in a year who wasn't dressed in buckskin," Ebenezer Tuttle whistled.

The dress was a stark contrast to the clothing that the women on the frontier or that the Native Americans were wearing. Her dress was even different from the dresses that his female relatives had been wearing when he left back home. The wide panniers, conical stays, and figured silks of the eighteenth century had melted into a neoclassical dress that revealed the girl's natural body, with a high waist and a lightweight draping muslin dress.

The dress was a reproduction of what Isaac imagined was what the fashions of Ancient Greece or Rome might have looked like. The draping shawl she had draped over her shoulders evoked antiquity. It was white like Isaac imagined that a Grecian woman would have worn. The slim, vertical line of the garment reflected a neoclassical geometry expressed.

As he came closer, he noticed that in addition to the very high waistline, directly under the bust, the signature feature of this womenswear was the prominent use of fine cotton muslin, the dress had a lightness and drape that could not be accomplished with wool or silk. The fabric could only be muslin.

The dress's neckline was quite low and square. The low neckline was filled with a tucker providing a touch of modesty.

Could it be like his dream? As he came almost near enough to look into her face, the girl turned her head downstream to watch the men on a flatboat remove their moorings and begin their long trek down the Mississippi. She wore a wide-brimmed bonnet. Her hairstyle of curls billowed beneath the crown of her woven bonnet. Her hair was arranged in ringlets and curls entwined with bandeaux, and ribbons.

The girl reminded him of Rebecca, but then he always seemed to have Rebecca on his mind as of late. The girl turned her face back downriver. He imagined the girl was Rebecca, but what would she be doing in St. Louis? She was supposed to be back home. She wasn't supposed to be here. Could it be?

He looked again. Her face was better focused now. The girl was Rebecca! He didn't wait for the boat to be tied to the moorings, but immediately jumped out onto the dock.

"Hey, Isaac, are you forgetting something?" Tuttle called out. He had been about to throw the mooring rope up to Isaac, but Isaac paid no attention to the boat's moorings or the other men returning with him.

Richard Warfington put his hand on the young man's shoulder. "Let him be. He's been wanting this moment for months."

Chapter 26-Rebecca

Rebecca watched the men on the flatboat as one man removed the hemp rope from the moorings. He threw the rope on the deck and jumped on the boat behind it. She watched the men dip their poles into the water to propel the flatboat downriver.

Rebecca heard oars upriver behind her, and she looked. Several canoes and a larger boat were coming toward her. A young man seemed to be watching her from its bow. At first, she was repelled by the gaunt dirty frontiersman who probably hadn't seen a white woman in months. Then she realized that the face of the man resembled the boy who had left Pennsylvania so many months earlier.

The man jumped from the boat and onto the dock.

"Isaac?" Rebecca called over to the scraggly bearded man.

He smiled his familiar smile and nodded. "It's me! What are you doing here?"

"I heard that there was a boat coming down the river and I was hoping. . . I know that sounds forward of me. I was hoping that you might come back with the barge."

"And here I am! And here you are!"

"You came back, Isaac."

"I did. I was on my way back to Pennsylvania. Why did you come all the way out here to St. Louis?"

"Why do you think? I'm guessing that we're thinking the same thing."

"I think we have the same ideas of what we want, don't you Rebecca?"

"And what would that be?" she asked.

He put his hands on either side of her waist. "I think you know."

"Yes, I do," Rebecca replied. The smell of the man who had been away for so long was revolting, but Rebecca did not let that keep Isaac from taking her into his arms.

He kissed her and as he did, he heard someone clearing his throat behind him. He jumped back when he realized that his cousin Andrew was standing behind her though he had not seen the young man earlier because his eyes had seen only Rebecca.

"Welcome back to civilization, Isaac," Andrew said. He put out his hand to Isaac.

"Andrew! You're here too! How were things down south." Isaac took his cousin's hand, then his entire arm, and pulled the other young man toward him into a hug.

"So good that I am returning south in a few days."

"How did you...?"

"I went up to Pennsylvania this spring to deliver supplies and Rebecca and her parents insisted that they hitch a ride back here with me. They have all been looking forward to you two getting hitched for a long time. Your mother even sent the family locket."

On this cue, Andrew took a small old wooden box from his leather pouch on his belt and handed it to Rebecca.

Rebecca opened the box to reveal the old golden object. She smiled. "I guess they were right, Isaac, we were just the last to know."

"But we do know now, don't we?" Isaac smiled back.

"Yes, I have no doubts," Rebecca replied.

They were married within the week. For their wedding, Rebecca insisted that Isaac shave his beard and get his hair cut and of course, he took a long bath to soak the year's grim from his body.

As he looked in the mirror before walking out into the church sanctuary where they were to be wed, he hardly recognized the man in the mirror. He wore his hair in a short natural tousled look known as a la Titus. His buckskin was replaced by pantaloons made of jersey that provided an incredibly close fit and was cream-colored. Napoleonic uniforms influenced the trousers' design. This design originated in the 1790s. These trousers were now in fashion, tightly fitted, and far less comfortable than the buckskin breeches he had worn on the plains. They extended to the ankle where they fastened buttons. His shirt had a pleated front.

Rebecca had seen to the details of his wardrobe. According to Rebecca, this type of neckwear was a crucial element in a man's wardrobe. The main form was the cravat, a large square of fine muslin or silk, folded cornerwise and carefully tied. Properly wrapping and tying the cravat was a main concern of well-dressed men, and Rebecca insisted that Isaac study several available manuals to help him determine the correct method.

He couldn't believe the height that his new top hat provided. He laughed when he thought about how he would be an easy target to the Sioux if he wore this in the plains. The eighteenth-century bicorne hat that his Uncle Phillip wore with a turned-up brim on two points was still seen around St. Louis, but Rebecca had insisted that he have a top hat, the now dominant headwear. She insisted that he wear that kind of hat made of felt to the wedding.

His boots were the ultra-fashionable Hessian boots defined by their cleft tops trimmed with tassels. He felt so different from the young man who grew up in buckskins and looked forward to returning to them again. He was happy to give it up and have Rebecca and civilization. She deserved this moment. He knew that he would probably dress this way whenever she wanted him to come to St Louis, but he would be back in his beloved buckskins soon enough.

Just after the wedding, Isaac received his pay for his services with the Corps of Discovery and his in-laws gave them a sizable wedding gift. They used the money to purchase a piece of property near Boone Lick.

To the south and the west lay the Ozarks and to the north and west were the Great Plains. It is here at the mouth of the Missouri that the two greatest rivers in America are joined. It was here that the two of them would make their home.

They settled in a small, deserted log cabin located on the property. With Isaac's help, Rebecca made it into a pretty little home with lace curtains in the windows and a tablecloth on the table. They put a vegetable garden behind the house, and Isaac raised horses, oxen, donkeys, and mules.

28

Chapter 23-Isaac

March started in the same way February ended. Captain Clark was busy making maps, while the blacksmiths repaired guns for the Mandan in exchange for corn. The rest of the men repaired the boats for going downstream to St. Louis and building canoes for further up the Missouri.

Because the temperatures had moderated the next day, and the river began to break free in places. Mr. La Roche came to visit. He had merchandise to trade with the tribes on the Assiniboine River.

He informed them that Simon McTavish, the head of the Northwest Company was dead. Simon McTavish had come to America from Inverness-shire, Scotland, before 1772, and was a fur trader in Albany, New York, and moved to Montreal in 1775. He was one of the original partners of the Northwest Company in 1779, and became head of the company "in fact, if not in name," and perhaps the richest man in Montreal. The New Northwest Company was founded by men from the original Northwest Company who broke with the old company in 1798–1800, because of disagreement with McTavish's policies. His death in 1804 would make the merger of the two firms possible.

The next day, Isaac shielded his eyes and watched some ducks flying north, a sign that the main party would soon be able to move on into the unknown and he would be heading back east.

Would Rebecca be back at home waiting for him? He had not heard from her in over a year. He wouldn't have missed this journey for anything. The mistake he had made had been in not getting the promise from Rebecca that she would wait for him.

Isaac sighed. Well, if she had made that decision, He had been a fool not to get a promise from her back when he left, but he hoped that if she had made that decision, at least, she would be happy.

Chief Black Cat of the Mandan and a Hidatsa warrior came to visit. Several other warriors came with corn. Some of the men were employed making coal for the blacksmith to use and some made towing lines for the canoes they would use on their trek upriver. Some men who were not making canoes went to Fort Mandan for provisions. Isaac continued his work the next day.

A Frenchman and an Indian crossed a river carrying a letter for Mr. Tableau.

On the fifth, smoke filled the air, the Indians were burning old dead grass so that the buffalo would have fresh grass to eat sooner. The horses stolen earlier by the Assiniboine from the Menetarras were returned. Little Fox of the lower village of the Menetarras came to visit. Shannon cut his foot with a woodworking tool, the adze, while working on one of the canoes. The river rose a little that day. Spring was on its way.

The weather on the sixth was colder than it had been for several days. The Coal visited the fort with a sick child. Captain Lewis gave the child some of Dr. Rush's pills. Charbonneau returned that evening from the Hidatsa tribe and informed Captain Lewis that all the nation had returned from hunting. The expedition's Menetarras interpreter had received payment for his services from the Northwest Company for his services with them. He received braces of cloth, two corduroy coats, one vest, two hundred musket balls and powder, tobacco, and three knives.

Even though the next day was another cool day, several Mandan came to visit, and others came to see the blacksmiths with items needing repair because they knew the craftsmen would not be there that much longer.

The most notorious chief One Eye visited the captains. He had a formidable, and largely bad, reputation. Traders and travelers alike described him as ugly, brutal, lecherous, bad-tempered, and homicidal, but they did acknowledge his leadership ability and prowess in war. However, when he chose to accept someone as his guest, he protected that person with all the force of his character and reputation.

He was less than cordial to Lewis and Clark.

The next day was cold and windy. Snow fell again on the eleventh and Isaac wondered if winter would ever end.

They had every reason to believe that Charbonneau, their interpreter, had been corrupted by the Northwest Company, and he was determining whether he still intended to go with them. They allowed him to take time to decide whether he wanted to go or not, but they did not want him to take his Snake wife, just his Shoshone wife because the Snake wife was thought to be conspiring with the Northwest Company.

The captains assumed the Hudson's Bay and Northwest companies wished to sabotage their expedition to secure the Indian trade exclusively for Great Britain.

The next day, Charbonneau decided he would not go with them under the terms given. He pitched a lodge outside of the Garrison and moved out. Gravelines was hired in his place. Whether for the journey or only while they were at Fort Mandan Isaac did not know.

In the days that followed, all hands shelled corn including Isaac. He was willing to do whatever he could to help them on their journey.

The following day they set out all the Indian goods to air and the Mandan showed a lot of interest in what they had, but they weren't trading any more to them. They needed their trinkets for the many tribes they would meet who could be placated with the goods.

Mr. Joseph Garreau, a Frenchman who lived many years with the Arikara and Mandan, showed them the process those Indians used to make beads. This Mandan and Arikara art was derived from the Snake Indians the Arikara took prisoners.

Joseph Garreau first visited the Arikara with Jacques D'Eglise's expedition in 1793 and remained with the tribe. Whether he was a Frenchman or a Spaniard, Isaac didn't know, and he doubted that the captains did either because he spoke English, French, and Spanish as well as Arikara and Mandan. He was an interpreter and trader among the Arikara and Mandan.

Isaac watched as some Mandan women made beads.

The glass bead-making process began by crushing some glass of many different colors into a fine powder. The women placed each color into separate containers They then washed the pounded glass in several waters throwing off the water after each washing. They continued this operation as long as the pounded glass until the water ran clear. Next, they used a three-gallon earthen pot which would not disintegrate in the fire. A platter was kept nearby also of the same materials but sufficiently small so that it could fit inside the pot's mouth of the pot. The pot has a notch in its edge through which to watch the beads when in blast.

They had some well-seasoned clay with enough sand to prevent it from becoming too hard when exposed to the heat. This clay had to be tempered with water until it is about the consistency of common dough. Of this clay, they then prepared enough little sticks of the size they wanted the hole through the bead to be. They did this by rolling the clay on the palm of their hands with their fingers. With this done, the women put those sticks of clay on the platter and exposed them to red heat for a few minutes when they took them off and allowed them to cool. They heated the pot to keep out any filth it might contain.

Next, they made small clay balls weighing about an ounce to serve as a pedestal for each bead. While these were still soft, they poured the glass beads over the face of the platter at a distance from each other to prevent the beads from touching. Using little wooden paddles of three to four inches in length sharpened or brought to a point at the extremity of the handle. With this paddle, they placed as much wet pounded glass into the palm of their hands as necessary to make the bead of the size they wanted. They arranged these beads with the paddle in an oblong form, laying one of those little sticks of clay crosswise over it. They pounded the glass with the paddle and roped it in cylindrical form around the stick of clay and gently rolled it in their hands until they were regular and smooth.

One of the women introduced another color. She perforated the surface of the bead with the pointed end of her little paddle and filled the cavity with other pounded glass of the other color forming the whole as regularly as she could. A hole is now made in the center of the little pedestals of clay with the handle of your shovel sufficiently large to admit the end of the stick of clay around which the bead is formed. The beads are then arranged perpendicularly on their pedestals and a little distance above them supported by the little sticks of clay to which they were attached. The platter was placed on burning coals or hot embers and the pot reversed with the aperture in its edge turned towards covering the whole. Dry wood that was mostly rotted was then placed around the pot and completely covered it and lit the wood on fire. The woman watched her beads through the aperture of the pot, so they are not destroyed by being overheated. She ensured the bead acquired a deep red heat and then it changed to a paler or whitish red. When the beads begin to become pointed at their upper ends, he threw the fire from about the pot and allowed the whole to cool gradually.

The pot was then removed, and the beads were taken out. The clay which filled the hollow of the beads was picked out with an awl or needle, the bead is then fit for use. The Indians were extremely fond of the large beads they created. They used them as earrings, or in their hair and sometimes they wore the beads around their necks.

The next day, Ordway ushed a French man into the captain's quarters.

"Captain Lewis, this man has a message for you from Charbonneau."

"Very well," Captain Lewis said. "Well, out with it, sir."

"Yes, sir. Charbonneau says that he is sorry for the foolishly acting as he had and he begs that the captains would be pleased if he could accompany you. He said that he was agreeable to the terms you proposed."

"Very well," Captain Lewis said. "Tell Charbonneau that we would be happy for him to come along with us as our interpreter."

The river rose a little that day and, in several places, it flowed freely. Spring was a whisper away.

Charbonneau then moved his stuff back and pitched his lodge near the fort. Charbonneau was officially enlisted as the interpreter of the trip.

The next day Captain Clark packed up all the trade goods into eight packs equally derided to have something of everything in each canoe.

The next day, Big White and Little Crow visited them. They brought with them a man and his wife and a sick child, who Captain Lewis treated medically. They told the captains that the Sioux and the Chippawa had gone to war and one other party going to war shortly. Sergeant Gass informed Captain Clark that the canoes were finished, and more men were needed to draw them to the river which was about one mile and a half from where they built the canoes. On the twentieth, they dragged the canoes to the river. Another step was completed.

The next day was clear and pleasant. The wind was from the southeast, and Indians from several tribes continued to bring them corn. A Hidatsa chief came to visit the officers with Mr. McKinsey and Mr. La Roche. The captains gave him a medal, an artillery coat, a shirt, and a knife. Rivet left alone in his canoe. Mr. McKinsey and Mr. La Roche left the next day.

Swans and geese were flying north. It wouldn't be long now. Isaac and Warfington were making cages for four black magpies, a prairie dog, and a sharp-tail grouse that they were taking back to St. Louis.

During the night of the twenty-fifth, the river broke up and nearly carried away their new canoes. At about 2 o'clock they returned with the canoes, but before they had landed the ice started so that they had to draw them out with speed. They hauled four of them had not got down to the fort, but they took them on shore so that took no Injury. All hands turned out and took them on the riverbank and carried one down to the fort. The ice stopped and jammed up. The ice started several times but stopped running entirely before night.

On March twenty-seventh, they had all the canoes corked, pitched, and lined over the cottonwood, with wind shakes, the name for cracks in the wood caused by the wind. The Mandan usually used these windshakes to feed their horses on cottonwood sticks instead of corn.

The ice stopped running on the twenty-ninth because ice blocked the river upstream. The corps and the men going south were all preparing the boat to set out. The Indians watched the river to catch drowned buffalo that broke through the ice while trying to cross. They harvested many buffalo this way every spring.

The next day, great quantities of ice passed, and the water level in the river dropped. The ice obstacle had broken away in the river upstream. The river rose thirteen inches during those twenty-four hours. The Indians jumped from one cake of ice to another to catch any buffalo that floated downstream. Many of the cakes of ice that they traversed upon were not more than three feet square.

On the last day of the month, several gaggles of ducks and geese flew over by now only a small amount of ice was floating. All in the party were in high spirits.

29

Chapter 24-Isaac

April first began with a thunderstorm. Of course, there had been a lot of snow, but this was the first rain they had seen since October. They put the boat and the canoes back into the water and expected to send the boat south with dispatches soon. Six Americans, including Isaac, three Frenchmen, and several Arikara chiefs were going back to civilization on the boat.

Six canoes of several French intended to ascend a short distance so they could trap the beaver which was in great abundance higher up were going up the river with the expedition. The Corps of Discovery would continue their expedition with their Interpreter and hunter Toussaint Charbonneau and his Shoshone wife Sacajawea and infant son Baptiste. As a former member of the Shoshone tribe, they hoped the woman would be more of an asset than her husband in the land where the expedition would pass. She would act as an interpreter to her tribe. Twenty-six Americans and French, York, and a Mandan would take that trip north. They had provisions to last for four months.

The next day was cold, and the captains worked all day writing dispatches for Isaac to carry back to St. Louis. The river was nearly overflowing its banks. On the third, they finished packing the boat to leave the next day.

Mr. La Roche and McKinsey's clerk to the Northwest Company visited them. Mr. McKinsey wished to receive pay for his horse lost in their service during the winter and for the horse stolen from the men during the winter by the Teton Sioux. All day they packed up sundry articles to be sent to President Jefferson.

Isaac picked up the last of the nine boxes they planned to bring to President Jefferson. He handed it to Corporal Warfington.

"I can't believe this is the end for us," Isaac said. "It's as though we were a part of history."

"We are a part of history," Richard Warfington said. "Are you sure you don't want to continue upstream to the Pacific? I'm sure that option is still open to you"

Isaac shook his head. "No, I know I am doing the right thing. It's time for me to go back."

"Do you think Rebecca. . ."

Isaac shook his head. "I don't know. I hope she hasn't chosen that man my family warned about."

"Do you think you made a mistake making this trip?"

Isaac shook his head again. "No. I wouldn't have missed this for the world."

"Then you have no regrets."

"None."

"Then everything should work out."

"I hope you are right."

Richard patted him on the shoulder. "Everything will work out."

Isaac didn't have Warfington's confidence.

Isaac looked up at the boxes secured to the boat. Those boxes held many memories for Isaac. In those boxes were the remains of antelope, black-tailed mule deer, a martin skin, a white weasel, squirrels from the mountains, a white and grey hare, prairie dogs, red fox skins, a magpie, burrowing squirrels, mountain rams' horns, antelope, yellow bear skins, insects, and mice.

They had cages of living specimens of prairie dogs, magpies, and a prairie hen. They had a sample of a plant with roots that was highly prized by the natives and was used as a remedy for rattlesnake bites or mad dog bites. They also carried a Mandan bow, a quiver of arrows, an earthen Mandan pot, some Arikara tobacco seed, buffalo robes, an ear of Mandan corn, a carrot of Arikara tobacco, and articles of Indian dress.

They were returning with special notebooks that Captain Lewis had taken with extensive notes about the fauna and flora of the Missouri River Valley. Included in these volumes were astronomical and weather observations. Some material represented a list of rivers and creeks. A list of mineral specimens was also sent back from Fort Mandan. There was also a list of Indian presents and "necessary stores" that the Indians requested for the future. Isaac was part of all of it.

Over the past three days, they had packed up all these boxes that the returning members of the expedition would take down the river. The weather couldn't have been better. On the sixth, the officers decided they would start their voyage that morning, and everything necessary was ready when a messenger arrived at the fort, from the Mandan Villages. Arikara were on their way to make peace with the Mandan. Captain Lewis decided to stay that day, to see if what the messenger told him was true.

Ten Arikara chiefs came to the fort to negotiate the treaty that evening. They put all their baggage on the boats to leave as soon as the treaty was complete. Finally, on the seventh, they were packed and ready to travel back down the Missouri River.

The boat was leaving first, and Isaac was getting anxious to return to civilization, but he would have to wait. Before he could return to St. Louis, Captain Lewis wanted to be able to share the results of this meeting between the Arikara and the Mandan relayed to President Jefferson as soon as possible.

That day was windy, The Interpreter they sent to the villages returned with the chief of the Arikara and three men of that nation. This chief told the captains that his tribe sent him to discover the disposition of the Arikara settling near them. He had not yet made those arrangements. He asked the captains to speak with the Assiniboine, and Crow in their favor. The Arikara wished to follow the American direction and be at peace with all. He believed that all nations in this quarter were well-disposed except the Sioux. He said that the Arikara would join with the Mandan and the Minatare in a defensive war against the Sioux who robbed them of their lives and property to the point that they could no longer live near them.

To this chief Captain Clark said, "I am glad to see you. I view this nation, your nation, as dutiful children of the Great American Father who would protect them with his good advice. We have already spoken with the Assiniboine and hope to speak with the Crow if we can see them on our continued journey. As for the Sioux, the President will not let them have any more good guns and will take measures to prevent them from murdering and taking property from the Native Americans who are willing to serve the United States. To you, I give these mementos of peace."

Captain Clark gave him a certificate for his good conduct, a small medal, a carrot of tobacco, and a string of wampum.

"Thank you so much, Captain Clark. You have been very generous. I have a request, if you may so oblige me."

"And what is your request?" Captain Clark asked.

"I request that your boat would take a lame warrior back to our nation when it goes downriver."

"Corporal Warfington would be happy to assist with this, wouldn't you, Corporal."

"It would be a pleasure," Richard Warfington replied.

Everyone was satisfied with the decision.

This Chief then handed a letter from Mr. Tableau informing the captains of the desire of the grand chiefs of the Arikara to visit their Great Father and requested the privilege of putting on board the boat three hundred pounds of skins and adding four hands and himself to the party. The captains agreed to this. Fifteen Indians joined the men on the barge to defend them against the Sioux if there was any problem with them.

After making all the preparations for their departure, the boat and the crew left with orders to return without delay to S. Louis. A small canoe with two French hunters accompanied the barge. These men had ascended the Missouri with the corps during the past year. The barge crew consisted of six soldiers, Isaac, and two Frenchmen. Two Frenchmen and the wounded Arikara warrior also took their passage in her as far as the Arikara villages. There they expected Tableau to embark with his peltry who in that case will make an addition of two to four men to the crew of the barge. They gave Richard Warfington, a discharged corporal., the charge of the barge and crew, and confided to his care likewise our dispatches to the government, letters to our private friends, and articles to the President of the United States.

Joseph Graveline, an honest and discrete man, was an excellent boatman and was employed to conduct the barge as a pilot. They expected the barge and the captains' dispatches would arrive safely at St. Louis. Mr. Graveline, who spoke the Arikara language extremely well, was employed to conduct a few of the Arikara Chiefs to Washington, DC who promised to go downstream in the barge to St. Louis with that purpose in mind.

As the crew on the barge prepared to leave, John Shields gave Isaac a buffalo robe. "I'd like you to take to my wife, Nancy. Can you do that for me?"

"Of course," The men slapped each other on the back.

"It was great having you with us, Isaac. I will miss you, brother," the elder man said.

"Are you coming?" Richard Warfington asked Isaac. "For someone who is in a hurry to get home, you certainly are taking your time."

Isaac sighed. A part of him, his father's part of him would always want this kind of life, but he knew that his heart was with Rebecca if she would still have him after all this time.

On April 7, 1805, Richard Warfington led the crew including Isaac, Private Dane, Private Ebenezer Tuttle, Private Isaac White, Peter Pinout, and the two former expedition members. Private John Newman was brought back in disgrace for being a mutineer and Moses Reed was sent back because he had tried to desert the expedition. Corporal Warfington turned the keelboat downstream as the permanent party faced their canoes westward. Warfington had charge of the precious journals and other records of the first year's travel, botanical specimens, and preserved animal specimens—plus a live prairie dog and six live magpies. The keeled boat took only about 47 days until May twenty-third to travel downstream the distance that had taken 173 days, including pauses to visit the Yankton and Lakota Sioux and bury a friend, to travel the same distance upstream.

Cygnet chose the pen name Cygnet Brown because her maiden name is "Swanson" (a cygnet is a baby swan) and Brown is her married name. She grew up in Northwestern Pennsylvania and began writing stories in Mrs. Watson's seventh-grade English class. Because of the experience, she wanted to become a professional writer, but life got in the way. She is a veteran of the US Armed Forces. She served on active duty Navy from 1981-1987 as a Neuropsychiatric Technician then in the reserves until 1999. She married, became a mother to three children, stepmother to another, and became a nurse. She resumed writing in October 2008 when she fell in love with her characters. She graduated Magna Cum Laude with a bachelor's degree in liberal arts in 2014.

Cygnet Brown currently lives in the Missouri Ozarks. She loves to research and write history from a fictional perspective. She never knows when she'll uncover a historical tidbit that sparks another story in The Locket Saga.

When *God Turned His Head* was the first book in her historical romance series *The Locket Saga* written in 2010. Other books in *The Locket Saga* include: *Soldiers Don't Cry, The Locket Saga Continues, Book III: A Coward's Solace, Book IV: Sailing Under the Black Flag, Book V: In the Shadow of the Mill Pond, Book VI: The Anvil* and now *Book VII: Two Rivers.* She has at least six more books in the works for this series.

She has also written a contemporary romance: Because of Ryan.

In 2013 she published her first nonfiction book Simply Vegetable Gardening based on her 40 years of gardening experience. She has also written *Help from Kelp, Using Diatomaceous Earth Around the House and Yard, Gourmet Weeds, Oregon County, Wild and Scenic, Living Today, The Power of Now,* and *Write a Book and Ignite Your Business,*

See updates as she completes more books at her Website: http://www.cygnetbrow.com Ms. Brown is the owner of *Ozark Grannies' Secrets LLC.* She has written for *Mother Earth News magazine* and online article sites. Ms. Brown is a retired public school teacher and the author of the blog: Author Cygnet Brown https://1authorcygnetbrown.com/